'Here clearly is a wri[...]e
and talent to explore, [...]f
[...]'
Christopher Wordsworth, Guardian

'Unnervingly assured at the deft interweaving of comic
and philosophical observations . . . Charlesworth succeeds
in reaching the heart while being brutally funny; no
mean gift'
Patrick Gale, Daily Telegraph

'A writer of significant accomplishments, among them a
gift for describing her characters as if they themselves had
taught her how to place them perfectly in context'
Jonathan Keates, Observer

'A novelist of very considerable talent . . . She writes with
such assurance that the reader is compelled to believe
what she says and to find it important'
Allan Massie, The Scotsman

'The skilful blending of realism and allegory, the deft
plotting . . . and the sharp intelligence of the writing
recall Muriel Spark. Ultimately, however, the author's
style is her own'
The Times Literary Supplement

Also by Monique Charlesworth

The Glass House
Life Class

Foreign Exchange

MONIQUE CHARLESWORTH

SCEPTRE

First published in 1995 by Hodder and Stoughton
First published in paperback in 1995 by Hodder and Stoughton
A division of Hodder Headline PLC

A Sceptre paperback

10 9 8 7 6 5 4 3 2 1

British Library Cataloguing in Publication Data

Charlesworth, Monique
  Foreign Exchange
  I. Title
  823.914 [F]

ISBN 0 340 61695 4

Typeset by Hewer Text Composition Services, Edinburgh
Printed and bound in Great Britain by
Cox & Wyman Ltd, Reading, Berkshire

Hodder and Stoughton
A division of Hodder Headline PLC
338 Euston Road
London NW1 3BH

For Lorie Charlesworth

Summer

Hilary Lennox found himself staring gloomily up at two tonsures, a double crown and one greying middle parting. The occupants of the single aisle seats were reflected in the long strip of overhead mirror which snaked down the Train à Grande Vitesse that was taking him all too speedily towards the Loire.

By tilting his head right back, he was presented with a long-chinned pixie version of his own face, a fall of middling brown hair over eyes so dark they were almost black, a bumpy nose. He thought of himself as a bit on the thin side. Was he attractive? Was not knowing one of his charms?

The view on the other side was worse. In the four-seat part slouched a spotty French lad about his own age, who was hunched over his GameBoy, poke-poke-poking at the controls. Opposite him, legs firmly clamped apart, sat his dear old mum. She was a small fat person who had been knitting a pink thing ever since they left the Gare de Montparnasse. At the end of every row she did a little grimace which made the hairy wart on her cheek waggle. This was her way of propelling her large rainbow-striped glasses that crucial millimetre back up her snout to the ridge where they felt really comfy.

Because he could not stand to see her do it one more time, he looked out of the window, where the waggle and specs reappeared in spectral reflection. Spot-face kept his head down, but every now and then he'd splay his fingers and blindly feel over for the raffia bag which lay on the table and burrow in until he found a bag of corn snacks or sweets or some other spot-inducer and slowly rustle out the contents.

Meanwhile in his corner seat, Father slept on. His way of coping and very understandable too. He was a repressed little man with wire-rims falling off and sad furrows down his cheeks, his wedding ring embedded in his finger. And this tribe of pokers and clackers probably represented a typical French family. The Beauregards would be like this. Except, since they were country folk, they would be less sophisticated. Ha. Hilary was struck by the unfairness of it.

There he was, seventeen going on eighteen with exams behind him and the prospect of a year away ahead, a great biker's jacket and a personal self-improvement programme. There was no point being too specific with the whole gleaming universe of opportunities and choices right ahead, but his aims included some sketchy thoughts about tennis and a few to do with reading matter. Mostly, he was concentrating on how he would set about getting his leg over as many girls as possible.

It seemed impossible to Hilary that a day would come when he neither woke nor fell asleep thinking about sex. Age would unsex him, as it had his parents and his friends' parents. Meanwhile, it didn't even take girls to arouse him – anything, from the touch of certain fabrics to the shiny smooth polished surface of things could do the trick. Surprising, really, that he ever managed to give his attention to anything else.

So what was he doing spending two weeks with some acned Frog? His mother had pulled rank on him. Amanda had announced that he would go and had refused to be precise about why. Mostly, she had cried. Hilary couldn't refuse her anything when she cried. She did this as if it didn't count or matter at all, when the reverse was true. It was apologetic, that was the funny thing, that something could happen and be life and death stuff, enough to turn the world's least weepy woman into a running tap yet she treated it as a little ongoing embarrassment. It was so strange and potentially catastrophic that his thoughts wouldn't stick, they preferred to veer off to some safer topic.

For what his mother usually fixed up was girls. These were always truly terrible girls, the lumpen daughters of her contemporaries. Even in middle age, even though seriously bleached and caked with make-up and ultra tweaked, these women weren't dogs. How come so many of their daughters had drawn the short straw?

This time, Amanda had announced that she had fixed up 'something special' for the summer. He'd made his dubious face, wiggled his jaw.

'If it's a May ball, forget it. I've been fixed up before. You tell your girl friends I'm out of the country or dead or something.'

'Oh, darling, there's no girl involved here,' she'd said, fiddling with the coffee machine. 'It's a really wonderful opportunity. A foreign exchange for you, in France, two weeks with a really marvellous French family.'

'Bloody hell – you're kidding.'

Tight-lipped, Amanda had risen and carried the milk jug to the fridge, closed the door with that slight excess of pressure which meant real annoyance and returned bearing the coffee pot and two cups. Silently, she'd shoved one over at him.

'I don't like that language, Hilary. I'm trying to arrange something, well, rather special and I think you should listen first, hear what it's all about and then you're in a position to decide.' She'd begun to pace from the window to the door. 'Look. Here's a free, all expenses paid trip to France for two weeks, which'll do wonders for your French, darling. Then you host the return visit for this young man – well, of course I'll do most of that. And that's it, simple.'

'But I'm nearly eighteen. Kids do these foreign exchanges. I've just given up French, haven't I? So what's the point? It's just stupid.'

'I want you to do this.'

'Look, don't think I don't appreciate – look, Mum, it's just not on. I don't want to. I'm sorry, but it's no.'

She'd stood still then and stared out of the window. Then she'd drawn one of those bad-news, deep shuddering breaths.

'Mum?' No reply.

'You said I'd get a whole year off if I got into university, right, and I worked my arse – very hard, and, look, this is my year. I'm too old. Come on, you know it's a silly idea. OK?' It was his reasonable voice. He'd come up close and put his arm round her, had given her a hug.

'Huh, huh, uh, Hilary.' There'd come another of those breaths, only worse, and she'd turned her face away and she was crying. She'd shaken her head at him and motioned to him to go away and then she had remained quite still while tears flowed out and rolled down her face. He'd held onto her, waiting for her to find the words to reassure him. But she'd been unable to say anything at all. Crying, like a mad thing. What the hell was going on? There was nothing you could do. It wasn't the first time, either.

The time before, it had happened like this: Hilary had come into the sitting room and found his mother sitting on the sofa crying, quite silently, without moving a muscle, while beside her his dad turned the pages of the evening paper. Hilary had half turned to do the sensible thing, which was to push off, but then he couldn't. He had come to kneel beside her. He had fished a tissue out of his pocket. Carefully, he had tried to dry her face. That had made her cry more than ever and given her the impetus to go out of the room with his arm round her. His dad read on, had not looked up once, while he was leading his mum away. Not once, he'd not looked once.

The green clear land flowed by, a gentle seesaw of lush fields with small copses, embankments succeeded by picture-postcard farms, all nicely wooded and cultivated. The gardens of la belle France. Madame continued to knit. At the end of the compartment, the door slid open and the inspector appeared.

He progressed towards them pursuing his calling with slow dignity. 'Tickets, Messieurs, Dames.'

Hilary's multiply-perforated computer-generated slip of a ticket was appraised and returned. He was travelling in the période bleue. How appropriate. Madame put down her knitting. A killing look was flung at the inspector who forced her to pause, to plunge deep in the raffia bag and find her ticket. She fumbled and sighed and dawdled about it. It got right up the inspector's nose.

You could see that he was a careful man, it was in the way he spoke, polite and precise. No breath of impatience ruffled his calm face. His uniform was pressed, the red enamelled badge shiny on the peaked hat, a careful tiny mend in the special oversized pocket for the notebook of authority. He took his time scrutinising the ticket and its accompanying reservations bit.

Did Madame have the special rail traveller's certificate of the troisième âge which had enabled her to buy her ticket?

Voilà, Monsieur.

He looked at it with his special hot brown inspector's eyes, which had seen it all before. Madame's certificate was out of date. He would regrettably have to tear it in half – for it is no longer valable, Madame. Politely, he returned the two halves to her. Next he whipped out his book and ran his manicured inspector's finger down its index, flicking through and then taking out his pen. Not for him the chewed stub of pencil behind the ear. The inspectors of the Société Nationale des Chemins de fer Français had proper pens. He made her wait a good long time.

The inspector rolled his beautiful pen through his fingers and proceeded to fill in a form rapidly, but pleasantly enough, finally tearing it off, handing it to her and requesting the sum of two hundred and forty francs – that being the difference, Madame. Between the ticket purchased with the invalid certificate and the full price. For the three of them.

Spot-face paused in his game. Hilary thought, but no doubt he was imagining it, that Papa in his corner paused an instant in his stentorian breathing, to shut his eyes tighter still.

Madame appealed with a shrug of her hands to the denim-clad young Chinese mother whose little boy sat on her lap to be fed continually. The young mother busied herself opening another Coke. The man beyond with the mustard coloured shirt and matching socks, whose vast feet jiggled incessantly to the sound of his Walkman, heard and saw nothing. With heaving bosom, Madame appealed to the inspector in the name of reason, of sense. If she had known that the ticket was not valid, she would of course have replaced it. It had been valid on the aller journey to Paris three days ago and was not now upon the retour. Quel malheur. And so on. She would not have made the trip to Paris – no, she would not have dreamt of going to visit her sister-in-law, frail and dying though she was, had she known. She was on a mission of mercy. Her fingers meanwhile clutched the brown leather purse very tight.

Ah. There was a long pause. The inspector drew breath. Was Madame refusing to pay the sum due?

She snapped her mouth shut and the purse open and counted out the notes in various thousands and millions, as the older generation was wont to do, which aptly illustrated what, in her eyes, the cash represented. Hilary continued his inspection of the gardens of France. The inspector counted the notes and nodded and then went about his business with just the faintest air of a twinkle about him and Madame knitted on at excitable double speed and Hilary sighed for pure pleasure. So. Being young, abroad, being alive was not so rough and this little aperçu sustained him all the way onto the platform at Saint-Pierre-des-Corps and across the platform to the waiting navette, the little silver shuttle that took a couple of minutes to run passengers over to Tours.

The train chugged to a halt in an old-fashioned arching terminus of a station with a seventies interior. He got off the train behind two brown-legged American girls in shorts with rucksacks and allowed their handsome, Identikit knees to carry him to the exit. So where was the French lad? God, that must be him, a weedy-looking boy with his mummy. Hilary walked up, extended his hand. Toujours la politesse.

'Bonjour, Madame Beauregard. I'm Hilary,' he said.

The boy made a strange face and backed off. 'Eh, alors?' he said, pulling out his lower lip into a rubbery 'ape face.

'OK, OK, sorry.'

So it wasn't him, the goon-faced twit of an oinkhead. Hilary looked around. There, standing under the huge archway, was one of the most gorgeous girls he had ever clapped eyes on, a beauty perhaps his own age with a long shining fall of silky hair, cut off jeans and a sexy little T-shirt. She was standing talking to someone in an old Peugeot and now turned, slipped a pair of sunglasses over blue, blue eyes and came towards him. He stared like an idiot.

The Peugeot slammed at full speed into reverse, shunted back into a parking space and stopped and a large middle-aged man got out. He was the ageing hippie type with longish hair and jeans and a pugilist's nose. Hilary's head swivelled to watch this lovely creature enter the station with him a dozen steps behind. Her lover, uncle, father? She was Beauty to his Beast, but they had similar colouring. She was upon him – she passed, inches away. Star quality. He sniffed at something amazingly wonderful and erotic in the perfume line which trailed behind her, which was worth whatever it cost, whatever.

Hilary now understood that it wasn't just the shape which counted, no, there was the incredible texture, the brown all-over colour of the skin, the incredibly fine-textured, faintly blue-veined piece of silk from which the master tailor had cut. The planes that shaded into other ones, lines that intersected with heart-breaking accuracy, geometry worth a lifetime of study. There was a caterpillar scar on her left knee, a round injection mark on one arm, two delicious imperfections that merely underscored the heavenly rightness of the rest of her.

He turned to watch her walk onto the platform. Even the back of her head was something. She was perfect from every angle. She was, quite simply, the most beautiful girl he had ever seen, anywhere, every line of her a poem – no, a bloody ode. She was gone and he closed his eyes, to commit her to memory. For later use.

A couple of minutes later she walked out again and stood no more than a few yards from him, looking up and down the road. The line of taxi drivers in their cream vehicles drawn up outside ogled her openly. One of those saps wolf-whistled, the clown, as if a girl like this would even know blokes like that existed. And where had the hippie gone?

Feasting his eyes, Hilary smiled at her in hope. Her face was impassive behind those sunglasses. He winked. She looked at her watch. He took a step forwards, laid his hand dramatically upon his heart, gave her to understand in sign language that his heart was hers and no mistake. Not for nothing had he done his Malvolio two terms ago at school. There was a tiny movement around the mouth – aha, a twitch. He bowed dramatically and edged a fraction closer. The closer you got, the more flawless she was.

There was the hippie. Over her shoulder, Hilary saw the big man ambling into the Informations kiosk and joining a good long queue. He stood, tapping his feet behind a whole horde of tourists and a dwarf-sized old lady with a very fat pug. Hilary reckoned that he was probably going to be stuck there for ten minutes if not longer. Certainly he was good for five.

Hilary sidled up to the ravishing girl in order to explain how crucial it was that he see her again.

'Bonjour, Mademoiselle,' he said. The explanation of this great need, which all but emptied his small reservoir of French, was because she had dealt him a terrible wound. A biggie. Une grande plaie. Right here. In his heart. He took hold of her hand, just for an instant, to indicate the area of the wound but she pulled it away. It must be a wound, you see, or why would his heart flutter so? Like a thousand butterflies, all beating their little wings. Mille papillotes. He made wings of his arms.

Her lips curved up deliciously. He pressed on. In England if there was a medical or social emergency, then anybody present was expected to help. She, who had dealt the wound, was responsible. What was she going to do about it? She could not refuse help in an emergency of this sort.

'C'est la vie ou la mort,' he said.

She was studying him now over the dark glasses, the

smooth brows, as gleaming as the rest of her, arched with gentle irony. She nodded her head gravely.

'Il vous faut un médécin, peut-être?'

No. Yes, anything.

If so, there would not be a problem, she would go and fetch one straightaway, to sort out this poor young man – and now, watching for his reaction, she smiled. Touché – and she laughed. It was a gurgly, real thing, this laugh, with her head thrown back to expose that kissable throat.

This was the moment when Hilary felt his heart break or melt or at any rate do something it never had before, something it never would again. It felt important and irretrievable and final. That wonderful sound.

No, he said, he thought that what he needed was a nurse. Une nourrice. Only a lovely young girl could help him. Oh, she said. When she smiled, one dimple appeared in the right cheek. Things were progressing sweetly and enjoyably and so Hilary, rummaging in his bag for a piece of paper and pen, found the name and the address where he was staying. Carefully, he copied it out. He presented it to her with a flourish. Here, he said, and I forgot to tell you my name, Hilary Lennox. This gave him an opportunity to shake hands, or rather to capture her hand for a second.

'Hilary is a girl's name,' she said, looking at the paper.

'Girl or boy, it can be either.' He loved the way her eyebrows flew up and down as she read what he had written. Now she took off her sunglasses to inspect him closely. There was a long pause while she looked at him and he stared back, dazzled.

Oh dear, she said, what a pity. As luck would have it, she knew the place and knew the people who lived there. They were not at all nice. So she had a suggestion for him. Why didn't he come and stay at her house? Hilary's face now bore the dazed expression of a small boy, all of whose Christmases have come at once.

He was by no means sure that he had understood her properly.

'Chez toi?'

'Yes,' she said, with glorious simplicity. Hilary thought for a bit.

'Me?'

'Yes. Why not?'

'Why not?' Indeed. Rapid thoughts buzzed through Hilary's already intoxicated head. 'You know,' he said, 'these people – well, actually, they're nothing special. I don't know anything about them. I mean – why not?'

She gazed at him quizzically, waiting for him to make up his mind.

The hippie approached, explaining to the world that the navette was unmissable for une personne alighting at Saint-Pierre-des-Corps. The guard on the platform would have directed her to it. It was, however, always possible for a person to have dozed off, not to have got out at all, since the TGV only halted its restless flight for two minutes precisely – zoom – and his hand took off along an imaginary runway.

'Papa,' the beauty interrupted, laying her hand upon the hippie's arm. 'I think you must meet this new friend of mine whom I have invited to stay. He is English. Isn't that delightful? Papa is wanting that I must speak better. You were saying again today, weren't you, how important it is for me to improve my English?'

Hilary shuffled his feet in fascinated embarrassment and watched Papa's face, which certainly was a study as he took in this outrageous piece of news. His eyes closed in a pained expression, opened again and looked Hilary up and down in a way which suggested he was not impressed. Then the big man shrugged his shoulders as if to say, what can we do against this sort of thing? Yes, what?

He beckoned. Hilary smiled a touch nervously. Papa drew

him over to one side, put his gorilla's arm round him in a slightly alarming way and leant to whisper in his ear. 'Au revoir,' he said. The centime dropped. Right, thought Hilary, fair enough and he shuffled back to his bag.

'Wait, Papa, did I not tell you? May I present to you Hilary Lennox?'

There was a long pause, during which Papa did an expressive double-take, twisting his head round and back again and then throwing it back. A great roar came out. He lunged for Hilary, who nervously tried to sidestep him, dodging only to be caught by the daughter. She held his arm. She put those luscious lips next to his ear. Her warm breath was the most delicious thing in the universe. It melted every bone in his body.

'This is my father, Dr Charles Beauregard. And I am Michèle.' Hilary looked at her. She looked at him. Papa caught up with him for a serious handshake cum hug and over his heaving shoulder, Hilary continued to stare at this remarkable girl. When she really smiled, like now, the corners of her mouth curved up in the most – the most deliciously fascinating way and she burst into peals of laughter and a second later, as the full wonder of it struck him, so did Hilary.

There was no Michel nor ever had been. Glory be, she was an only child. For some minutes they babbled Euro-semantics and gender-benders about Hilaire and Hillary and Belloc and Clintons and Michels with and without an e and Hilary explained that his mother was very bad at distinguishing between the masculine and the feminine.

'Aha,' Charles said. 'Is she? That surprises me, I would not have thought so,' and everybody laughed. Hilary was laughing like an idiot at anything anybody said – he was so high that there had to be some release. As they all got into the car, Hilary could not help noticing that the delicious Michèle did not stop looking at him. As he looked at her. He repressed the urge to bray with pleasure.

Charles drove just as Frenchmen were said to, using the stop-go method. Bursts of speed alternated with screechings of brakes, the whole accompanied with gesticulations and comments flung freely from the car. He lit the first of many Gitanes, driving with one arm hanging out of the window so it was available for the kind of Gallic insult that demanded the upraised, phallic clenched fist. He smoked continuously, eyes narrowed against the smoke.

'OK, Hilary, what did your maman say about me? Did she tell you much?'

'Hardly anything,' he said. Sitting in the back, with his gaze fixed on the back of Michèle's head, he saw against that halo the handsome façades lining the Boulevard Heurteloup which they passed with surprising speed for such an old vehicle, before hurtling up a ramp improbably signposted both 'BORDEAUX' and 'PARIS' and onto the motorway. The idea that he hadn't wanted to come was a distant dream. Mothers were always right.

'She said I'd have a wonderful time and she was right.'

'Come on, what else she say? You know, she is an extraordinary woman, yes, yes, very, very special.'

'She's great, yes,' he said, seeing in the driving mirror Charles's inquisitive eye fixed upon him when it very definitely needed to spare the odd glance at that lorry just ahead which they now pulled out to pass with inches to spare. Hilary's own gaze could not stop wandering back every couple of seconds to feast upon Michèle. Her long hair hung down to just a couple of inches above his knees, which would have been eternally and achingly grateful to be swept, just once, by that fringe. Her smooth brown shoulder, which he could have reached out and touched, shimmered just a few inches away.

'OK, OK,' said Charles. 'You can tell me after.'

When they left the motorway and drove past a large pond, the road came out in a long sinuous roll of cornfields. The ears of grain were exactly the same ripe yellow as Michèle's hair. Charles pointed out the landmarks, two ancient walled farms dating back to who-knew-when, slowing down and swerving slightly. Down that way you could just see the beginnings of the park of the local château inhabited by the Count of something or other, very spry for his age, the place was littered with his middle-aged bastards, all manfully striving to keep up the family tradition. Le tout countryside sported the worthy nobleman's distinctively pointed and cleft chin.

And this way was the house of the notaire, a pretty seventeenth-century moated house, most unusual – the poor man had had a terrible growth here, just here, and Charles pointed at his shoulder, half turning round dangerously while Michèle also turned, laughing, for Papa knew everybody for miles. Hilary saw at this funny three-quarter angle how amazingly similar they actually were, in terms of cheekbones and colouring, as similar as two people could be when one was gorgeous and the other pretty worn out – and he yelped and pointed as a tractor loomed up between the two similar heads.

Charles veered away and they stopped, just in time. Perfectly unfazed, Charles leapt out of the car, lit another fag and went to chat to the rustic perched high on the machine. They launched into a discussion about whatever incomprehensible thing it did, complicated by the equally incomprehensible thing the disease of some mutual acquaintance was doing.

Listening to the rise and fall of their voices, Hilary seized the chance to lean forwards in the gap between the front seats, thus coming within two inches of Michèle. He allowed his senses to frolic, to revel in the smell of her. That skin, that perfume. Dizzy with desire, he saw the old bloke jump down into the road. Charles was examining his machine. Now – and anyone who had spent even a few minutes in a car with Charles would have known that this could not be a good idea – he was climbing up into the seat. He sat in a commanding pose. The engine throbbed. He fiddled with levers and switches. The old bloke was bent double with laughter when the big man couldn't get it into gear, then unexpectedly drove the tractor backwards at speed. He was still guffawing as they once more drove off, swivelling his head to keep his weeny bull elephant's eye on target for an eyeful of Michèle.

The house, ten minutes further on, was a handsome manor house on top of a hill, with cornfields undulating right up to it. They bumped through the corn down a track which led off from the main road. Over to the left Hilary spotted a monument historique announcing itself. A rather impressive-looking old ruined château. There was just a glimpse of this as the Peugeot hoppety-bumped at speed over tractor ruts and then through some gates and past an orchard so it wasn't until they had actually driven round the building that Hilary saw that what he had taken for the front was the back.

The house had a formal entrance here, a big flight of steps sweeping up in wings from the long garden with its beech-shaded drive. It had been built on the crest of the hill with a commanding view of the village which lay at the bottom in a snaking cluster of red-roofed houses. The whole business was as pretty as a picture.

Standing very upright on the flight of stone steps and thus dominating the whole shebang was a beautiful woman in a white silk frock whose face, as Hilary neared, expressed an almost comic disbelief. As he shook hands with Louise Beauregard, Charles and she launched into a very rapid exchange to do with his being un garçon and Hilary wondered for one intoxicating moment whether he might have

been going to share a room with Michèle and was there any
hope of this substantial house being equipped with only two
bedrooms, or of the other rooms being suddenly struck by
rot or damp or deathwatch beetle. While the vision this
offered danced through his head, he studied his beloved's
mother. If you were interested in the daughter, you should
always look at the mother.

There was a lot to consider. She was quite tall and had
an older version of Michèle's beautiful face and a lot of
dark hair which was pulled back into a chignon which
exposed the nape of her neck and her small ears, all of
which were very nice indeed. The rocks in those ears
looked pretty substantial to Hilary. Certainly, his mother
didn't have anything like that, nor the fancy enamelled
pendant watch nor the three or four jangling bracelets, all
of which seemed real enough. Nor, of course, had he ever
seen his mother wearing what he took to be an evening
dress in the day time or standing at the front door to greet
people in this regal and, let's face it, pretentious fashion.

Louise paused for a moment in her discussion with
Charles and stared at Hilary who now expressed his hypo-
critical regrets at being a boy. There was quite a lot of 'Quelle
difficulté, je regrette' and a lot more of 'Pardonnez-moi,
madame' before she calmed down a bit which gave Hilary
time to look from Madame to Michèle and take in how
brilliantly terrific it was to be a boy in this particular corner
of the world. There were a good ten minutes of this while
Hilary hung about the steps with his bag at his feet while
Louise went into the house, came out again, stopped having
a go at Charles and started instead having a go at Michèle
for not being more hospitable.

'You poor boy,' Louise said, 'You must let me show
you the house,' as though he'd been forcibly stopping
her from doing that. She swept him in and, silk skirt
swishing, rushed round the house in a voluble whirlwind

tour. Hilary was encouraged to shake little fingers with a greasy-pawed Madame Moulins on her knees in the pantry. Various bottles of home-preserved fruits were pointed out to him. He was led to inspect the salon and dining room and even the surgery with carved wooden whatsits on the panelling before being led up an elaborately painted trompe-l'oeil staircase and through various bedrooms and bathrooms. Louise, always two dancing steps ahead, threw open cupboards to reveal piles of linen and towels and cloth whatsits. Hilary couldn't have cared less for the whereabouts of the sheets and bolsters and drawn-thread work antimacassars, any more than he cared about the confit de canard or the preserves. Hilary was fully occupied examining Michèle. The French girl smiled very sweetly at him and he smiled back.

Finally they reached the guest room, conveniently adjoining Michèle's, where Hilary and his bag were deposited and where the sight of various feminine items such as bowls of potpourri and cotton-wool-ball-type stuff all laid out sent Louise Beauregard off downstairs to do a reprise of the whole boy-girl thing with her husband. Hilary did wonder then as he lay on the bed and stared at the ceiling (this, like the walls and even the chest of drawers, was completely covered in flowery paper) whether Louise wasn't perhaps a teeny bit off her trolley.

Amanda Lennox would never have shown anyone round her house – people his age were expected to find their own way around without fuss. Nor did she seek approval for her kitchen stuff, though she was as keen as anyone on that department. Hilary hung his feet over the end of the bedstead which had been designed for a French midget and had a bit of a think about this whole exchange business. It was deeply unlikely that his highly organised mother could have failed to work out that the Beauregards had a daughter and not a son at all and, indeed, vice versa. He only had time to decide that it was probably Charles Beauregard who was to be blamed, or rather thanked, when a knocking on the door woke him and it was dinner time.

Various things became clear at the dinner table. Louise Beauregard was no slouch in the cooking department. One course succeeded another, not to mention one clean plate after another and a bewildering assortment of glasses, doo-dahs, knife rests and such like.

'Things are very simple here,' Louise said. 'We will have just a little pasta to start, then a little meat and a little salad and perhaps a sliver of cheese. That is it.' And she shrugged, self-deprecatingly. The pasta was homemade and meltingly delicious with olive oil and wild mushrooms and pungent scraps of rubber – these turned out to be scrapings from a simple bit of fresh truffle from the forests here. The fillet turned up, seared on the outside, tender pink inside. Cheese meant a goat's cheese, simply rolled in volcanic ash, a sheep's milk one and then of course the ordinary buffalo milk jobbie, not to mention the simple unpasteurised brie that kept rolling off its corner and oozing onto Hilary's plate.

Hilary wondered as he drained his glass for the fourth time whether they would eat (and indeed drink) like this every night. French people were very different, clearly capable of no end of good living. Then there was the way they dressed up. Louise's white silk number revealed its everyday status compared to the little black job she was now sporting. Michèle had also changed into a simple silk shift thing which didn't seem to leave much leeway for underwear anywhere. This supposition had forced him to undertake a detailed albeit surreptitious inspection.

The phone rang and it wasn't a patient as Louise feared, but Hilary's maman. He stood waiting for the phone as Louise spoke volubly of her surprise and so on and smiled at him meanwhile, to show that she was perfectly reconciled to, if not thrilled by, the whole thing. Hilary could imagine his mother in the sitting room at the other end, struggling to understand the flow of words.

'Darling,' Amanda said. 'Good grief.'

'Mum, yes, it's great, you see she's just pointing out that I'm a boy. And guess what. Michèle is an elle – is a girl.' And what a girl she was, he could see her gorgeous long legs crossing under the dining table through the double doors at this very moment. Oh, girl.

'Oh, darling, silly me. You're not disappointed, I hope, it's not going to spoil your stay? Charles found you all right, though, all the same. How is he, darling? Shall I have a quick word? Shall I? Hilary?'

He was still laughing at the idea of the disappointment he might be suffering. 'No, yes, God no, it's fabulous, Mum. Look, I don't think he can talk right now, we're eating. I don't want to be rude to Louise. Call you soon, OK, Mum. Give my love to Dad – byee.'

Back at the table, he saw that Charles was stroking Louise's hand appreciatively. All through the meal husband and wife had discussed the food and where it had been bought and how it had been cooked in immense detail. Appreciation was due, was offered and received in a way Hilary couldn't imagine at home. Also the pair of them lit up every other minute. This was equally unimaginable in the Lennox household, where Nicholas permitted himself a cigar only on such festive occasions as his birthday and Christmas.

Charles, fag in mouth, went to make the coffee and offered a Gitane to Hilary, who puffed and coughed unenthusiastically. Through a blue haze he looked from the gorgeous girl to her parents and wondered why his mother hadn't told him what they were like. How was it possible that she hadn't known about Michèle? Because the more he thought about it, the more unlike her it was and he leant forwards then and caught Charles Beauregard's eye.

'When did you arrange it, for me to come here?' he asked.

'On s'est rencontré à Pâques,' he said. 'Oh, quite by chance.'

Easter

Amanda Lennox stood at the top of the black run, facing down the steep gully. The day was overcast and chilly. Yesterday's mush had frozen. A young man skied past and she watched him begin to skid. His arms jerked up as he tried to save himself. He was halfway down before he came to a spraying halt, almost bent double with the urgency of stopping on the sheer ice before he cannoned off the edge. Slowly, he straightened up and then slid again, toppling over backwards with windmill arms. When at last he regained his footing, he stood for a long time at the edge of the piste and looked down the steep and treacherous way.

Her husband came up beside her, glancing her way and half waving. She opened her mouth to speak, but Nicholas carried on. She watched him go down in his usual manner, not so much stylish as capable. Down he went, slow and steady. At the very bottom, he stopped and looked up at her and then he beckoned. He did it again, then a third time. He put his hands to his eyes, staring up at her. Surely he knew that she was terrified.

Amanda remained where she was, the whole of her body trembling. She was tempted to break into loud, hysterical laughter, but a couple came past so she watched their careful descent instead. Their skis scraped loudly on the ice and they shouted encouragingly to each other, they waited and pointed out good places to turn. These sounds reverberated up, amplified by a funnel effect. She had come to a point where there was no option but to continue. Far away down below, Nicholas waved again. She leant on the sticks and watched them all down, safe. Again, Nicholas beckoned. No option, she said to herself. She had come to a certain point. But she could not go on. Behind her, unreachable, the chair lift swayed its way to the summit carrying its pairs of skiers, two by two, and then came floating back through the sky, empty. Away up beyond, the Matterhorn rose up to challenge the sky.

She took a deep breath and pushed off, without hope. At once her skis slithered unstoppably down the narrow path and she tried to control the urge just to sit down, to give up. Little stones in the ice, freezing air, her body refused to face forwards. She was leaning back, the skis getting faster, out of control. She began to fall, awkwardly, full of self-loathing, arms flailing. As she fell, she screamed silently.

There would be bruises all along her thighs. Shaken, winded, only slightly hurt, she lay for a long time on the ice, invisible to those below and, more dangerously, to those above. Her teeth chattered. Her nose was runny. Eventually, after a struggle, she extricated a tissue from the recesses of the stupid salopettes. It came away black and damp from mascara and tears. What would happen if she never came down? She stared at the brownish patches where the hill was struggling to break through.

A stranger stopped. Was she OK? Kind eyes, a helping hand. Amanda smiled for him and began to get up again and there was her husband still watching, the beckoning hand angry now.

'Nichts kaputt,' she said. But it wasn't true. As she rose up, the slope seemed so terrifyingly steep that it made her heart lurch. The world wheeled about in front of her and then shuddered to a halt. A moment of pure fear. Some kind of separation from this was imperative. She was not going down. Never, he couldn't make her. In sudden exaltation she released herself from the struggle. She stepped through a door and slammed it shut and locked away all the misery behind it.

And so the whole slithering cowardly descent was carried out in tearful haste by somebody else. Nicholas's wife underwent the ignominy of a second fall, of sliding right off the path and having to scrabble, hot-faced and shivering, for a lost ski. Amanda remained standing where she had fallen and risen again. She watched the poor wife tumbling down, seeing before her, clearer than ever before, the dangerous consequences of a lack of nerve. She skied that slope in her head as she would have done if she had had the luxury of being alone. She was elegant and she was fast. Singing in her head were the words alone and free – alone and free.

By the time wife, chilled and stained, caught up with him, Nicholas was chatting to another bloke, an Englishman they'd bumped into in the restaurant at the top. 'You took your time,' he called out to her, all jovial and hail-fellow-well-met. 'Wasn't that fun?'

With a wave of the hand, unable to reply, she skied past, digging the sticks in and spurring herself along. He turned and followed and soon caught up and passed little wife in the make-believe jolly race. Wife averted her blotchy, ugly face. When he was ahead, Amanda skied elegantly. As they went down to the valley she felt, for the first time in years, some of the joy that skiing had once given her, that sweetness of propelling yourself forwards wherever you might choose to go.

'Jourbon Ellrigab, va ça?' said Nicholas. Bonjour Gabrielle, that meant. 'Amanda taught me how to ski, you know,' he said, leaning against the little bar in the hotel and talking a little too loud as he always did after a few drinks. Twinkly-charming and ogling the handsome French barmaid. He often chatted up women in her presence, just as he always mentioned his wife in those conversations. She knew that he never looked at a woman except when with her. She knew that he didn't actually fancy other women. Unlike most men, he did like them. The barmaid had been telling them all about backwards language, which she spoke with incredible fluency and speed and which Amanda was completely unable to grasp. Nicholas, who wouldn't speak normal French, with characteristic perversity had cottoned on to this.

'He's such a quick learner,' said wife in her schoolgirl French and Gabrielle swiftly replied with some kind of bar-maid's heavy double entendre that she could well believe that. The three of them laughed, Nicholas throwing back his head and roaring with his face rosy and full of pleasure. Such pretend intimacy delighted him. 'He's better than me – at skiing, I mean,' she said. Nicholas haw-hawed. Gabrielle looked at him as she turned away, looked at her too. Don't you dare judge me, she thought fiercely.

If he was in a good mood, dinner would go well and she could think her own thoughts. There was the whole evening to be got through before she could lie awake and think. She had travelled light years already, had got through the lawyers and the divorce courts and custody of the children and become a free woman just while soaking in the bath. Poor wife, a mass of bruises and bumps. Amanda was already so very distant from her. She relished her new capacity to laugh at the absurdity of it all. Her situation, as his wife, was so strange. She was tempted to go back, to touch Gabrielle's shoulder as that solid creature polished the glasses, to say, 'It's not how it seems. Really.'

The minestrone was good, better for being cooked by somebody else. Wife said as much, nicely, and buttered her roll and smiled and meanwhile Amanda thought with astonishment what an elaborately structured life had evolved over the years without her having exactly chosen any of it. She rolled it back in her head, as Gabrielle did her sentences, and found no sense in it. She had given up her career as a doctor and had children instead, and Nicholas had become the successful surgeon she had always wanted to be. Yet in return for very menial tasks, housekeeping and cooking and childcare, she was rewarded with very high pay. Unthinkable that wife might give in her notice when this barter system provided expensive holidays and good clothes and a half share in a house envied by those who did not have to clean it. There would never be cash for her to spend, without asking, and sexual intercourse was on demand for him but not for her. On the other hand, there were the two children, much loved. There were plays and outings and cultural events, but also a dull series of conventional evenings with people just like them, for whom she was expected to cook with gourmet flair. There was the occasional company of Nicholas, that solid husband, that brainbox, who had competed for her, who had been her chosen one. They spent perhaps five or six days a year alone together. For a further three weeks they might be ostensibly in the same place but never sharing it. Nicholas always ran ahead, one way or another.

He raised his glass to her across the candlelight, pleased with her. 'Are you happy, darling?' he said. 'I so much want you to enjoy this.'

'You know I am,' said his wife quickly, gulping a little, for kindness was hard to bear when it seemed genuine. Amanda wasn't having that. She swigged down some wine and let it rise to her head a little. Stupidly, she had often bemoaned the extent to which her husband lived in his head, unconscious of other people. So many nights when he sat to think and she had resented it. Wife was such a fool. And now, unable to think of a single remark she could conceivably address to him, Amanda understood the urgent necessity to be left alone with one's thoughts.

Leaving Zermatt had always been hard, but this time the journey down could not depress Amanda. The prospect of freedom made her light-hearted. Secret knowledge transformed the world. All the way to Zurich she stared at the lovely scenery and watched the snows melt away without regret.

She hated flying but even this worst part was now bearable. At the airport, wife did tend to make heavy weather of the skis, huffing and puffing and manoeuvring her trolley. Lightweight stuff, yes, but she found it tricky, like all the jobs that Nicholas allotted to this anxious soul. The skis stuck out, they stabbed at corners and threatened shoulder bags. How hilarious wife was, how absurdly her trolley plunged and heaved across the shiny concourse of Zurich Airport in Nicholas's wake. Amanda found her so easy to impersonate that she had begun to ham a little, to play up that dizzy dame. A parody of a parody, Amanda playing wife.

Nicholas always had his part by heart. He had the heavy suitcases and the money and the tickets and on he surged, all weight and frothing behind. Amanda let wife lag a little, so she wouldn't have to listen to him. His chuntering drove wife bananas, poor thing, but Amanda quite liked the way it showed Nicholas up. It was a kind of long-range extended nutter's mutter which flowed after him, full of expression but incomprehensible. People looked.

Brainbox had evolved a number of little games of his own. Ways of killing time, since he couldn't bear to waste it. Right now he was pursuing his self-appointed task of translating tannoy announcements, all the flight numbers and destinations, into what Amanda rather thought was ancient Greek. That would probably be for the benefit of his imaginary companion, Philip of Macedonia. Occasionally

Philip's son Alexander joined them. Not often, though, for Nicholas thought he lacked the statesmanlike qualities, the sheer gravitas, of his less famous dad. Sometimes Nicholas could be heard chortling to himself as he polished a rather risqué bon mot in Latin for the benefit of one of the bawdier and more murderous Roman emperors. That suited Nicholas to a T, to embellish a dead language for some imaginary dead old man. Not just any old man, mind, only despots and prime villains were worthy of the effort. Brainbox never cared what other people thought even if he noticed them, which, being him, he didn't. He didn't look to see if wife was following. He knew she was.

Amanda was trailing slightly behind as she turned the corner and wondering if she could let wife lose her balance altogether, just by removing the hand which was stopping the skis from rolling. Tempting though this was, she decided against it. Wife was so vulnerable and she did not want Amanda's exaltation to be spoilt by wife's tears. One of the strange things that still happened was the kindness of Brainbox, which could come quite unexpectedly just when his usual irritation was expected. His gentleness, so characteristic of the old, unformed Nicholas she had married, just broke her down. Wife had wept in many public places recently, too many. Fortunately, Nicholas had decided not to notice or, if he did, not to care. He could be in the same room and could even sit beside his wife on the sofa while tears flowed unstoppably down her cheeks and carry on reading the paper. Perhaps he had loved her once, but he had not kept faith. Instead, he had encouraged her to play the wifely part without ever defining terms and conditions. To behave as though everything was in order when, being so intelligent, he surely knew better, this was a grave fault.

Something caught her eye. Just ahead of her walked a big, shaggy looking man, walking arm in arm with a woman.

He looked very familiar. Her heart gave one huge thump, then carried on at double speed while her brain relayed the rational message that of course it couldn't be him. But her internal organs set up a bowel-twisting little dance. The man who couldn't be Charles glanced sideways at the newspaper stand, then veered over to it. Her stomach churned. It was him. She stopped dead.

On went Nicholas in full polyglottal flow, expecting wife to be present and willing as she always was. Amanda was immobilised, watching Charles Beauregard. Twenty years since she saw him last. There was a huge lump in her chest of misery and longing. Breathe, go on. She forced out an exhalation. Better. A sharp pang of need and desire sprang into the air, it crackled live and electric across the space.

He stopped dead, as if stung. Dear God, he knew. He turned to look, saw her, said something to the woman and came towards her. He shimmered across the waxen floor, a glorious mirage. As he took her hand, he examined her face very carefully. In those few seconds before anything was said, she received a simple but important message. Whatever she felt, he felt too.

The woman's high heels tapped over to where Amanda and Charles stood quite still, staring at each other.

'Amanda, how wonderful this is. May I present you Louise,' said Charles. 'My wife.'

His accent was just as strong as ever. He remained holding her hand and she had to retrieve it to shake hands with the elegant woman he had married. This person said 'Enchantée' and Amanda replied 'Bonjour, Madame' and could not help noticing how exceptionally well turned out and attractive his wife was. She was conscious of being observed in return. Jourbon Damma. The backwards language flowed.

Inside her shoes, Amanda's toes curled with the urgent

need to exchange essential information. Yes, she had married that man, the one from then, whose name was Nicholas, who was over there somewhere, ha ha. They had children, yes.

'Deux enfants,' she said. Hilary was seventeen and the little one, Edward, nine. Her French was dreadful, his English worse. Stubbornly each strove to speak the other's language. She wanted to explain that the poverty of these communications was to do with the fact that the woman he was seeing now was not the real her. Inside wife with her nervous smile was the real Amanda, who was repressing the urge to lie down with him there and then. Any surface would do, the airport floor would be fine, if necessary. Or, there again, why lie down? Incredible that for so many years she had forgotten how it felt, to feel desire for a man. Her heart pounded painfully.

'My Michel is nearly seventeen,' he said. 'They like each other, les jeunes.'

'Oh yes. Oui, I'm sure. Young people do,' she said inanely.

The elegant wife was plucking at his arm, their flight was being called and Amanda realised that something had to happen. She couldn't possibly stand never to see Charles again, no, she very possibly couldn't stand to watch him walk away without lifting up her head and howling her loss and regret like a wolf. She had a vision of herself lying rigid and resentful alongside the skis on the trolley, being pushed away by Nicholas.

'Look, Amanda, I tell you this,' Charles spoke with great meaning. 'You send your Hilary to visit us, then we come visit you,' he said. 'Young people, they do it. Always. They like each other. You like it? We do this definite, yes?'

'Yes?' she said, without quite grasping the sense. From the corner of one eye, Amanda saw the swivelling head of Nicholas. Now he was a minesweeper, his manner on ward rounds, his face intent. This was how he searched his roses for greenfly. This gave her a jolt and made the blood flow into her face and concentrated her mind.

'A foreign exchange,' she said, 'Yes, of course, I know just what you mean. How wonderful, we must do it.'

'This summer,' said Charles. 'We do it. Yes. I call you.' He took from his wallet some little cards and pressed them into her hand. 'Write please your number. Address too.'

'Yes,' said Amanda. 'Définitivement, oui. And you will come to England, what a good idea, how lovely, Nicholas will be thrilled. My husband, Nicholas. He is mon mari,' she said smiling at Charles's rather beautiful wife, as though the word husband somehow legitimised the outrageousness of the plan, as though there were any possibility of this woman accepting it. Very carefully, she wrote down her name and address in capital letters. She tucked his second card into her purse.

Charles's wife smiled and nodded back in a very polite way. It became clear that she didn't understand English. Amanda took her hand and shook it with enthusiasm, unable to banish her foolish smile.

Nicholas had seen them and was bobbing his head in recognition and as he got near he inverted the stretch of his mouth into a smile. He was bound to be annoyed. For Nicholas punctuality was, if not the chief of all virtues, certainly one of the braves.

Charles's wife was looking at her watch, tugging at her husband's arm, with all the universal let's-go signals.

'This is Charles Beauregard and his wife, um, Madame Beauregard,' said Amanda, speaking very rapidly. 'Hilary's going to stay with them this summer. It's all fixed up.'

'Why, hello there,' said Nicholas with false bonhomie. Written all over his face was distaste at being pushed into shaking hands with complete strangers. His eyebrows telegraphed astonishment.

'You remember Charles, darling?' Wife put on her brightest tone. 'Of course it's years and years. Before we got married. Charles did six months at Guy's. Mon mari est médécin,' she added for Madame's benefit. She began to feel wildly exhilarated.

'Ah,' said Nicholas. 'Enchanté.' It was by no means clear that he did remember, but Amanda saw that this explanation put a different complexion on things. So, more glossily, did Madame Beauregard. 'Madame, I'm sure I would have remembered you,' he said gallantly.

Madame nodded and smiled. The goodbye handshake went on for a bit longer and he continued to look and smile admiringly as the Frenchwoman led her husband away, just as Amanda watched and absorbed Charles. She committed him to memory. She could hang on, for the summer. Now there was something worth waiting for.

'What was that you said? Amanda. For heaven's sake.' Nicholas shuffled with irritation from one foot to the other.

With deliberate slowness, Amanda put what he always called her scarf thingie on, carefully wrapping the long trailing ends round her neck, securing the whole fragile enterprise with a small knot. Then a bow. She made it all right and tight. As secure as it could ever be. She found that she was still smiling.

'About Hilary? Amanda?'

She gave her full attention to pulling out the ends of the bow.

'What do you think you're doing?'

'Putting on my scarf.'

'Don't be obtuse. Those people, who are they?'

'Look,' she said with a faint edge, drawing from him that and-what-have-I-done-now irritated look. No, she thought. Why should I tell him anything? 'Come on, darling. You know how you hate to be late,' wife said, very nicely, and set off at a good old whack. He came rumbling along behind.

'It'll never work,' he said.

'What?'

'Hilary won't want to go and stay with complete strangers.'

Things tended to come out in a rush and a muddle when she got seriously annoyed. That was why she didn't argue with him any more, because she always managed to defeat herself before the battle started. Amanda drew a deep breath. She wasn't going to argue. She was just going to do what she wanted.

'Amazingly lucky for him,' she said, mildly.

'Amazing,' Nicholas said in his deeply ironic voice, 'is thinking that Hilary will agree.'

'It's arranged.'

'Without asking him?' Nicholas snorted derisively. 'You're very confident. He'll have made his own arrangements by now.'

'Oh no, I don't think so,' said the sweet voice. 'He'll just have to unarrange them. It means I'll be able to concentrate on Edward, before he goes to summer camp, while Hilary's in France. Ed needs attention, you know how wild he is. Oh, and I've invited the parents to stay, when they pick up their son. We'll do a weekend thing, I expect.'

For years she had been setting up such joyless arrangements and he had always accepted that that was what a wife did. It was curious to see how little meaning the words offered compared to her powerful inner sense of what was actually going to happen. She could deceive him because, for a complex man, he was so simple-minded.

Nicholas's brow furrowed in disbelief. They were nearly at the front of the queue. 'What did you want to do that for?' He loathed guests in the house.

'Tickets, darling.' She smiled as nicely as she could at the

– what did they call them? – the ground hostess. Nicholas muttered on and she shut her ears to him. Amanda thought that if they had arrived at the airport two minutes sooner, or later, then she would not have seen Charles. The little hairs on the back of her neck felt strangely sensitised by this idea. That she could by such a narrow margin have missed him made her feel dazed with the luck of it, the incredible, extraordinary, wonderful bit of good fortune. She had already determined to change her life. Nothing was going to stop this from happening. She let her mind drift away back to Charles and how he looked and sounded. It was essential to preserve as much as possible for the coming months. Her heart continued to thump madly while she began to think about what it had felt like to be held in his arms, so long ago.

Summer

'We ran into your maman and papa at Zurich Airport,' said Louise. 'We nearly missed our plane.' She'd been impatient, hearing their name echo tinnily through the public address system. *Please proceed immediately to Gate 34. Monsieur and Madame Beauregard. Immediately, please. Your flight is about to depart.*

They'd been the last passengers for the flight, they'd done their usual gallop down the stairs and onto the bus which had ferried them in solitary glory onto the plane for Paris. Familiar though this was from twenty years of being married to the erratic doctor, whose time was not so much kept as heedlessly thrown away, his wife had yet to come to terms with it. Then, when Charles had made casual mention of the foreign exchange, Louise had moaned gently. He knew very well how she hated guests and how nervous they made her. How could he?

'We hardly know these people.'

It had spoilt weeks of the summer, knowing that this was coming up. Having been brought up in a modest household where callers were subjected to intensely formal meals, she always felt that she would have to be on her best behaviour and that her best could never be good enough.

'Oh, I know them very well. English people are not like us. They are very relaxed.'

Charles had said this, or something like it, several more times in the intervening months. 'Her, the wife I know very well. You know it will be pleasant to have another child in the house.' Or, 'It's a big house, they will do whatever they like and you'll see, you'll have less to do, not more.' He'd smile or pat her hand, sounding so considerate, getting his own way. He always did. He had a particular tone of voice which stopped her from arguing.

There was something in him, some force that could not be resisted. She leant forwards and kissed the top of his head, thinking that this was almost the prime characteristic which defined him and it was precisely the factor which made him so very attractive to so many people. The reason, she supposed, for his success.

So. He'd arrived safely. So. Back in England, Amanda sat looking at the phone in the bedroom and waited for her rage to abate. Why had she not strangled her idiot son at birth? Her hands were trembling with annoyance and frustration.

She was staring ahead vacantly. Eventually through the open bathroom door she caught Nicholas's eye; he was well advanced upon his tooth-brushing routine. He liked to gargle with various green liquids and did so pre- and post-brushing. This second gargle would culminate in his singing up and down a scale with the stuff in his mouth and then doing a mega spit, at the end of which he would carefully examine his output for streaks of blood. Recent root canal work had alerted him to the need to preserve that which he had, drilled and filled, but still his. The spit came. The examination was a pass and now he looked at her with a bit of a gleam in his eye, evidently mistaking her interest for, well, interest. Without meeting his eye, Amanda reached for the remote control and flicked on the telly. Motor racing.

'You don't want to watch that.'

'I don't mind, really. I know you enjoy it, darling.'

This expressed precisely how Amanda felt about sex with her husband. Except that she did mind. Actually, if precision were required, it would be more accurate to say that he generally seemed to enjoy it and she almost never did. Once things had been different, but now they weren't and she always had minded and always would.

'You are sweet.' Kiss, kiss. His breath smelt of spearmint. He lay beside her with the earphones on, in order not to miss a single roar or whine as the bloody cars throttled up or down or did whatever they did and Amanda pretended to read her book. She was working out when she could call France tomorrow and making a mental check list of the questions she needed to ask to establish precisely when Charles might be in the house alone. Just what she would say to him she didn't know. It would be sufficient to hear his voice. She would have been very happy to hear him recite the phone book, indeed just listening to him breathe would be a fine, sweet pleasure. To feel his breath against her face, now that would be the summit of desires. To feel his cheek against hers. To feel.

Her imagination leapt nimbly on to other desires. Desire didn't begin to cover it. This was lust and it was unmanageable. It was so powerful a force that it leapfrogged all the usual fidelity and loyalty stuff that got in the way of this sort of thing, it lightly jumped every hurdle to do with her own physical two-children's worth of sag, those inhibiting lumps and bumps. Achingly strong, her lust even flattened those reasonable, indeed essential worries about the consequences. She didn't care. Whatever happened, it was worth it. Amanda was not beautiful but knew that he would find her so, that she would be so. He was beautiful to her. Her hubris was such that she even knew that it was impossible that she could feel such desire and Charles feel nothing. He felt what she did; that much was certain.

She closed her eyes. She lay very quietly and thought about Charles. There was so much to consider that she would ration him, she'd start with neutral territory. There was the unusually elegant way his ears slid onto his altogether delightful head with two tiny, lovable creases. Then there was the strip of velvet skin which ran behind those ears. She dwelt in some detail on Charles's honey-coloured skin and tried very hard to remember how it tasted and how it might be both sweet and slightly salty. That was the place to start tasting him, the tender flesh just near the nape of the neck. She thought about the particular timbre of his voice, so gentle and so sexy with resonances which shook her from head to toe. His mouth, the humorous curve to it.

With eyes shut tight, she began to imagine his body. This game involved a careful invocation of memory and imagination, thinking carefully about what she knew and remembered and then about how it would feel to stroke him and where, exactly, she might choose to start. So many places to start, only one to finish. She would not yet permit herself to think so far ahead, she would not touch him until near the end. Amanda sighed.

No, to begin with, she would lie next to him, very very quietly, and for a long time they would kiss, they would deliberately prolong the sweet agony of waiting, though the imagined taste of him pulsed through her entire body.

Resisting the urge to touch herself, Amanda found that the now imagined touch of his bare flesh was enough, more than enough to make her quite giddy. Now came the speculation as to which particular set of reciprocal nerve endings he might choose to start with.

The game was arousing and dangerous and completely addictive. Amanda breathed in and out, to still her pounding heart, which continued its painful thump. She felt a great throb of heat rolling off her body and realised with astonishment that just thinking about this man was nearly sufficient to bring her to the point of orgasm. Not now – not yet. She would resist, until she was alone.

Nicholas shifted. This ridiculous state of arousal was somehow affecting her husband. She took another deep breath and froze. His hand reached under the covers.

'Darling,' he said in a tone of pleasurable surprise. The lust she felt for the Frenchman was about to benefit an astonished Nicholas whose exploratory finger touching her thigh felt an exceptional pulse of heat and lifted in disbelief, only to return, to rise, one centimetre at a time, delicately to penetrate its rippling source. She heard herself let out the long-held breath. Her disloyal body could not prevent its response and so with eyes tight shut she succumbed and thought and felt only Charles.

Hilary and Michèle were sitting at the old wooden table in the orchard staring at the stars and the moon over the château and waiting for Charles to bring out the coffee. Hilary was intoxicated. There was the wine, of course, but over and above that the night and the place and the ravishing Michèle. She was giving him that thoughtful look again, the one that brought back to mind the idiocies he had uttered at the station. These were the kind of heat-seeking missiles which were bound to home back in on him sooner or later. Hers was also the sort of look which made any number of fresh idiocies inevitable if Charles didn't get a move on.

Michèle leant forward and put her hand on his arm and half whispered with her warm breath into his ear with an assurance that was far, far older than her sixteen years. The touch of her hand throbbed through his entire body.

'Hilary,' she said. 'Will you do something for me?'

'Yes, of course, anything.' He swallowed. Battalions of messengers were racing up and down his body letting all the other nerve endings know that something was going on in the arm region and that there was a warm mouth very very close to his ear and a whole warm, silky gorgeous girl attached to it.

'I want you to pretend something, that we are having a little romance. You know. Just for fun and to fool the parents?'

Hilary nodded while he sought words which would handle the situation and enable him to deal with this shameless and totally acceptable advance without issuing wild whoops or war cries. Call this a favour? Thank you, God. He was in heaven.

Bursts of Gilbert and Sullivan erupted at intervals from Nicholas's shower. He had left the bathroom door open. Amanda, passing grimly with a pile of towels, saw her husband throw back his head and let the water run down his face while he carefully soaped and re-soaped all orifices. Nothing like a clean man. Nothing like a happy chappie. Nothing quite like an accredited red hot lover on a glorious summer Saturday morning, who would soon come trilling downstairs and give wife a special resounding and above all self-congratulatory kiss over the muesli. Would he wink? Yes, she rather thought he would.

Amanda had that night experienced something closer to real passion than she had felt in years. She felt very dark, both replete and sexually unsatisfied. She lusted, oh unreasonably, for Charles. Desire had woken her early that morning as it did every morning, beaming in with the dawn. Not fair, not right, when it also kept her awake at night. She was dreadfully tired, yet this combination of sensations was interestingly strange. I think I hate him, Amanda thought, and I'm alive. I've not been alive for years. She leant against the door of the airing cupboard and Nicholas, descending in his bathrobe, saw her standing there and winked.

'Love you,' he said and wife, quite unable to frame any kind of reply, smiled.

Down the path they wandered in the direction of the village, hand in hand, Hilary and this girl, who fitted him so well. Their arms swung to the same rhythm, she was the perfect height, as she was the perfect every-glory-be-everything. As soon as they were out of sight of the house, Hilary would make a move. The big tree, that was the place.

'Mm, Michèle, wait,' he muttered. Baise-moi, he had discovered, meant fuck me. Not that that idea was intrinsically bad, but it lacked subtlety. A person could by stages work up to that same excellent idea. But as soon as he got within striking distance of that delicious, that adorable, that incredible mouth she sprang away like a terrified gazelle. For Christ's sake. He wasn't going to rape her. One kiss. Goddamit. Romance included kisses, right? She had kissed him two days ago with thoroughness, with every appearance of pleasure.

Breathing heavily, Hilary tried to work out what it was he was doing that was so terribly wrong. People kissed in France, it wasn't contrary to the Napoleonic Code. The village was full of rustic snoggers, they were at it, open-mouthed, slobbering each other like expiring carp in the aptly named Café Necker in the village square. While he, the chosen one, didn't even get to give her the sort of kiss she got from Mummy.

'Tu viens?' she said, skipping merrily ahead. It made no sense. If he was so repellant, why did she grab his hand at every opportunity? This, it had to be remembered, was a girl given to removing her bra in order to sunbathe in full view of total strangers with a devastating effect upon his anatomy. He wasn't going to be able to spend the rest of his time here lying on his front which was already noticeably paler than his back. He was permanently aroused and ludicrously frustrated, oh, but totally bewitched.

She took his hand again. The back of his hand grazed her jean-clad thigh. OK. No need to think, after all. He concentrated on making this happen again. His knuckle, sensitised, was a new erotic zone.

A toot, at the bottom of the drive, signalled Charles in the old jalopy, off on his rounds. Were they coming with him? Hilary looked at Michèle. He didn't have a brain or anything like that. Whatever she wanted, they did. She nodded at her father so they both got in and then at the last minute Michèle leapt out. Ah, she had forgotten – shopping for Mummy. You go, Hilary. She blew him a kiss and his head turned, a sunflower revolving on its stalk, seeking its sun. He watched her in the rearview window for as long as he could.

As Charles roared about the countryside, he sang old Prévert and Brassens ballads extremely loudly. Hilary was picking up the odd phrase and now and then joined in. They both enjoyed this. Occasionally Charles would put his arms round Hilary and hug him and this, to Hilary's amazement, was something he didn't mind. He'd never been hugged or touched by a man before. Charles smelt wonderful, of strong tobacco and a faint hint of aftershave and clean skin with a kind of after-hint of Louise and the teeniest trace of Michèle and it was perfectly obvious that he wasn't feeling him up. He didn't have designs on Hilary, unlike the multitude which Hilary had on his daughter. Would Michèle let him just hug her like that, lean up against a tree perhaps and just lightly feel the delicious length of her – hmm, if he didn't try to kiss, but just felt? Hilary, closing his eyes to think a bit more about this one, was startled by a roar in his ear. Charles was singing again.

This man, so utterly at ease in his own skin, had a mission to frighten passengers out of theirs. Hilary gripped the dashboard as the doctor once more overtook on a bend and at reckless speed, sustaining one high, cracked note for the duration of the adventure. Charles seemed to be addicted to danger or, rather, to running risks in everything that he did. These relaxed him to about the same degree that they tensed Hilary up.

They now turned at fairly unreasonable speed and with some protest from the tyres into a long unmade road which led up a thickly wooded hill to the modern house of the elderly Demoiselles Dupont. They had a farm but the house, a modest two-storey building sitting on a little hillock with a garage beside it, was pretending to be a suburban house. Fancy wrought-iron railings separated the garden from the animals and hens and stuff beyond, which were all housed in the kind of romantic barns and outhouses that any Brit would have chosen to make into the house.

Charles was there to cut their corns for the two elderly ladies. The elder of the two, the one with the quivering neck, came on tippy-toes to open the front door, walking along a long snake of towel which led from the front door into the salon. There, Hilary was introduced to the second one, who was dressed just the same and was distinguishable from the first only in being less wobbly and in smiling more. He had come to like the way you were properly introduced and shook hands with people in France and they said something polite to you (often about the English weather and how you weren't missing it, ha, ha) unlike the British system of generally not bothering and pretending the other person didn't exist or, if you ignored them, would go away.

The ladies sat down on their green brocade sofa waiting and waggling their four parchment-coloured feet. The towel they had laid out beforehand was exactly the same colour as their flesh. Charles Beauregard was ransacking the battered old case for the tools of his craft, failing to find a suitable implement in its capacious depths. They knew their man. Number one sister smiled flirtatiously and whipped back a green cloth and there, laid out ready, was a whole battery of clippers and parers. Now, as one, they lifted their four feet onto a special bolster.

Hilary, once he had got the idea of what this little operation involved, let his attention stray and stood at the window watching through the railings a cockerel floating about the yard in the back and generally hassling the hens which were scratching away in their run. He was thinking about life and the universe, which mostly meant thinking about Michèle. The cockerel chased a nice fat hen up the run into the hen house. Good luck, mate, thought Hilary. You and me both. But the bird was too stupid to enter the hen house though Hilary at the window mentally egged it on. If the bird made it, so would he. The dumb cockerel just stood there.

Charles sat on a little footstool in front of the first mademoiselle and massaged her foot while she whispered into his ear and the second mademoiselle said four or five times that the chiropodist did not have his gentle touch. Then the doctor accompanied the two mesdemoiselles into their bedroom for an examination of whatever else might need looking at. Though he was never summoned for anything other than feet, Charles had implied that there was often some other, more delicate service to be rendered which, unlike corns, could not be mentioned over the phone.

Since he never produced a bill, for these services Charles was rewarded with a fine old bottle of Armagnac from les caves of Papa Dupont. He seemed loath to take it, but they went on insisting. Another rummage in the bag produced his packet of fags and his matches and he lit up and they all had a little drink which was generally the lethally strong fortified wine everybody offered as standard issue to round off the doctor's visit. If you were still alive and could drink this, then you'd make it. The demoiselles beamed and everybody clinked glasses and said 'Cheeyars' as a little compliment to Hilary and he said 'Salut' and 'A la vôtre'.

'My old friend Professor Vigne-Laval taught me to drink. Surgical spirit – bouf! Strong. Some doctors drink before the patient comes, some afterwards; he said you're a good doctor when you can drink with them,' and Charles winked broadly in Hilary's direction and the ladies giggled. This professor was the genius and mentor who had also taught Charles how to drive and drink and how to bed women, possibly all three pleasures simultaneously, and he'd supplied a bon mot for every one.

'OK,' he said, back in the car as they rolled up the windows to keep the dust out. 'Now we will have a little swim on the way back. Hilary,' always pronounced Eelaree, 'when I look at you, I think you could have been my son.'

This was the most intimate thing Charles had yet said and so close to what Hilary was thinking that it was eerie. He didn't know how to reply. It was a perfect day and the river, with its series of deep places and little beachy spots, deliciously cold. They parked the car on the road and walked to a place where Charles said nobody came and there lay in the shallows and talked. It was a fisherman's paradise. Hilary watched a shoal of small brown fish dart around inches from where he lay. Charles interlaced his fingers and caught one for an instant before letting it dart off to join its fellows. For such a massive man, with a substantial belly and a great bull's neck attaching the big head to the torso, he was very gentle, exact in all his movements. He knew when to be silent and when to sing. Everything was simple for him.

'I don't always like my father,' Hilary found himself saying. 'I mean I respect him and all that and I suppose I love him but he never lets you forget who's the boss. He has to win, that's his problem.'

'C'est toujours comme ça – all men have to win,' said Charles, for that was how they were made. His father was a good man, Amanda had told him so.

After that they swam in deeper places. Hilary was a natural athlete and Charles hopelessly unfit but gifted with brute strength. Resting naked on the bank beside that great mass of flesh, Hilary felt very young. Charles smoked, naturally, and wore his most serious face.

'Ta maman chose him as a father for you, this fine doctor, Hilary. She could have had any man. She wouldn't look at me, no, I begged her, but she would not let me give her a baby.'

Hilary tried to speak, producing a squawk which came out as a gurgling 'Hurhahmmmaaaaagh?'

'How do you think a woman like that gets to know a man like me? Just drinking coffee in the coffee bar?'

'But you're not like that – she's not like you – you're completely different. Mum's not that sort of woman.' He started again. 'Look, I hear what you're saying but believe me you're completely wrong. My mother is – is – très comme il faut.'

'Amanda?' Now Charles simply roared with laughter, so much so that his cigarette butt shot out of his mouth and buried itself in the undergrowth, a fire hazard which then had to be recovered. While he found it, he afforded Hilary a disconcertingly frank view of his hairy buttocks and balls hanging down – the same view, perhaps, that his mother had enjoyed? No, Hilary couldn't believe it. For Christ's sake.

In England, the conventional mother crept furtively towards the telephone.

The Lennox's house in Sussex was agreed to be absolutely charming, a perfect little Queen Anne house surrounded by lovely gardens. The manicured lawns were the pride of Nicholas Lennox, who at this moment was singing a Gilbert and Sullivan aria extremely loudly as he drove the motor mower back and forth. Every now and then he glanced over his shoulder to admire the newly minted velvet stripe. Amanda could see him through the narrow window in the hallway as she lifted the telephone.

A couple of feet away and very well hidden from both his parents crouched nine-year-old Edward Lennox, cradling a large water gun. Amanda, as she dialled, smoothed her hair. There was a series of clicks and stutters and then a considerable pause before she heard the ringing tone. She cleared her throat several times.

In the house on the hill, a woman picked up the phone.

'Oui, bonjour?' This was Madame Moulins the cleaning lady.

'Bonjour, hello, ici Madame Lennox. Bonjour, Madame Beauregard.' There was a pause, then the woman at the other end said something quite rapidly which seemed to imply that she was not Madame Beauregard, but that she would fetch her. Or so Amanda assumed.

'Ne quittez pas' meant don't hang up. These were the only words she could be quite sure of understanding. So she stood there, staring out of the window, saying 'Shit, shit, shit' to herself, over and over again. Why was it so hard to get through to him? All day she had thought about the timing of the call and planned in her head what she could say. So many useless days when she had not heard his voice.

At this moment, young Ed leapt out of the viburnum hedge in his Ninja turtle fighting stance and blasted his father in the face with a powerful jet. The machine swerved sharply, destroying the beautiful symmetry of the lawn.

Amanda, hearing Nicholas shouting but missing the cause of such fury, was shocked by the sudden gargoyle looming of her husband's wet and hysterical face which came from nowhere to rage and gibber at the window. At this nightmarish vision of uxorial revenge, she leapt up and in her guilt dropped the receiver which swung and banged backwards and forwards against the hall table.

Pointing and frothing, Nicholas rushed by. Amanda ran to the front door where the cause of the commotion and the full extent of the carnage upon the lawn became all too clear. Nicholas continued to chase after – and fail to catch – his jubilant, dancing demon son. As he went, Eddie was laughing fit to bust, flailing one hand over his head and shrieking 'Ex-ter-min-ate' over and over again. This was his favourite way of mocking his father's authority. Amanda found herself pacing forwards and backwards at the front door in impotent rage. It took a while before she – or they – quite realised that she was screaming 'You're destroying me' over and over again. Amanda knew it only when Nicholas came up to her and took hold of her shoulders.

In France, Marie Moulins shuffled back to the phone, picked it up, shook it, then shouted at it. 'Oui, oui, Madame?' she bellowed a number of times. She continued to repeat this louder and louder before finally putting down the phone with a shake of her head.

On the river bank, Charles shook his head at Hilary.

'C'est ça,' he said, laughing. 'So you think a woman like your mother doesn't fuck?'

2

Louise carried in the usual plate of eggs with swimmy yolks alongside thick slices of bacon and as Hilary thanked her he wondered if she'd still smile at him so nicely if she knew Charles had slept with his mother. Look at these prisoners of the kitchen. That these women had been young once and had experienced the passions he did was both obvious and grotesque when the object of those passions sat in front of you, dipping a vast tartine into a big bowl of coffee and shoving the sodden brown mass into his gob. And was his mother intending to relive the experience? If she'd had it? He swallowed, hard. Please. He was overreacting. He peppered the first egg.

'Chérie,' Louise said to her daughter, 'don't go out just yet, the Dutroncs are calling.'

'He's so boring. Oh, all right,' and sulkily Michèle snatched another roll, buttered it on the wing. Out she marched, bowl of coffee in one hand, bread in the other, opening the door, oh yes, with her hips, the most delicious roll of all.

'You know, for a woman her age, my mother is very shy.' They hung around the orchard. 'Is your mother shy?'

'Yes. No.' When he was twelve she'd beaten off a big black dog that had bitten him by hitting the snarling beast with her hands. Then she'd gone into the road and stopped a passing car for help, insisting that the driver take them to a hospital. He couldn't even begin to explain her.

Two heads came a bob-bob-bobbing past the apple trees. Michèle's warm breath on his cheek, whispering that Monsieur Dutronc was the mayor. 'He is the owner of the ironmonger's down the hill and very old. You watch, how he holds the hand of his wife all the time. You see, she is his new wife. Come on, then,' and she pulled him gently by the hand.

In the salon, Hilary shook hands with two small gnarled folk with almost identical pointy ears and smiling brown faces. They could have been twins. He settled down for the statutory hour of sweet nothings and the old chap's visit to London in 1934 or was it 1949 and/or his membership of the Résistance. Most of France had belonged, well, many in the neighbourhood – well, certainly in this village. Bravely Dutronc upheld the honour of his people vis-à-vis the English. Of course one could not speak with certainty of the newcomers and the mayor shook his head sadly. Michèle winked at Hilary.

'Monsieur Albert?' she said and Louise tutted and Dutronc spread his hands as if to say, who knows? He had a way of pausing before he spoke as though he was thinking very hard about the reply and as though it would be worth waiting for.

'Who knows?' he said at last, with the air of a sage. 'About Monsieur Albert – who knows?' So who was Monsieur Albert?

Madame Dutronc, whose manner reminded him of those nodding dogs with rigid bodies you got in cars, gazed with brimming eyes of love at her husband while keeping stumm herself. Louise disappeared to the kitchen, abandoning them. There was a very long silence. Hilary cleared his throat.

'Vous avez beaucoup souffert,' he said, 'dans la guerre.'

Madame nodded and smiled. Behind her back, Michèle cast her eyes to the heavens and suppressed her laughter.

'Ah,' said Dutronc. 'Ah . . .' There was a long silence. 'Non. Non . . . J'étais jeune,' and he squeezed his wife's hand. Young people did not, could not suffer. That was for the old. She brimmed and nodded. Hilary had noticed this sort of thing before. That was how they thought, in vague generalisations. The language lent itself to a sort of charming blither. La vie est pour vivre, they would say – la jeunesse, ah, long pause, c'est pour les jeunes.

The little something came back and proved to be a fortified wine and coffee, black and very strong with lots of sugar lumps. Routine dictated that Louise would offer round prettified plates of petits fours which were to be admired rather than eaten. These, duly admired and politely refused, circled while they went on to discuss the weather in England (very bad) and people's babies (so ugly nowadays) and what French republicans thought of the Queen (remarkably little) – subjects on which Hilary was evenly ill-informed. Monsieur Dutronc paused and laboured through his hour, determined to show them all what a man of the world he was.

After they'd all embraced the air four times and the old couple had trotted off, Hilary discovered that this was the cut and thrust of politics, petits fours style. The elections for mayor were imminent and Dutronc was counting on the Beauregards. This visit affirmed as much. Dutronc represented the old guard, the villagers of yore, among whom the doctor and his family held an honorary position. Representing those unreliable and by implication collabo-rationist newcomers was the pharmacist and opposition candidate, the selfsame Monsieur Albert.

Only half an hour later the petits fours recirculated. The opposition candidate so far forgot himself and the etiquette of canvassing as to snaffle up the entire plateful of goodies as though he were starving. Monsieur Albert was a pharmacist but his father had been a communist and worked on the railways all his life and had always worn a jumper and scarf hand-knitted by his wife. Jean-Jacques was passionate about the terrible mistake his father had made. In old age he had had to survive on almost no pension while his sharper workmates all got promotion and were better off and index-linked, though less clever than he. He had recanted, but too late. To live nearly your whole life according to a false belief was bad enough, but to realise it was tragic. Hilary, agreeing, preferred this man of passion to the old bloke with the hippy-happy smile and the charisma bypass, even if he did have three first names and an absurdly fluffy wife with the yet more ridiculous name of Héloïse.

'I'd go for him,' he said when he'd got Michèle on her own. 'He's got some oomph in him.'

Michèle knew better. 'He's nouveau riche and Papa says he has ambitions because he has no children,' she said dismissively. 'Everyone knows it's Héloïse who makes the money. People who like my father won't want to vote for him.' This was illogical, quite barmy.

'You mean people prefer the old one with a new wife?'

'Of course. And the remarriage business, you know, it helps.'

'What happened to Dutronc's first wife?'

'Madame Dutronc picked and fried a basket of poisonous mushrooms and ate them – with butter and herbs. Very fat and greedy she was, she ate them all on her own. Nobody liked la prétensieuse. Elle se donnait des airs. Dead in twelve minutes. Six weeks later he married the other one. They love each other like crazy.'

And people want to vote for him after that?'

'Why not? You don't get it. Dutronc is what he is. But Jean-Jacques creeps around being nice to everyone. But really we all know he just likes money. It is a big business, you see, the sale of drugs. That's why he comes courting Papa, because he doesn't prescribe drugs so often. So really, Jean-Jacques can't stand him.'

And the mayor doesn't like money, then?'

'Bouf,' he loved that sound, the expelled hot air. 'Of course he does. But he isn't a hypocrite about it. Come on. Let's go to the village.'

Again, Michèle took his hand. Hilary had plans. These centred on a particular segment of the drive which just took them out of view of the house. Every inch of gravel was as familiar to him as his own house, if not more so. Here any number of rich emotions had been expended, here more had happened in four days than in a lifetime in Sussex. So at the big tree, on cue, he took Michèle in his arms and sort of leant with her against it for a glorious, giddy instant, delicately, resisting the urge to lean too hard and definitely he should not grind his pelvis into hers.

For four seconds this warm, lovely creature allowed him to hold her in his arms and he felt the whole length of her lightly touching him. Then Michèle chuckled and did her usual trick of shoving him off. She hopped off ahead, laughing and skipping. As though she hadn't a care in the world. If lust could be said to grind a person down, then he was just a small heap of pulverised ash at her feet, a molehill attached to a giant, painfully throbbing and permanently erect member. Sighing, the legs attached to the organ walked it down the hill. He could watch her for ever, from any angle, even the way the little bit of ankle he could see between the jeans and the shoe was made. The extraordinary elegance of those bones deserved study.

Louise watched her daughter and Hilary drift past the window and then set off down the drive hand in hand and, without thinking, remarked to Madame Moulins how charming the young couple was. Marie, who was on her hands and knees scrubbing the flagstones, now rose panting and groaning to her haunches, where she remained, breathing heavily, for ten or twenty seconds. From this position she rose slowly, levering herself up with both hands against the kitchen dresser.

Louise, who knew what was coming, wished she had bitten her tongue. Marie would hang her head as if in contemplation of those big raw fingers, slack with exhaustion, for a further ten or fifteen seconds. Then, wiping her hands on the towel that she wore permanently slung round her right shoulder, she would lumber to the window. By the time she got there, the young couple would be long gone. So she would give her employer one of her special seemingly blank but actually faintly accusatory looks and, instead of returning to her former and entirely self-imposed labour of cleaning the floor by hand (any number of long-handled implements had been provided for this purpose), would need to have a glass of water and a bit of a sit-down and a moan about her legs. This, generally, was accompanied by such suggestions as sit down, Madame, you have a rest, don't you worry, I'll just catch my breath. Why am I so stupid, thought Louise. Why don't I know when to be quiet?

As Marie slowly sipped the water, Louise would offer her coffee or a tisane. Marie would refuse with loathing. She was there to work, that was the implication. Yet she would always sit down and have lunch with the family, managing to put away each course, not refusing second helpings and even – for it would never do to leave that little bit – greedily polishing off all the leftovers as she did the dishes afterwards. The plates were scoured before they got near the water. This disgusted the more abstemious Louise.

And then it occasionally happened that later in the

afternoon Marie would have one of her funny turns and need to sit down and naturally Louise would offer to make tea or a tisane and somehow over the years it had become a matter of course that Madame would offer Marie a little something. Marie always demurred at length but sometimes after a lot of persuasion might eat a little piece of tarte aux pommes, say. She ate very slowly, needing like a child to be urged for each mouthful. In this martyred manner she always managed to finish every last morsel offered, infuriating Louise who had insisted that she take it. She was as greedy as Louise was inconsistent.

All afternoon Louise danced around her, torn between the desire to get rid of her and the feeling that she ought to get better value for money. Sometimes, in her haste to see the back of Marie, Louise would find herself running her down to the village in her little car. Every time, she could not help noticing the old plastic carrier bag that had been coming up the hill empty and going down full for years. She'd never looked in it; she had her pride, after all. And it was no good, no good at all Charles saying that she should simply not give her lunch or, more contentiously, sack Marie. Charles didn't understand that, tedious and indeed horrible though she was, Marie was utterly reliable and always came and needed the work. How could Louise, with all her blessings, sack a horrible fat old woman who was poor, whom she disliked and whom nobody else would employ?

Slowly Marie sat down, breathing heavily, looking down at her fat fingers. The whole thing now followed its allotted course. Today, however, Marie was in a particularly vituperative mood. It couldn't be the legs, though they were bad enough. Whenever she felt more than usually put upon, Louise thought about how dreadful it would be to have been born with such shapeless tree-trunk legs and to have to clean as Marie did. Sometimes her own slim, long legs could reconcile her to the tyrant of her kitchen when nothing else could. Louise sighed. Ten long years since she'd first looked at Marie's legs and for their sake excused the inexcusable.

Over the sip of water, Marie was making a snuffling noise. That was her way of expressing derision. 'Why do you permit it, Madame? An English boy. Everybody knows about the English.'

Louise said nothing. It was so stupid, to try to reply to something as pathetic as this. It wasn't as if she cared what this stupid woman thought. Only a complete idiot would listen.

'Ah, poor Madame, you smile but of course things are far from easy for you,' said Marie, smiling herself with false sympathy, 'How does even the most careful maman protect a young girl like Michèle, one with her, you know, her . . . well, and then to have a young man like that right here in the house.' She shook her head knowledgeably and clucked and sighed and Louise drew a long breath at the cunning of this double, no, triple insult.

'Oh no, Marie, you're joking. I mean to say, really, you can't say these things.' Louise turned on her heel and went out of the room. Seconds later (she could be nimble when she scented blood) Marie heaved into the hallway ready for battle and snuffling louder than ever, her hands crossed on her substantial chest in a praying position.

'If only you knew all that I know, Madame,' she said rapidly. 'But the good Lord has spared you much, indeed he has.' Her bosom heaved, she made a sign of the cross. Louise paused, turned, looked at her.

'All that you know? What exactly do you mean?' she said sharply. Mention of the divinity made her nervous. 'What do you know?'

'I – I?' said Marie, whom injured innocence ill fitted,

starting to wheeze as prelude no doubt to one of her little attacks. 'I? What should I mean?'

Louise ground her teeth. At moments like these she understood how easily a person could chop up another person with an axe. A good sharp butcher's knife would do it, though it might be more enjoyable to run that person over with one's little car, back and forth on the gravel, reversing over the silly old fat head until it popped.

Hilary understood nothing. Not even at the hour of the apéritif when much Frenchness explained itself, in vino veritas. Half an hour before dinner, when for two hours, nothing had been consumed, Charles would emerge and do his stuff with a bottle of cassis or fraises des bois and some white wine or champagne, depending on the general mood. He drank a lot without ever getting drunk. Two or three glasses before dinner, and plenty more with it and brandy or whisky afterwards, a little digestif to settle the stomach. Coffee came with plenty of sugar cubes and perhaps one might have a little je-ne-sais-quoi in the marron glacé line. Hilary, nothing loath, stuffed his face from dawn to dusk.

Why weren't they porkers? Michèle tucked in as did Louise and they both had more curves than the Grand Corniche and not an inch of excess. That old saw about living to eat held full sway in this household. I eat, therefore I am. Full intellectual vigour was applied to the discussion of what to have and where to buy it, hours went on cooking and serving it, clearing up and starting again and the whole point was that it all had to be fresh every day, or else honour wasn't satisfied.

When, thinking to emulate Charles, Hilary expressed some interest in what they were having for dinner, Louise took him into the kitchen. There for ten minutes she explained precisely how to bone and stuff a duck with full mime effects, gesturing around and skewering an imaginary quacker.

The thing about Louise was that she just didn't have that mechanism which told you when people were making a polite inquiry and when they were really seriously needing to know the precise number of pine kernels you crushed in a basin with how many leaves of tarragon. She also unnerved Hilary by looking directly into his eyes in a very serious way, as though she genuinely cared what he said or thought and was very possibly committing his words to memory. These in his experience were the well-known signs of off-your-trolleydom, particularly the female sort and particularly unnerving when the face staring at yours was as lovely as hers still was.

Yes, Louise was very, very watchable, particularly in the kitchen and he much preferred her in her big butcher's pinny tied up round the waist nice and tight with a little bow in front to the way she was when got up in one of the immaculate silk numbers. There was something quite interestingly erotic about Louise palpating a chicken breast or coming across the kitchen towards you with a handful of liver dripping through her fingers. It was a treat to see her faintly flushed and daubed with flour with a little wisp of hair escaping at the nape of her neck, Louise nicely mussed with her hands deep in a bowl doing a bit of pastry-crumbling or whatever. Cooking was a sensual art, no doubt about it. In her case there was just a shorter than usual hop from kitchen to boudoir, from stew pot to sex pot. Lucky old Charles, eh?

Mentally, though, he couldn't quite get her straight. In other respects she wasn't afflicted. Unlike his parents' pals, she never volunteered views on how much bigger he would or wouldn't be or on what it felt like to be young/old/growing up/past it, with it/having it/not having it. Nor did she find herself hilariously entertaining, hee-hawing at her own jokes. She didn't do anything really in the joke line. Charles was the fun and games merchant. Louise was pretty quiet, not speaking except when spoken to. She didn't lecture him either, except when he made the mistake of asking about something – and then, unlike his mother who could boomerang from dirty smalls and A level revision round AIDS and back to car borrowing and room tidying in one swoop, she stuck to the subject.

Louise was refreshingly indifferent to whether or not he washed or had washing or needed anything, nor did she ever expect him to nip down to the village for a pint of milk or a newspaper. She seemed to expect nothing at all from him and to be absolutely thrilled whenever she got a bit of praise. When you thought about it, she was remarkable. Just like her daughter.

'One day you will be old, Hilary. Même toi. You see these old fools, they disapprove of everything, but it's just that they have forgotten. Many of them never had any fun anyway, poor salauds. They haven't lived at all and now they're dead above the neck and below the waist. What's life without passion? Always play for high stakes. Live on the edge. Your mother, now, she completely understood that,' and he shook his head remembering and looking with pity at the old guys who hung about the place. What did he remember, exactly?

Charles had taken Hilary off for the afternoon to play boules. They stood in a shady bit of dust, throwing their balls around. Charles never stopped going on about his feelings. What a combination that'd make: the body of Michèle and the emotions of Charles. Hilary told himself that he couldn't seriously be thinking what he was. No. Well, he could, but not at those moments when Charles would keep going on about Amanda.

Hilary was concentrating on trying to discover exactly

what it was she and Charles had got up to all those years ago. The finer part of him didn't want to know, but there was a pushier, lower part which was very nosy. That part had decided that their goings-on – if they had gone on – presaged him and Michèle having some. Of course his mother had slept with men. Twice. She had two sons, didn't she? Obviously, there had been some sort of friendship with Charles. Some sort of something. There was no hard evidence. Let's just rephrase that, yes? No proof that it had included sexual intercourse. Sexual intercourse was high on his personal agenda. Why should his mother have been any different? Because most girls, nice girls, pretended that they were?

'Charles,' he said, 'where exactly was it that you met Mum?'

'In hospital, of course. Didn't she tell you?'

'Sure, sure, of course she did. It's just that some of the details have slipped my mind.'

Charles ambled up to the end of the boules ground, examined Hilary's ball, paced back slowly. His mother had told him nothing.

'She was so sexy, it was unbelievable, it took your breath away. Tu comprends?' He fumbled for a cigarette, lit it, exhaled slowly. Hilary smiled and nodded. He could not imagine it.

'Oui,' he said.

'I wonder if you really know what I mean. Women, you see, in some ways are profoundly unknowable. So much is intuitive. Women experience real pain, mental and physical in childbirth, for example, more than a man has in a lifetime and they can be so strong. I've seen them do incredible things. But in other ways they are hard to understand. When I touch a person, with my hands, like this,' and he laid both hands on Hilary's shoulders and pressed down on them, firm and hard, so that it almost but didn't quite hurt, 'I know whether they are lying or not. I can tell you from touching a person if they are really sick or not, if it is serious. The soul and body are linked, you see. Things like cancer, you can feel the heat through the flesh, man or woman. But mentally – ah, it is very different. When I look into a man's eyes, I generally know what he thinks, and he with me – but a woman?' He stared into Hilary's eyes and Hilary, dazed, stared back.

Caution had long since given way to a reckless abandonment of care. Amanda, ruled by needs she had neither the desire nor the ability to control, scarcely waited for Nicholas to go upstairs before she lifted the telephone to call France. Let him listen, she thought. Let him think whatever he thinks. Just leave me alone. Nothing Nicholas might say or do could matter.

Engaged. She put it down. Try again in a minute. Nicholas came down, went into the garden and sank into a deckchair. He waved to her to come out. She waved back and made some gesture, designed to imply that she had something to do. He lay back and closed his eyes. Something stirred. She looked at his upturned face, drinking in the sunlight with a strong sense of déjà vu. There had been a day like this. She closed her eyes to think – and then she had it. Fifteen years ago a patient had died on the operating table and Nicholas had come home for the bank holiday weekend and lain in the sun like this.

She had treated him as a convalescent, brought out cups of tea, had remained in the dark of the kitchen with Hilary teething and fretful, shushing him so his father could rest in the brightness outside, from which they were excluded. Nicholas was in pain and she thumped pieces of Play-Doh and boiled kettles and stole out to hang nappies on the line and stood, just as she was doing now, to watch the man outside. There was one helpless little creature pulling at her. Here's the train with the eggie on it, down the little red tunnel we go. For Nicholas wanted to give up. He wanted to jack in the career, the house, go away, be something different. She had said all the obvious things. She told him that he saved lives, that his training would be wasted, that he was needed and so on. Silently she was screaming: what about me? One of them had to be a surgeon, or everything she had chosen was a waste of time. Yet this never occurred to him. So, in her bitterness, she said nothing. Not then, not later when he went back to work quite normally without any further discussion, for she was frightened to give him the slightest opening. Silently, the train continued down the track and there was no knowing what other direction it would have taken or where else it might have ended up.

Amanda moved through the days in a kind of dream state, conscious of how strange it was that to the outside she appeared to be the same. Nicholas had noticed nothing different about her, nor would he while dinners appeared as usual. If anything, she was more attentive than usual, inquiring about his work and showing an unprecedented interest in his tedious college of physicians politickings. She wanted him to talk so she could let her mind drift to Charles. Time alone, that was the precious thing she yearned for, time to sit and think. Perhaps she was a better wife to him now than before. Perhaps being disconnected was the secret of happiness in marriage and everybody knew it but her. Every day a new secret seemed to reveal itself in her private consciousness. She noticed the looks people gave each other, felt the meanings behind words.

It was Ed, whom she had put down as intrinsically incapable of noticing anything outside his own, highly selfish, personal boyworld, who gave her pause. 'There's something different about you, Mum,' he'd said in a thoughtful manner. 'I know. You're not telling me off so much.'

Amanda saw that this was true. She was so filled with her inner, secret life that she didn't have the time to feel as annoyed as she had before, things had a new perspective. So that was how spies managed. It was perfectly possible to lead a double life, providing you kept it all in your head and told nobody anything. Silly little wife with her dull moments and her chores was good at protecting Amanda that way.

The phone rang only twice before a female voice answered. Amanda asked to speak to Charles. 'C'est Madame Lennox,' she said.

'Oh, what a pity,' the voice said brightly. It was Michèle. Her father and Hilary, she said, were out playing boules. Amanda sighed heavily, said goodbye, put the phone down and turned with leaden tread back to the kitchen where there was, as ever, dinner to cook, and where she snapped a tea towel at a fly and got it, for a change.

'Boules-shit,' she said.

Louise was in a temper, she paced up and down in front of her dressing table. As she took off her clothes and creamed her face, she was replaying the scene for Charles's benefit.

'Your problem is that you have no problems,' said Charles in his weary voice. This infuriated Louise.

'Of course,' she said snappily. 'I of course have no problems, know nothing and am nobody. Why should anybody care? Why should the daughter of a hairdresser from Rennes even aspire to know anything? Evidently even a stupid country woman knows more than me about everything, including my house and my daughter and has better manners. And is perfect in every way.' She started to brush her hair with violent strokes. Charles groaned. She rounded on him.

'Life is very easy for you. You have a position in society. You don't have to get excited about stupid women, you can keep your famous calm. You and your beloved Professor Vigne–Laval have all the best lines. But even an ignorant country woman is permitted to tell your wife what's what.'

'What did the old bag say that was so terrible?'

'Oh, she is always cunning, I told you, it was all spite and innuendo. Nothing. But it was what she implied. As though the whole village knew that Michèle was some kind of tart.'

'Sack her,' said Charles.

'I hate it when you speak like that.'

'What do you want me to say? Why do you listen to her? Is this all you have to complain about?'

And so on and so forth. If there was one thing Louise couldn't abide, it was being told how perfect things were and how wonderful. He never listened to what she said.

'Speak up for yourself. Answer her back,' he growled.

'That's what I am doing,' she said, 'and you DON'T LISTEN!'

'Dear God, what do you think I am doing? What more do you WANT?'

'I want to be taken seriously. Not treated as a nobody. A nothing.'

'You aren't a nobody,' roared Charles. There. This was how it always ended up, with him shouting at her. She went on trying to explain that he didn't realise, that he didn't really care. He just thought he did. Charles rapidly became quite demented.

'SHUT UP,' he said, 'JUST SHUT UP AND DO AS I SAY.'

He continued to shout on and rave that she WAS a SOMEBODY and must assert herself and so on until she was bludgeoned into silence. They stared at each other, each breathing deeply. Louise was flushed, hectic, trembling. Charles pushed her down on the bed, crushing her with his substantial weight, none too gently. He smoothed back her hair, kissed her when she protested. He was as aroused as she was, as she always was, by their arguments. Whatever the subject, they always had the same outcome.

A startled Hilary, woken by the din, was sitting bolt upright in bed. His room was directly above the parents' one and he could hear them screaming at each other, at it hammer and tongs, with emphasis on the hammer.

The shouting stopped. He could hear the springs of the bed going dzigga-doo, dzigga-doo. Quite slowly at first but yes, inevitably, speeding up. In the sudden silence the noise of the springs was very loud. Dzigga-dzigga-doo, doo. And, getting louder and louder, came an accompanying noise. It was a gasping, throating sort of moan. This might well indicate the utmost throes of pleasure. Or not. Dzigga-dzigga – aahh, dzigga-aahh, dzigga-aahh. Aahh . . . He lay down on his side. Firmly, he pressed the pillow over his free ear.

The next day, when Michèle and he rambled off on their usual walk, she took him down to Café La Fourchette and didn't come in. 'A tout à l'heure.' A little wave and a smile and off she went swinging her shoulder bag and did not invite him to accompany her.

Hilary, drinking the usual Coke at the usual table, waited and when she did not return he grew impatient. Twenty minutes passed, thirty, forty and he refamiliarised himself with the mental gymnastics that went with this sort of clock-watching. Ten minutes at the cleaner's, maximum, twenty to buy fruit for Louise, five minutes to press the flesh here and there, another fifteen minutes to remember to go back and pick up the daily baguette and so on. Then it was an hour. He stared into the windows of the Boulangerie Lardon opposite, watched the continuous flow of baguette-buyers with no Michèle among them. Then it was an hour and ten minutes.

Not the most generous of calculations could account for

the hour and forty minutes she kept him there, returning empty-handed and smiling. He felt stupid about it, he felt that the time had been stolen from him somehow. He'd been conned.

'You were gone a long time.'

'Was I?' They walked up to the house. The bag went on swinging and swinging.

Dinner was a quiet affair, served by a pensive Louise who funnily enough seemed to have exactly the same problem on her mind.

'Hilary? On s'est amusé comment? This afternoon? You know, you forgot the bread.' Louise dragged deep on her inter-course cigarette. Hilary glanced at Michèle, who continued to rip apart her piece of bread, giving him a bright and slightly inquisitive look, as though she didn't know herself.

'Nothing much, the usual,' he said.

'For instance?'

'The café, a walk. You know.' He shrugged his shoulders.

'Did you meet anyone?'

'No.'

'Not anyone? Are you sure? None of your acquaintances in the village?'

Hilary shook his head. He looked at Michèle, who smiled boldly back at him. Oh, her mouth.

'Nobody at all,' he said. The phone shrilled out and Charles leapt up, while Louise ground out the stub with her usual extra thoroughness, frowning as she always did, each phone call the harbinger of annoyance. Charles returned a moment or so later and clapped Hilary on the shoulder.

'Vite, vite, come with me. Call out. Maybe you can help.'

Did they want coffee? Louise was on her feet, brandishing the pot as Charles left the room.

No, he called and they were off, Charles snatching up the old bag near the front door, loping across the gravel. Hilary hurried behind. Bang, they were away, the wheels skidding slightly on the gravel. Through the bright window, he saw the two lovely women moving about the table picking up plates. In the large, elegant room, they were like figures on a stage set. Did they speak to each other when he wasn't there? Did they exist at all? Perhaps they would disappear into a void. Perhaps it was the same one that had swallowed Michèle this afternoon.

They were through the village and out, picking up speed. The headlights flickered along thick white bands painted on grey bark all the way along the avenue of lime trees. The night lay waiting, caged beyond the bars.

'Thanks for taking me,' said Hilary. Charles smiled and lit up and the car filled with the acrid, comforting smell of his Gitane. If he weren't Michèle's father, Hilary would have asked him for advice. He thought about asking for it anyway. They were going to see a pregant woman, Charles said. Slight problems, nothing serious but the husband was worried. It was not far away, but difficult to get to.

The long tree-lined avenues rose and fell, hill after hill, through early-to-bed villages with their shutters drawn tight and then they turned off onto smaller roads. At last they came out on a road so rough it was scarcely more than a track. They were crossing a plain with only a few lights in the far distance. The Peugeot bumped along more and more slowly. Charles cut the lights and engine.

'Now we walk,' he said. 'Look'. He was pointing to the stars, brilliant in the inky dark. The night was quiet and warm and there was no sound but their own footsteps and an occasional rumble of a motor in the distance, where the road snaked by. Charles had a torch but they didn't need it for the moon lit up the track. On they went, silently. Hilary felt how small he was in the world. He listened to his boots crunching and felt the pressure of the slight unevennesses under his feet, the wind in his hair. These were delicious sour-sweet minglings, like sugar dissolving to relieve the acidity of lemon juice, new sensations transmuting the old bad ones.

Up ahead they saw a light swaying from side to side. The man holding it was keeping a lookout for them and he hallooed as he heard their footsteps. Charles hailed him cheerfully. The farmer spoke rapidly in a local dialect Hilary couldn't fathom, pulling at Charles's arm. He was nervous and jittering. Charles laid his arm over the man's back, half escorting him into the house that lay ahead. Hilary understood him repeating the word 'douleurs', pains, which the man pronounced as though in Latin. 'Dolors,' he said. 'She has bad pains, very bad,' and he shook his head from side to side. In the light, they shook hands and Hilary saw that he was in his early thirties, bony and sallow with a long face with flared nostrils. Hilary sat downstairs and kicked his heels and looked at things while the man led Charles up the stairs. The room was all brown: a brown piece of carpet on brown tiles, eight chairs round a table, a huge television set, a dresser. Hilary looked at the wedding photograph, which showed the man with his wife who was pretty and small and young and dolled up in a big frothy white dress. He towered above her, unsmiling, the long upper lip drawn down.

In a matter of just a few moments Charles was down again, looking for the phone, dialling, rapidly speaking. He was saying it was an emergency, an ambulance was required. He began to explain how to get there, interrupted by the farmer, adding and changing instructions. Patiently, Charles made sense of these, incorporated them. 'Get here as fast as you can,' he said. 'She hasn't long to go.' The man began anxiously to pluck at Charles's arm as he put the phone down, saying no, doctor, surely not, she's not even seven months gone, and it was startling to see his nervous smile reveal his huge yellow teeth, real horse's teeth with big gaps between them. He was terribly ugly when he smiled.

'You know, Monsieur,' Charles said, very calm, very polite, 'sometimes babies cannot wait. Sometimes it happens like that.'

The two men went back up the stairs and as they did so a whimpering cry floated down. For an instant Hilary thought it was the baby, but of course that was ridiculous, it was her, the woman upstairs.

A few minutes later Charles was back, phoning the hospital again. Emergency, he'd said, and couldn't they hurry – just get a move on? The farmer came clunking down the stairs.

'They'll be as quick as they can,' Charles said. The man stood very close to him, staring at him with huge scared eyes. He swayed slightly and looked as if he might faint. Charles looked at his watch, threw Hilary a glance.

'What will happen, what is going to happen?'

'Do not concern yourself, it will be fine. I think the baby will come soon, will come early, but probably not before the ambulance comes. They have been warned, they have all the equipment. You know, my friend, trust in your wife. Nature has designed woman well, inside and out. My old professor, Vigne-Laval, used to say that nature was the artist, and man merely the paintbrush – women are designed to make babies.'

'Tell me, what will happen?' the fellow repeated, pawing at Charles's arm. He was not capable of taking anything in.

'First we will get everything ready. Come with me.'

Back upstairs they went and now Charles set the man to work, calling for fresh linen. The big wrought-iron chandelier shook as Charles's heavy tread passed back and forth overhead. Five minutes later, he came down again and opened his bag, stared thoughtfully into it. The farmer tumbled down the stairs after him and stood too close, looking from Charles to the bag. His hands were shaking.

Charles rummaged at length, thoughtfully. He pulled out a packet of cigarettes, offered them, was refused, went outside for a smoke. Silently, Hilary and the father stood and watched his broad back through the window, until another cry from up above drew the worried man back upstairs. Hilary went out.

'Will they come in time?' He was whispering, though there was no way she could hear, upstairs.

'I doubt it. Come on, you can help. She's nine months gone, but he doesn't know that. I won't tell him either. The waters broke this morning, she didn't dare tell him. Lying in a wet bed for twelve hours . . . She's half dilated now, it won't be long. She's very narrow, too, and I have so few instruments . . .' He sighed heavily and shook his head and blew an elegant smoke ring to the heavens. 'Poor little thing. Let's go. You find me towels, lots of them, and boil up some water. Put it in anything you find, jugs will do or bowls. Ça va? You're not going to faint, are you?'

Hilary smiled and nodded and turned to go back into the farmhouse. He caught the merest glimpse of Charles's bowed head and the flash of a hand as it formed the sign of the cross. A shudder passed from the crown of his head right down his spine, the touch of an angel's wing.

It got worse. He'd seen hospitals before, plenty of them, had hung around waiting rooms and chatted up nurses, but he'd never been close to anything like this. The bedroom was gloomy, filled with dark furniture which seemed to come from another time. The young woman lay on the bed propped up on pillows and moaning. She wore a silly nightgown, a pink thing with ribbons, above which her white face and terrified big eyes seemed all the younger.

As each pain came, she gripped her husband's hand and screamed and her whole body tensed and arched upwards. At the end of the contraction, she lolled back and the whites of her eyes rolled up. She seemed to be exhausted already and she kept asking for something, but her accent was so thick he couldn't understand. Yet she spoke with such urgency. Hilary strained to make it out while her husband sat silent and grim, staring at her face.

Hilary came in and out with jugs. He found ice. He ransacked the big old-fashioned wardrobe in the room for towels. That was the only time she appeared to notice him. A contraction ended and she struggled up to a sitting position and stared at him.

Then she fell back onto the pillows, letting out another of those terrible cries, which sounded as if she was being pulled apart. Her calf muscles knotted up with cramp each time. Bunched, like athlete's legs, they looked to be in agony. When that happened, Charles at once began to massage her feet and legs. How huge her belly seemed, unnaturally distended. Hilary looked away. Tears were running down her face.

At the next opportunity, Charles gave the instruments he had to Hilary to boil. When he got back with a steaming bowl full, Charles was sitting beside her. He was like a cat, the way he got himself so precisely into a small space. He was talking soothingly and Hilary saw that he was trying to stop the father from panicking and frightening the mother yet more. The three of them took a deep breath. Charles exhaled slowly and counted with a raised finger, meanwhile resting his big hand on her head. Hilary found himself copying him, counting in his head. She took a breath. She was trying, she was, but every time she turned away to her husband and saw his scared face, his terrible yellow rictus of a smile, she began to whimper again. The pains were now very bad.

'Excellent, very good,' said Charles cheerfully, beckoning Hilary to come out with him. Outside the door of the bedroom, he whispered to him to go down and put the lantern out, next to the car, for the ambulance men, then to find the very sharpest kitchen knife. He was to sharpen it as well as he could and as quietly as possible and then boil it and bring it upstairs. Hilary's heart was knocking painfully against his ribs, he was in a sweat of fear. He had to swallow before he could speak.

'What are you going to do?'

Charles touched his face tenderly, as a groom touches his bride, as a lover touches his beloved. Poor frightened, small Hilary let his face rest in that warm hand for a moment. 'Probably nothing. I might have to cut her a little, to let the baby out. The ambulance will never come in time. I have an old scalpel, but no new blade.' He smiled ruefully. 'Be quick with the knife, but don't let our friend see. He's in a bad state.'

Hilary hurtled downstairs. He ran, his breath panting loudly in his ears to the car and back. He clattered through the kitchen, pulling out all the shelves until he found it, a wooden-handled knife with the slimmest and meanest of blades. He put a pan of water on the stove to boil and searched on. An old-fashioned grindstone. He turned the wheel, it groaned. Another terrible scream rang out from upstairs. He nearly sliced off his finger, but just stopped in time. With one trembling hand, he stilled the other. He held the blade in the boiling water for a couple of minutes and then like a murderer stole upstairs with it behind his back.

The girl lay on her back and round her open knees stood a circle of old-fashioned smoky storm lanterns. Heat and light shimmered off them in the big, dark space. Beyond the lights, like sentinels, stood two huge jugs of water, steaming, beside the piles of towels which Hilary had banked up. The farmer sat rigid on a chair beside the bed, staring in horror at his wife's contorted face, while she gripped his hand so hard that the knuckles were white round squeezed red sausage fingers. He kept saying how sorry he was, how sorry.

The room was filled with her, with the hoarse sound of her moans which stiffened into screams each time the pains came. She was still asking for something. As he slipped the wicked blade into the disinfectant, Hilary understood. She was begging her husband to kill her for she could no longer endure the terrible pains. He kept shaking his head and saying forgive me, forgive me.

Hilary began to pray, continually, in his head, along the lines of please God, make it be all right, please God, please.

As he moved across, he saw the incredible sight of the baby's head, or rather part of a head of dark hair appearing between her legs, an impossible bulging curve of head that couldn't possibly get through there, couldn't.

Charles seemed to be pushing down on her stomach with one hand, his ear pressed to one side of her belly, listening to the heartbeat of the foetus. It looked as if he was trying to push the baby out. Jesus. It must have hurt like hell. Hilary watched, with clenched fists. He was sweating himself, like a pig.

The noise was now terrible, screams punctuated by moaning gasps as she drew breath, only to scream again. She was drenched with sweat, her hair plastered to her head, she writhed and twisted. That a woman could endure it – it was unendurable. That a man could do this to a woman – that was also unendurable.

Charles reached out for the knife. 'Be quick,' he said. 'Quick.'

Carefully, Hilary fished out the knife and put it into Charles's hand. Please God, please.

The father saw the knife. He stood up and moved forward

a few paces and then fainted dead away, crashed onto the chair he'd been sitting on and smashed onto the floor. Hilary tugged at his boots, shifting the dead weight a couple of inches along the floor to lay him out straight. He was so heavy, a dead lumpy weight he could barely move. Was he dead or concussed? Neither of the other two seemed to have noticed. Hilary knelt beside him, saw that he was breathing and stood up again.

Charles was cutting her, and again, blood spurted out everywhere in a crimson gush, terrifyingly, and then savagely he reached right inside her body and still he was cutting at her and Hilary stood there, frozen with fright. The butchery was appalling. He felt sick and giddy. All at once, the baby slid out of her body and the mother stopped screaming instantly. She knew.

Something was terribly wrong. The baby was a boy, a tiny skinny thing covered in greasy wax stuff but his skin was a horrific bright purple. It was a colour so unnatural that Hilary had never imagined skin could be like it. He saw the severed cord and then the marks where it had been wrapped round the baby's neck and pulled tight. Now he understood.

With incredible speed and gentleness, Charles took the little thing and laid it down on the towels and bent over it.

'Take the cord,' he said to Hilary. 'Gently, don't pull, just hold it, the afterbirth must come now. It is a boy, Madame, a lovely boy, the image of your husband, a wonderful boy. Just one moment, Madame, I will give him to you.'

There was complete silence. The young woman just lay there, waxy-faced, strangely still. Yet a moment before she had been so loud, so violently in motion. Her eyes were fixed on Charles's broad back. She stared at Hilary and her face was so white and stricken, her look so appallingly full of pain, that he could not bear it and knelt down, out of her sight, still holding the cord. The bed was a mass of blood, otherwise he would have rested his head against it. He was so very tired.

He was very careful to make no noise but could not prevent tears running down his face, which they did, on and on, unstoppably. She was silent. He kept his head well down, so she would not see. There was another huge contraction, he could feel it through her whole body, but still she made no sound. It was the afterbirth coming out, a great white spongy mass at the other end of the cord which like some hugely sophisticated electrical cable was a complex spiral cord with red and blue in it. He curved it all round carefully into one of the bowls.

The only sound in the room was Charles pummelling and stroking the baby. In the new quiet, the slapping noise was very loud. He was cruel, Hilary thought. Why hurt the little thing, even though it could feel nothing? Hilary wanted to say stop, it's dead, we all know it's dead, let it be. He was crying too hard to say anything.

Charles began to hum. It was a strange noise, a kind of sing-song incantation. Then he was talking, quietly under his breath, and then louder. 'Come, little one, that's right, that's good, that's better, oh, that's very good, that's the way, come, little one.'

On he went and on. Through the bones of his head, through his flesh, Hilary heard the voice and concentrated on it, so gentle and so kind. There came the sound of a little cry, which turned into a wail. Hilary drew a great sobbing breath, gulped, smeared the fresh tears which would not stop falling with the back of his bloody hand. He began to sob out loud, uncontrollably. The baby cried again. He found himself saying thank you, thank you. Thank you, God.

The little mouth opened, drew another breath and began to wail even more loudly. The eyes were squeezed tight shut in the little purple monkey face and, carefully, Charles wrapped him in a fresh towel and presented him to the mother. She took the baby in her arms and stared at him. Incredibly, the little thing stopped crying for an instant and opened up its little eyes, which were a watery blue, and stared at her. As though it knew who she was. And the way she looked and looked back at the baby boy made Hilary want to laugh and cry all at once.

They heard it, distantly, then ever nearer, the siren wailing in the distance. They had forgotten the father. Charles now picked up one of the jugs of water and poured some of it on a cloth and dabbed at his face. As he came to, Charles helped him to his feet, wiping him down. Surreptitiously, Hilary washed his own face.

'You fainted, Monsieur, very understandable. Look, you have a little boy. Premature, but nice and big for his age so he will be fine. We must get him to hospital though, and your wife also needs some attention. She has been so very courageous. Come along, mon brave, you help Monsieur.' He winked at Hilary.

Hilary supported the farmer down the stairs. He was groggy, but all right. The ambulance men were at the door and organising matters. Within minutes they had taken the little family away.

Hilary and Charles stood at the farmhouse door and watched the tail lights bumping slowly down the track. Charles yawned and stretched and went back inside and helped himself to a glass of brandy. Hilary had one too, which made him shudder and then warmed him. The terror was subsiding.

They drove slowly through the lovely pre-dawn. Clouds of mist swirled and eddied across the fields. Over the horizon a faint streak of light heralded the day. They turned onto the tarmac road.

'It was a miracle,' Hilary said. 'You made that baby live.'

Charles shrugged his shoulders. 'Did you know it would be all right?'

'I hoped.' He smiled. He had prayed, too. Hilary felt like embracing Charles.

'So did I.' God, yes, and how. Especially over the knife.

The day grew and grew and Hilary found that he was no longer tired, but exhilarated. His hand hurt. That, too, was good. He sang 'Jerusalem', belting it out, all the way through, at the top of his voice. Charles put his hand on his arm, delicately.

'J'étais bien content que tu étais là.' He sighed. 'That poor man. Somehow, I can't see it being his baby. Who knows. A man, you see, never quite knows. That is the prerogative of the woman.' He fumbled for a cigarette. Hilary struck a match, held it for him.

'I loved your mother very much, it was a most passionate affair. I could never forget her. I never have forgotten her.' He cast a sideways glance at Hilary. 'I feel how much you are like her. Perhaps that's why I feel as I do. Cela te gêne?'

'No. Go on, I want to know. Really, please. I don't even know how you met.'

'Look, I tell you, for maybe six months, I was a student in London. It was for fun, it was the place to be. All young, all medical students all together. Your mother was beautiful, clever, everybody was in love with her. She chose me, it was incredible, wonderful. Then, I asked her to come to France and stay with me, I had two years to go in medical school. She said no, she had to be free.' Charles was driving slower and slower.

'You see, she understood me very well. I wanted her, but the fact was, I also wanted to be free. Later she wrote and said she had met your father, she was going to marry him. Well, I didn't like that at all so I went to England and saw her. I met Nicholas. I don't think I liked him very much, nor him me. But I saw that he was clever. Brilliant, some said. I could see that he, who was going to become a great doctor, was an eligible parti. Whereas I, you see, was erratic, a bad student. I wasn't even faithful to her. Of course I didn't tell her that, but she knew. I loved her, but I was not the better man. So I said that to Amanda that she was right. Partly it was true, partly I wanted to hurt her. I knew, you see, that she still loved me.'

He sighed heavily, lit a new cigarette from the stub of the old one. The car stopped at the roadside. Hilary stared out at the sunflowers, all on automatic compass and swivelled the other way.

'If I had not been a naughty boy, you might have been my son. She was clever, your mother. It was her choice – not me. She made the right choice. She chose your father.'

Charles started up the car again and they moved slowly off. Hilary looked at the sun shafting across the early morning mist and the promise of a brilliant day. He thought about his mother, who had never finished medical school, who had married the wrong man and had his babies, screaming in pain like that woman. She had had choices, more than most people did, because she had brains and looks. With all that, she had got it wrong.

He couldn't see that clever, beautiful, free-spirited student at all. He didn't believe in her. His mother was a nice conventional woman who dressed badly and was a good mother and who spent her days doing things for other people. And on and off so unhappy that she cried in the middle of the day for sheer misery. She had been destroyed. The world was a tragic place. There was the smallest gap imaginable between getting things right and getting them hopelessly wrong. It all made him feel old and incredibly sad.

'I'm not so sure,' he said. 'That she was right, I mean.' His voice came out very small. 'I'm not sure if she is happy,' and he said this quietly, because it was clearly very wrong to tell this man that. Charles, accelerating as he cheered up, laughed and it seemed that he hadn't heard that bit. Hilary felt a pang at his own disloyalty.

'Oh, I didn't do so badly,' Charles said. 'I had a lot of fun instead and later on I met my lovely Louise. Besides, at the time it seemed to give me an excuse not to go on. I knew, you see, that any healing powers I had lay in these hands. They couldn't teach that in a lecture room.'

'So why did you go on?'

'I didn't.' He shook his head. 'I never qualified. It was easier for me to find a way to have the papers forged,' he said calmly. 'That was how I got registered. After all, it was necessary for me to have the papers somehow. To have a dossier, a certificate number.' He shrugged his shoulders in a very matter-of-fact way. 'You need that to practise as a doctor.'

'It's usual, then, in France?' Hilary swallowed. He didn't know what he was supposed to say. Was this some joke? Charles then explained that of course it was not usual. Nobody knew, not Louise, not Michèle, nobody. Only him, Hilary.

'Je comprends,' said Hilary. His throat hurt.

'I knew that I was meant to be a doctor, you see. That was obvious.' Smilingly Charles reached over and gripped his shoulder for an instant in a playful, friendly way. Hilary covered his eyes as, turning the next corner, the sun hammered through the windscreen with painful brilliance.

3 ∫

Hilary caught glimpses of the old lady's frail body stretched out on the shiny stuffed counterpane, saw Charles bending over her, his hands soothing and stroking flesh that was dead white, only the forearms brown, like long gloves. The door had been left ajar. He paced about the tiny room, unable to stop himself from watching through those couple of inches. She had groaned to begin with, had let out a little cry, collapsing stiffly forward onto the bed. Now she was very quiet. When they arrived she'd kissed the doctor's hand before he could stop her.

Madame Ourlandes was eighty-nine and lived alone, having buried her contemporaries, her husband and all three of her children. Her house was tiny and wooden, with a verandah and a sprawling garden grown wild. There was a small area in front which was immaculately tended and she was generally there, weeding or planting, when they arrived. It pained Hilary to see her nearly bent in two as she carried the heavy watering can along the path. How shrunken her world was, how vast the wilderness she kept at bay. The house was very isolated, but Madame was not troubled. She had been born in this, her grandparents' house. She intended to die in it.

She let out little sighs of pain all the way up the stairs which she ascended with terrible slowness. You could see how she suffered. It was in every inch of her, in the deliberate positioning of feet and hands. Years of experience had taught her the least painful ways of doing things. Madame Ourlandes had acute arthritis and it had knotted her up, had taken further inches off her height, turned her hands and feet into big knobby branch stumps which looked as if they were made of wood. Her eyes, though, were alive and bright, her mind acute despite constant pain. She spoke in a very small voice, high and sweet like a child's. She had a way of giving you her utmost attention, of looking at you with wise eyes.

Three times a week Charles Beauregard came to the little house and soothed her with massage. She was his last call. Madame blessed him for it, kissed his healing hands. Gently, she took Hilary's hand between her tortured palms and whispered to him that God must bless the doctor and keep him safe. His calls soothed her to sleep and real rest which was precious for coming without pills. Charles always left her fast asleep. Like the old countrywoman that she was, she rose at first light, put herself to bed when it faded. She had no electricity and did not miss it. Quietly Charles and Hilary crept away from her house. Like thieves in the night they would tiptoe down the little staircase and gently close the front door.

Charles knew to park a little distance away down the quiet lane, for fear that the noise of the engine starting up would wake her. Her hearing was acute. 'When God calls me, I shall hear him,' she said to Hilary. He particularly wanted to see her face at repose, smiling, and wondered if she looked like that when asleep. He hadn't dared to ask if he could go in and look at her, but the idea grew in his head.

'She always asks me the same question. Why does God keep her alive, an old woman, no good to anyone, when he took her children?' Charles lit a cigarette, eased the car onto the road.

'What do you say?'

'It's hard. I don't know. She is a pure spirit, you know. She is nothing really but pain, inside and out. It has refined her down to the essence. Perhaps we need that – we others who are coarse and rough.'

'Is that what you say?'

'Ah, no. Never. I would not presume. No, no, I tell her I do not know her purpose but surely she has one. For we all have one.'

'But if we don't know what it is?'

'Ah, that is precisely the human condition. Not knowing. If we knew those things that God knows, we would not be human at all, but angels. Perhaps the precious thing about Madame Ourlandes is just that at her great age, with all her wisdom, she still asks such questions. My old professor used to say that there were three things you should know about a person. What they know, what they don't know, and then what they don't know that they don't know.'

They were quiet then, the warm air blowing in as dusk fell, the same mild air filling the room where the old woman slept at peace. It would be invaded by the real dark of the woods and countryside by the time they were home.

They had finished dinner when the phone rang and Louise's habitual shrillness softened at once into warmth.

'Bonjour, Madame, oui, oui, I can guess who you want to talk to – vite, Hilary, ta mère!'

Hilary, who felt both a compelling need to talk to his mother and dread of any more frankness from anyone, rose slowly.

'Mum,' he said.

'Hello, Hilary.' She sounded a bit flat. 'How are you, darling?'

'Fine, terrific. Couldn't be better.' He felt a bit flat himself. 'Something I wanted to ask.'

'Yes?'

Not easy, this. He turned over various ways of phrasing the next bit. Did you sleep with Charles, Mum? By the way? Or, mind if I ask a rather personal question?

'I was a bit curious, I just wondered how well you really know Charles? I mean – how, well, ah, well?' He let out as false a laugh as any he'd ever heard.

'Quite well, Hilary, or else you wouldn't be there, would you?' She laughed lightly.

Hilary asked himself how exactly he proposed to check out Charles's account of their relationship. *'You see, Mum, I'd like to know whether he tells the truth or not. Can we start with something non-controversial. Sex. You and him. Are we talking numero cinq? Numero seven? Hecky thump. So you did it all. I see. Thank you. Really glad I asked. Next question. Would you describe your old ''friend'' Charles as a liar? I mean, do you think of him as being a cheat? A fraud, a pathological criminal?'*

'Darling? Are you still there?'

'Sure, sorry, just a second, hang on.' His hand, holding the phone, was sweaty. Hilary knew that he, no chip off that old block, was incapable of Charles's appalling frankness. Through the glass door, he stared at Michèle, sitting at the dining table, as she leant forward and picked up a glass. The curve of her throat, swallowing, could move him almost unbearably.

'Hilary, are you there?'

'Course I am, Mum. Where did you meet Charles?'

'At Zurich Airport, darling, I told you,' she said wilfully. Another long silence. 'Aren't you happy, Hilary? You did say it was wonderful, before.'

'Fine, sure, yes.'

Once he told anyone Charles's secret, it would be in the air and somehow people would find out. And if Charles was betrayed, he, Hilary, would be responsible. He alone. Visions of an arrest, of Charles being taken away, danced through his head, the family ruined, tears on Michèle's face, hand-wringing, bailiffs at the door, silk dresses being carried away in bundles, Louise in rags and a shawl. Dickensian squalor and distress. And if he kept quiet, didn't that make him an accessory to the crime? Why had Charles told him?

'Hilary, what is going on, darling, this is long distance,' said his mother sharply.

'How is Dad? And Ed?'

'Ed's asleep. Well. I must be going. Goodnight, Hilary.'

''Night, Mum.'

Both receivers were plonked down simultaneously. What now?

'Pear tart with just a little Calvados? Or apple?'

In the kitchen, Hilary dithered about while Louise went into the pantry and selected from its cornucopia of good things. She slipped the tart onto a plate while he chose words and discarded them and then, because in a minute they'd be back in the other room, he blurted something out.

'Charles is an extraordinary man—'

'I think Michèle—' she started and stopped.

Think, Hilary told himself. 'Go on. Please.'

She turned the tart on the plate and turned it again until the position was right, for a thing had to be perfect or it wasn't worth doing. 'I think – mm, well. Michèle really likes you,' she said. 'I know a mother mustn't say those things. Never interfere, you know. But we are pleased you came. Good. What were you saying?' She picked up the plate with a kind of apologetic little swoop and dip and waited.

'Ce n'était rien,' he said. Of course he wasn't going to tell her anything.

* * *

Amanda looked at Ed. Head down, her boy went on forking stuff into his mouth blindly while attempting to extract a piece of paper which had unaccountably become stuck down the rim of his bird-watching binoculars. His extraordinary patience and concentration were only ever applied to his own very small and personal interests. Not unlike his father. Who, again, would not be home to dinner and had only just rung to tell her so. Another man might have been having an affair. Nicholas? She thought about it. On the stove, the pans were bubbling away. One by one, she turned them off. Not Nicholas. Incapable of it. He didn't have the juices necessary for passion.

Too low a flame. How could a man as clever as her husband choose such stupidity as a modus vivendi? She turned to look through to the dining table laid for dinner. She went up to it and gave it a malicious little shove. Silver-plated and spotless, knives and forks and serving spoons winked and trembled.

In the kitchen, Ed focused the binoculars on the wall telephone. They were too heavy for him and his hands trembled. Slowly and triumphantly, Columbus sighting land at last, he read off the number he knew by heart.

When the oven pinged, Amanda removed the fluffy, golden mass. Nicholas's favourite pudding.

'Soufflé, Ed?'

'Ech, echaah, ecch, aagh. Ugh, ugh ugh.'

The vomit noises went on for some time and were then transmuted into Apache war cries by her discovery of one remaining tub of vanilla-chocolate-fudge ice cream. She spooned it out, without bothering to rebuke him. Ed shut up after a bit and looked at her. She sat dreamily on the edge of the table and stared at nothing. He let the ice cream melt into a pool and then with loud gasps and slurps drank most of it. Inserting a straw into each nostril, he blew as hard as he could into the beige puddle. A sort of tune bubbled through. He looked at his mother. Still she did nothing. He did it again, much louder.

Nothing Ed could do really bothered her any more. He did the theme of Thunderbirds twice and then managed to draw the remaining liquid up into his nose. He held his head back to keep it in. He now waved at her, permitting it to drip out again, gesticulating meanwhile for tissues.

'Gotta bad gold.' Silently, Amanda observed the twin flow of matter. Without comment, she passed the box of Kleenex. She started to clear the dishes away.

'Bathtime,' she said mildly. 'Upstairs. Off you go,' She found no need to urge and coax as she used to, just as he found no reason to argue and refuse.

Amanda waited for Ed to get out of the bath, a process complicated by his recent discovery of modesty. The water seemed to run interminably. She had swum naked with Nicholas on their honeymoon, centuries ago. Clamped together, kissing, letting the bubbles rise as they did. Closing her eyes, she thought about how it would be to swim like that with Charles.

Inside the bathroom, Ed knelt damply upon the bathmat and gazed at the soapy meniscus which was on the verge of flowing over the rim of the bath. He had blocked the overflow with soap. He controlled the bath by judicious manoeuvrings of a trickling tap and the plug, which was held in the plastic beak of a long-handled parrot's head. This was supposedly designed to open and close when the grip was squeezed. Often, though, because it was a very cheap toy, it failed. This potential failure was what gave excitement to the project. The trick was to lift the plug at the precise second of the bath overflowing. He started the countdown in his head. If his grip slipped that was it.

'Come on, darling.' It was quiet in there. Amanda tapped on the door. For a long time there was silence. At last, she heard the sound of water gurgling down the pipes. A pink shrimp completely wrapped in a sheikh's robe towel, Ed sidled into his bedroom, closing and locking the door to keep her out.

Leaning against it, Amanda remembered the long gone era when she and Nicholas used to pay attention to what the other one said. She'd loved him then, or at least she'd thought she did. To be precise, she'd not had to think about whether she did or not.

'Ed, you ready?' She tapped on his door.

She had been amused by him, that had been the essence of Nicholas. Fun allied to sharp, dazzling intellect. Sexiness which was linked to words, the mind rather than the body. The pleasures of intelligence. Whereas Charles just emanated that extraordinary physical allure. Whereas Charles just . . . *was*. She closed her eyes, to aid concentration.

'Mum?' The shrimp unlocked the door and appeared, hair combed, pyjamas on, smiling. He jumped into bed. She tucked him in. With the astonishing display of passion which arose magically each night from the deep sea of his self-centredness, he hugged her tight and kissed her and told her how very much he loved her. She loved him, too.

'Mum? Why've you gone quiet? Are you happy now?'

'I'm always happy. Don't be silly. Time to go to sleep, darling,' but he propped himself up on one elbow and gave her his deep, disconcerting stare.

'You won't do anything dramatic, will you, Mum?'

'Why on earth should I?'

'You promised me you'd tell me when you were ready,' and he at once turned over and closed his eyes. Within a minute, he would sleep.

Back in the kitchen, Amanda thought about the immense tenderness she felt for her children, never more strongly than when sleep or absence freed her from them. Whatever it was that linked them to her, it was stronger than everything else. It was as powerful as life itself.

There on the table stood the concave collapse of what had once been a perfect dome. And what was to become of it now? She lifted up her fist and smashed into the middle of it. Bang, to the bottom, ouch, a frill of substance jumped into the air and she felt the stored heat from inside burn her hand. A satisfaction, of sorts. She let cold water run over her hand, watching each frothy splodge of soufflé fall from her skin, swirl round the sink and then carry on its journey, down the plughole and ever on, down to the sea.

Amanda ran a bath. She contemplated her legs which rose pinkly from the foam, long, yes, if a touch Rubenesque. She wasn't twenty any more, but things were generally speaking in the right place. Or not too far from it. Her hand, which had to be kept out of the warm water, which hurt it, splayed on the rim. She breathed in, watched the waist reappear and a rib or two and the breasts jut forward. Men liked bottoms and curves anyway. Men had always liked her. Funny. She'd forgotten that. There were many things, even very important ones, she had forgotten and which it was crucial to remember, if only she could remember how.

Over at the dressing table, she stared for a long time at her face, too pale with such light coloured hair. Such terrible hair. The bright blonde stuff was ridiculous and she would tell Georgie to tone it down. She pulled it back, frowned. She smoothed back her forehead with her hands to make the little frown lines and crow's feet disappear. She brushed her hair forward, back, then forward again. Carefully, absurdly, she applied make-up.

Not that terrible old nightie. Slowly, she extracted garments one by one from her cupboard, trying on this and that. She sprayed on scent. Still humming, she floated around the bedroom, finally arranging herself voluptuously on the big double bed. A woman ready for adultery. There was no place where she and Charles had not made love. Her parents' house, their faintly Spartan queen-sized bed, her skimpy single bed, the drawing room floor, the bath – closing her eyes Amanda tried to recapture the details of that memorable weekend of her parents' twenty-fifth wedding anniversary. While they made love with closed eyes in a darkened room (if they did it at all) in the Grand Hotel, Brighton, their wild child did better. Their good girl Amanda, left to guard the house. You won't be lonely, darling, will you? No, Mummy, I won't. You have a lovely time. Don't worry about me! I'll be glad of the quiet to work, Daddy. Sex was something that to this day they had never mentioned.

So long ago. Over twenty years. Amanda had been a good student, hard-working, always in the front row to be sure of not missing a word of the lecture. She had made careful notes with different coloured biros to underline major and minor headings and this, in medicine, was crucial, for nobody sought originality or inspiration. They wanted facts, dry and well-ordered.

That summer morning as she sat down, she had become aware that she was being stared at and had to turn round and there was Charles, two rows behind. He had smiled at her in so suggestive a way that she had blushed. And for the remainder of the lecture she had been unable to concentrate for his eyes on her back. She knew that he would ask her out and that she would go – that he wanted to make love to her and that she felt the same. All in one glance. Incredible.

Opening her eyes, Amanda was saddened to see her 45-year-old body reflected in the mirror where she half expected the long hair and the absurdly young face and Mummy's pearls. The little blemishes and marks of life, everything losing its lustre, even the gums beginning to retreat. She had been pretty, very – she knew it now, even if she hadn't then. Charles had made sure that she knew that she was beautiful; he had made sure that she felt all the important things. And the upshot had been that she had cut all her lectures, had six glorious weeks of passion and the following year had chosen to marry Nicholas. Charles had made her need a man. Why had she not chosen him? She frowned, thinking hard. She had known one day that she shouldn't marry him. On such a meagre basis, lives were decided. It had all started and ended on intuition. But why? How? When? Why couldn't she remember?

Pudding plates clattered (soufflé, his favourite, not a patch on Amanda's) and Nicholas saw that they would be out of the restaurant with nothing ventured or gained if he didn't get on with it. With something not unlike a prayer he leant forward. He looked intently at his dining companion. Fearful of being overheard, he lowered his voice.

'After all these years. First time I've done anything like this. You see, Amanda,' he paused, feeling uncomfortable and disloyal. He looked imploringly at the face opposite. 'It's hard to put it into words.' There was another long pause. Get on with it. 'There's something wrong with her,' he said.

'Physically wrong?'

'I don't know.'

'Has she seen her doctor?'

'No, no, that wouldn't be – you don't understand. She doesn't say a word to me. Not even hello. I was hoping you'd have some idea. Of what it's about,' and Nicholas waved his hands about, helplessly.

Professor Jameson lit his cigar and rolled it in his square-ridged scholar's fingers and then sucked at it, luxuriantly. He smiled in a kindly manner. Nicholas wondered if his wife was mad. It seemed a long time before his companion spoke.

'She doesn't speak to you? I see. Why do you think that is?'

A bluish aromatic cloud lay over the table where they sat. In frustration and annoyance, Nicholas spread his hands to signal that he didn't know and looked at them, his long, strong fingers, helpless on the tablecloth.

The pharmacist spotted them through his big plate-glass window, came running out of the pharmacy and right up to them, face wreathed in smiles.

'Wonderful news, Mademoiselle! My first little nephew.' He shook hands with Michèle, offered his faintly damp hand to Hilary. 'And you were there, young man. You see, I have heard the whole story. Fernand is my cousin, you know. You didn't know? Ah. On my mother's side. Second cousin really, almost a nephew. Well, he's a fine healthy boy, thank the good Lord. Mademoiselle, your father's a genius. Ça alors! What can't the man do? First of many, I hope. Young blood, that's what our family needs. And without the doctor, who knows what might have happened? Nearly a tragedy. What a man, no?' Drawing out a handkerchief, he blew his nose.

'Why are you so surprised about the baby?' Michèle's tone was tart. She got out a Marlboro and inched it between her lips. What was it with her and the smoking? 'My father's been doing his job for twenty years. He should know what he's doing.'

'No, no, no, Mademoiselle,' Jean-Jacques wagged a playful finger. 'That is so often not the case. You'd be surprised. Doctors get prescriptions wrong. They make mistakes, oh, all the time. Not your papa. You know, he doesn't prescribe a lot of medicine, not him, I should complain for that's my business but no, I respect him. Twenty years, you say? Twenty years. It's true, yes. Why, I have been here twelve years. I can tell you, Mademoiselle, I have not in that time made a fortune from your papa, but still I consider him the best doctor I know. The very finest. And you – you helped him, young man. I thank you.' He grabbed his hand again. Hilary shuffled bashful feet. The pharmacist's penetrating eyes, which occupied the exact midpoint between the shiny dome up top and the compensatingly hairy luxuriance of the moustache below, swam with unshed tears.

'Oh, it was nothing. Really.'

Bored, Michèle puffed restlessly on her fag. Hilary thought about the cord round the baby's neck, its purple skin. What if it had died? How would he be feeling now? Could a proper doctor have prevented the whole crisis happening in the first place? A real, qualified one?

'So, there was a real emergency, I hear. Well?'

Hilary began in his stumbling French to tell him the gruesome details, half waiting for him to say, ah, but that was the wrong thing to do, surely, normally a doctor does this and that. He might betray Charles inadvertently. Oh God. But Jean-Jacques went on listening attentively while Hilary gave him a blow by – no, a cut by cut account, while incurious, rude Michèle backed slowly away. When he got to the gory business, the pharmacist shuddered.

'Ah, poor Fernand could never stand the sight of blood and nor could I. Excuse me, please – twenty years, eh, that is something.' He backed smilingly off and, in increasingly morose mood, Hilary ambled on.

The problem was the daughter, not the father. Hilary had thought it couldn't be possible for him to exist in this state of permanent dizziness while she remained unmoved. Well, he'd been wrong. She could be indifferent to him and continue to play strange and cruel games. He had a permanent lump of misery in his chest, a hopeless feeling that he couldn't do anything at all, that he was doomed to follow her about and slaver at her heels like a dumb dog. And this incredible combination of raging, unsatisfied lust and total lack of knowledge of the other person added up to being in love. Love was the reverse of knowledge. What he knew about her, he didn't necessarily like. How could that make sense?

And yet it did if he thought about girls he liked but could not desire, as opposed to those whom he had made love to who were often not likable at all. Julia. She had allowed him to do some quite astonishingly bold things to her on her mother's kitchen table, a place that was deeply uncomfortable yet inarguably less cold and hard than the alternative, the quarry-tiled floor. Julia, who was athletic and bright and quite pretty, yes, and whose parents were in the house. He didn't like her particularly. Nevertheless, at Julia's instigation they had gone into the kitchen and boiled the kettle and steamed up the windows and put the radio on. Every now and then he had laughed loudly. For the benefit of the parents upstairs, who could never have allowed mirth to coexist in their minds with the kind of animal behaviour it was accompanying. Girls were in conspiracy with his prick, which chose instant gratification, however sordid, every time. The world divided into girls who never would and girls who definitely did, and while the latter existed on the planet, his hormones wouldn't let him waste time getting to know the other sort. Then there was the incomprehensible Michèle who managed to be everything at once and whom he could both love and hate with the same terrible intensity. Why was she so cruel?

Héloïse sat with her legs crossed in front of her gilt and curlicue dressing table laden with lotions and unguents. One fluffy mule was swinging, she hummed nasally to herself. Slowly, she rubbed cream into her forehead, then streaked it lightly down her nose. Dipping into the pot for another smear, she dotted it about her cheeks and on her neck. She threw her head right back and stared down her nose at her reflection. Then she patted her cheeks with both palms, fingers curling back. Jean-Jacques, approaching slowly, bending to kiss her neck, encountered a dollop of substance. It was always the most expensive of substances, too, always the tiny jar at 150 francs. The little minx. Not that he begrudged her a thing, she should have the very best, the finest. He bent forward again.

'Mon ange, be patient. Don't you want me to be beautiful for you?'

He did, of course he did. But beauty took so long and so many greasy creams and then he was frightened to approach her and often, too often, after another exhausting day, he fell asleep before the creams had been absorbed. Not tonight, though. The news of the new little baby cousin had put ideas into his head. These ideas were old friends. He twinkled at her in the mirror. She smiled back.

'Not long, my darling, my chéri.'

Waiting, he began to pace about the flat, thinking for perhaps the thousandth time that if there were a child, as there would be, of course, eventually, since there was nothing wrong with either of them, then they would move. It was very convenient to be right above work, but a child needed space and light and a garden. Life would change, for the better.

'Chérie,' he said, 'when I am the mayor of this town, I shall reorganise everything, every last bit of it. This place needs action. New blood. Old Papa Dutronc is past it, he's had his day. We need to put the place on the map. Make things happen. You would like that, wouldn't you, my darling?'

No reply came from the bedroom. She was concentrating of course. Trying out new products was part of the job. A woman had to look after herself, especially one as good-looking as his wife. Beauty was her profession, she made a nice little living from the parfumerie and the beauty treatments. Looking good was part of her professional armoury. Though the money never quite came out at what he thought it should be, considering the clientele and the prices she charged. It was just enough to give her a nice little allowance, nice clothes and her little fripperies. Not enough for the basics. Still, that was fine by him. It was a husband's job to provide for his wife. When they had children, when she had to give up her work, she would find him just as generous.

She would not lack for a thing. No silly, pretty thing she fancied should ever be denied his Héloïse. To this end, the pharmacist worked as hard as he could, always looking for new business opportunities, doing many menial jobs himself, always up early and to bed late.

'How to make one's mark, eh, that's the question, isn't it, my love? How to make people think. They just do the usual thing. Good old Dutronc, they say, fine old fellow and they vote for the nice old man. Without thinking, you see, what could be. Without progress. They don't realise what I am capable of. How to be known as a go-getter. Ah, that's the thing.'

Still muttering to himself, by now he was in the kitchen, opening the fridge door. There were face creams in here, too. A fridge should have some food. He gazed mournfully at the ampoules of collagens, the gels and vitamin supplements, the extracts of lamb's foetuses. Never any protein or vitamins in their more usual form. He fumbled through a couple of pieces of paper. A slice or two of ham, a little sweaty. A few green beans in a bowl. An old orange. His wife could not be accused of extravagance in this department. Jean-Jacques sighed. He was often hungry. Héloïse said that he needed to lose weight. He hardly had any belly at all. He sucked in his stomach, inflated a manly chest. What was that in the back, in that little Tupperware box?

As he carefully felt with outstretched fingers past the beauty treatments to the very back of the shelf, he thought about the new little cousin and the great good luck of

Fernand. What a hard time that poor Marianne had had. But a boy, a dear little boy. His Héloïse would be in the most modern clinic, yes, and early too. With the finest doctors in the land. What had Mademoiselle Beauregard said? Her father should know his job after twenty years. She was right. A good man, the doctor, though Jean-Jacques regretted his tendency to under-prescribe. But he had achieved a miracle. With a little shiver, the soft-hearted pharmacist thought about what the English boy had told him, about the purple baby and the cord and the nearness of disaster. Without the doctor, what would have happened to the baby? Dead no doubt, the little thing. Twenty years' experience. Healing hands. Truly, he was a good man. In a sudden access of generosity, the pharmacist decided that Dr Beauregard might be the man to deliver his and Héloïse's future son. A man to be trusted despite his great fault.

It was a sauce, a tomatoey kind of sauce. Jean-Jacques opened the lid and dipped a finger in. Not bad at all. It needed just a touch of pepper. He found a piece of bread left uneaten from supper and dribbled drops of sauce onto the bread. He was stuffing this rapidly into his mouth when inspiration struck. He called out to his wife.

'Listen, chérie, a magnificent idea. What if I organised an event to honour the doctor? Twenty years in the village.' He swallowed. 'You know, it's a pretty important anniversary – he must be the most popular man in the place. I think I am the first to think of it.' He got a spoon out, returned to the sauce. A little salt helped, too. 'What do you think, my angel? An inspiration, isn't it? What do you say to a dinner, a banquet?' She probably couldn't hear him. He raised his voice.

'For the doctor. A banquet. Ten courses. What could be more appropriate than for the pharmacist to organise such a thing? People will remember. They'll see it's something between professionals, those of us in the medical profession.

Something that would hardly do for an ironmonger. Ha.' He was feeling more and more pleased with himself.

'Did you hear, chérie? I said they'll see, then, a pharmacist is in that club too. A professional. Naturally it must be beautifully done. Only the best of everything. Nothing but the finest. Foie gras. Homard. Champagne!' His mouth was watering. Jean-Jacques tore off a large piece of bread, dipped it into the tomato sauce. He chewed and swallowed it rapidly.

'The cream of the place will come, not just from here, either. This will be a tiptop medical occasion. You know, I could talk to the big hospitals, get a list together. Surgeons, doctors, a professor perhaps. For you – a lovely new dress.' Pacing backwards and forwards in excitement, Jean-Jacques now dribbled the remaining drops of the sauce onto the last piece of bread. He could scarcely believe his good fortune. There was a kind of muffled bleating noise from Héloïse in the bedroom.

'You know what? I'll find out where our good doctor qualified and invite his contemporaries, to honour him. His professor, his best friend, all his colleagues.' He stuffed the last piece of bread into his mouth and with élan skimmed the empty Tupperware box onto the draining board.

'Did you hear, Héloïse? Dutronc will think himself lucky to be in such company. As for that sweaty pig of a baker, Lardon, he needn't aspire to it. They'll all see who counts and who doesn't. Me, I shan't be too proud to shake hands with old Limousin the farmer, no. People will see. What do you think, my angel?'

Lardon with his shiny big red face, his hairy back, his string vest, his overgrown loutish son, would not be invited. Young Lardon was a randy goat and notorious in the village for his womanising. He made eyes at every woman. Once, approaching the parfumerie, he'd caught the young man with his too-tight jeans and gaudy shirt staring in through the window at Héloïse and licking his lips. The thought made Jean-Jacques shudder. Disgusting though he was, the young baker knew his place. His father, who never met the pharmacist without embracing him as a confrère, was a very different proposition. Lardon with his coarse red face and his rank armpits needed to be shown who the real professionals were—

There was another bleating noise, this time much nearer. Rapidly, Jean-Jacques turned round, calling out, 'Did you hear, my darling?' He found himself just centimetres away from a green-faced ghoul with huge white eyes staring at him.

'Chérie?' He blinked. How silly he was. It was just the darkness of the kitchen, the thin unearthly light from the fridge, the greenness of the mask. His wife was pointing at the sink.

'You idiot,' she said. As she spoke cracks began to appear in her face. Fine green powder showered down her front. 'You fool, what have you done? My special mask. Human foetal tissue, very pure, and white of eggs and vegetable extracts. And you just throw it away, as though it cost nothing.'

Jean-Jacques' face quite suddenly took on a greenish hue all on its own, quite without any artificial aid. He staggered to the sink and bent over.

'Baargh,' he said. A long spasm shook his entire body. 'Burghth.' Then, with a great heave of his shoulders, to his wife's horror and disgust, his mouth opened and a stream of reddish liquid gushed out.

Descending as usual in the direction of the village, Hilary and Michèle passed the pharmacist toiling up the drive in a smartly pressed grey suit. He shook hands, explaining that he was coming to pay a call upon the doctor and Madame Beauregard. So he would find them at home, that was very good. He gave off an air of suppressed importance. As they reached the gates, Charles roared past. Toot toot, Mr Toad. He had the gleeful smile on his face of one who'd got away with something.

Thursday was market day, a little breeze fluttered the pennants on the stalls and the sun danced over the porcelain ornaments and glittered on a thousand butcher's knives. Hilary and Michèle wove their way along the high street. The place was stuffed with people as half the countryside took its basket for a saunter along the cobblestones and paused to say a newsy hello to its neighbours. The delicious aroma of chickens roasting on slow-turning electric spits made his mouth water.

A jostling bunch of grannies were queuing up to select their cheese and eggs at a vast caravan. You could scarcely see the assistants behind the pyramids of cheeses. Hilary couldn't resist a nutty Pyrénées cheese, grey-brown rind and inside pale yellow, delicious with the dark gold crust of his bread. A goat's cheese rolled in herbs followed. A woman selling foie gras gave him a taste of the aromatic pinky beige mass. Pure goose. Look, Monsieur, here is one with truffles. It was smooth and rich and irresistibly good even at six quid a tin and he bought a couple for Mum. Then he needed a bag and saw a granny's green string one which meant he could manage a couple of slices of smoked ham for the pleasure of the dexterity with which it was cut and then, because they were so pretty, a huge bunch of red and white striped radishes with feathery grass-green fronds. Louise would find uses for this stuff.

He'd lost Michèle. No, there she was over in the little square where the T-shirts and tops and swimsuits swayed brightly against each other. All the mademoiselles of the village seemed to be there pouting at the boys while they flicked their way through rows of sexy little tops. Yes, teeny knickers were big. You paid more for less, 'FF255 le set' it said against the row of evidently crowd-pleasing matching bras and pants in astonishing designs, all satin and lace in lurid colours.

Michèle smiled at his shopping bag. Like him, the shops were getting into the spirit of the thing. They had set up their own stalls in front of their windows, blocking the pavement and spilling people onto the street which offered the additional excitement of making cars swerve all over the place. This gave Hilary an excuse to take Michèle's arm and she, all smiling compliance, held on to him, so close that the wind flicked her hair in his face.

How perfectly the brilliant day combined its glories and then added one more, a warbling bird. A nightingale? He looked. No birds, no cages, but a crowd clustered round an agile-looking wizened old darling selling bird whistles in clay. He wore a wizard's hat. The whistles were shaped like birds and some of them were fired and glazed in brilliant colours. Their maker had laid them out prettily on shelves covered in velvet and he snatched up first one then another, putting two of them to his mouth at the same time and making one bird call to the other. He watched the crowd carefully and smiled at Hilary and beckoned him closer. The melodic warblings sounded genuine. Hilary bought one, it was just the thing for Ed. He blew on it. Tu-whit, to-whoo, it warbled. Owl-shaped as well, nicely made. Another item for the string bag.

Café La Fourchette was nearly full. Over coffee, he tried to explain to Michèle what Ed was like, with his bird-watching mania, his mad interest in all feathered things so oddly allied to total disrespect for anything else in nature. His totally destructive genius for practical jokes, his Superglue and tripwire antics. All the time he was waiting for the right moment. He'd know it when it came. Then he'd tell her about her dad. If he was to confide in anyone, it had to be her. She stared out of the window with those extraordinary eyes of hers, her air of having everything sorted out.

Would he, ever? Hilary worried, sometimes, that there wasn't much to him beyond a certain facility with book-learning, a good memory. He had thousands of opinions, ever shifting sands there, but what were his real passions, where were his commitments? He changed his mind about things all the time. Like, from minute to minute. And was it proof of his shallowness that whatever he started thinking of, he tended to end back with himself? He had half an eye on the greaser over the way who seemed to be attempting to stick his long yellow tongue down his girlfriend's throat while lighting a cigarette.

'Tu restes?'

His attention was recalled. 'Where are you going?'

She gave him her most dazzling smile as she stood up. 'Just a couple of minutes – I forgot to get something. Wait for me?'

Hilary nodded. Lightly, she touched his shoulder and then went out of the café and down the street, swinging her shoulder bag with her usual cheerfulness. He turned his attention back to el Fumato, who was now sharing his fag with his girl. Lovingly they blew smoke into each other's faces. Hilary now realised that what he'd taken to be a strawberry birth mark on the hussy's neck was the largest love bite he'd ever seen. A real whopper, a rosy red swelling three inches round. Old Nicotino was having a proud prod at it, presumably the most recent token of his esteem. She was slapping playfully at his hand, on which two guitarist's nails stuck out like horns, cracked, yellow and hard.

Amazing, really, all that Michèle knew about these people. Georgie, his mum's hairdresser, looked gay but wasn't. There was a girl in the shoe shop with huge tits. That was his local knowledge. Very subtle. But Michèle was pretty sharp in her observations and then all of a sudden he realised she wouldn't come back.

Hilary got up and went out into the main street, looked up and down it. What a fool he was. She wasn't in the Boulangerie Lardon opposite, nor in the mini supermarket. He looked up and down, but all the market stalls were in the way. He went up the street back towards the house without seeing her until he reached the turning in the road from which he was bound to see her if she was going up the hill to home. No Michèle.

He retraced his steps, passed the café going the other way. She wouldn't get away with it, not this time. Why did she have to spoil everything? Why couldn't he trust her?

Hilary speeded up until he was somewhere between a saunter and a jog. The village came to an end fifty yards on at the T junction. Beyond was an old stone wall which carried on for another hundred yards and beyond that lay the forest. Way up ahead, he saw a little figure in the distance which could only be her. Slender, jeans, the hair, moving quite fast. Panting a little, getting into a good rhythm, Hilary accelerated further until he was running. Another few minutes and he'd catch up. She was walking quite fast, the shoulder bag bouncing against her hip. He thought about whether he'd grab her, playfully of course, give her a fright. Though any second now she'd hear his footsteps and turn.

Another figure appeared out of nowhere, or rather out of the woods, and boldly walked side by side with her. Blue jeans, bright shirt, a man, tall and broad, dark hair though Hilary couldn't see any detail, it was too far for him to see the face. They were talking. Michèle was gesticulating. Some jerk. She was giving him the brush-off.

Straining a little, Hilary increased his pace. The man suddenly reached out and simply pulled Michèle off the road and into the thick woods. Yanked her, by the arm.

One minute there were two people in the road and the next second they were gone. Shocking.

Hilary shouted her name while he ran as fast as he could. He kept his eye on the place. It could have been no more than a minute before he was at the spot. He shouted again. Nothing to be seen. Panting, he sat on his haunches for a few seconds to recover and stared into the trees. Nobody. His heart was pounding. He felt completely panicked. A catastrophe was happening, she was being attacked, he was just sitting there in anguish. Rape, murder. Dear God Almighty. He felt his heart skip painfully with fear. Standing up, he took a deep breath, then another, to calm himself. Be sensible. Get your breath. She can't be far. She'll hear you.

'Michèle!' Not loud enough. He called again as he walked forward into the wood. No sign of anybody. And was this the place where they disappeared? He looked at the carpet of bracken and twigs. No signs of a disturbance. Had the man dragged her through here? No, he must be in the wrong place. He went on, then on some more.

Hilary plunged deeper and deeper into the woods as fast as he could. Running, though, was nightmarish on the uneven ground, with stumps of trees to trip you and hollows and dips. He went crashing through the forest, bursting through brambles and bushes which whipped at his face and body. It took all his concentration to avoid falling, jumping over logs, swerving through the trees and all the time bellowing her name like a wild man. No sound came back, nothing but the thump of his heart, the crisp noise of twigs breaking, a couple of startled pheasants, whirring aloft. His legs were hurting, his heart and throat sore, he was full of terror. So easy to get it wrong, the narrowest of margins between everything being all right and catastrophe.

There was what looked like a riding up ahead, its smooth

expanse of green pulled at him and he turned, sure that that was the way to go. It would be easier to run on. Jumping and swerving over a deep ditch full of bracken, he failed to spot a log. It tripped him. He lost his balance and cannoned into a tree, falling forwards, head first. The thick bark simply jumped out of nowhere and hit him, hard. Thump. He fell heavily and then lay like an idiot, amazed to discover that he didn't seem to be able to stand up.

Jean-Jacques had felt a little twinge of disappointment when the doctor drove past, when he waved but did not stop. No doubt he was on his way to see a patient. An emergency perhaps. For a little moment, he stood and mused. Should he turn back? And then it occurred to him that it might be no bad thing to have a private little word with Madame. Perhaps she had already arranged a party for the twentieth anniversary? And it certainly would be convenient to know the correct date without asking the doctor himself. Actually, he had no particular desire to meet the doctor who, good though he undoubtedly was, never quite hit it off with him. How could he, when the man so thoroughly rejected his métier? Not that he bore a grudge, for that was not his way. Why, he hardly ever said a word about it, not even to Héloïse. Doctors were his business after all, it was his job to support them.

Perhaps, and he rubbed his hands together at the thought, it could be a surprise? There was something glorious about the idea that Jean-Jacques Albert might enter into a secret correspondence with professors and specialists. He began to visualise the winks and nods, the special greetings. He imagined the old ironmonger shuffling up to him, when he knew. There was a man incapable of penning a good professional letter. He'd be well and truly out of his depth.

'Monsieur Albert,' he'd say, 'I'm getting on a bit. Out of

touch. I wonder – look, I know it's presumptuous to ask, but have you ever thought of doing my job?'

At the front door, Jean-Jacques spent a little moment combing through his hair, neatly removing the stray hairs and dropping them onto the gravel. He wiped his hands on his trousers and checked his face in the little mirror he always carried for shiny spots. Héloïse always fussed. His bald head shone, but there was nothing he could do about that. He picked a number of imaginary pieces of lint off his jacket and straightened up, putting onto his face what he hoped was a respectful but friendly smile. Madame was always immaculately turned out. And she was a healthy woman. Headaches, yes, aspirin was sometimes required. Sticking plasters, the usual female stuff. She was an infrequent visitor to the pharmacy. She had never yet brought in a prescription.

Finally, he knocked on the door of the doctor's house, coughing quietly to himself once or twice and resisting the urge to smoothe his fringe of hair. When nothing happened, he rang the bell.

'Madame! Ça sonne!' Nervously, he frowned and then again prepared his smile. He waited, swallowed. In another little moment, he heard the rapid tippety-tap of high heels hurrying towards the door.

'It is you, Monsieur. Come in, please.'

Madame Beauregard was wearing an apron, clearly she was busy in the kitchen. Jean-Jacques was ushered into the salon and there he paced from the doors to the far end of the room, continually threatening to knock into something and thus making himself nervous and alarming his hostess.

'Thank you, thank you, Madame.' He paused. Breathily, he sought the best way of explaining his plan. He noticed, as no man could help but notice, the delightful curves of Madame's figure as outlined by her robust but to him alluring garment, its strings pulled tight. It was a very long time since he had seen his Héloïse in one of those. 'I am thinking – I am thinking of organising a little event to honour your good spouse, Madame—'

'Ah Monsieur, excuse me, my stew will burn . . .'

Alone, Jean-Jacques did a number of turns upon the carpet. The most wonderful smells were floating through the open door, smells to make a man's stomach rumble and his mouth water. Back she came.

'You must tell me more, Monsieur,' she said. 'Please sit down,' and, reluctantly, he did. Jean-Jacques explained about the twenty years – his good fortune in finding that out. 'You see, Madame, one must never be too busy for the good things in life,' he said softly and it was true, very true, he felt himself how often he had made that mistake. So many good things that he had missed . . . he leant forward and softly began to speak his heart. 'Permit me to tell you of my dream.' His mind began to buzz. His plans began to seem a little understated. He would elaborate upon them. His head began to race ahead. 'Something exceptional, something the village has never seen. I am talking about a banquet – a magnificent occasion,' and Jean-Jacques sprang to his feet.

'A dinner fit for a prince – a king, Madame. An occasion to do honour to the doctor and to the esteem in which we hold him – the guests all very important personages . . .' Was she laughing at him? 'Of course,' he added rather stiffly, 'I am not in a position to choose who shall and shall not come. Your husband has so many medical colleagues, all his contemporaries. I have thought that perhaps, to save you the trouble, I should be the humble organiser. A mere functionary, Madame—'

'I would be so pleased if you would organise it. You know why I am smiling, Monsieur? It's because I am truly delighted with your idea.'

Pacing back towards the fireplace, Jean-Jacques spotted

a silver cup upon the mantelpiece. He went nearer and looked. Turned, looked at Madame. She nodded her permission. It was a trophy for lifesaving, awarded to the young swimmer Charles Beauregard.

'I don't believe it,' he beamed, shaking his head. He read and re-read the inscription, simply charmed by it. He couldn't put the thing down. If he had needed to be convinced of the rightness of the cause, this trophy would have done the trick. 'Ah! There must be a presentation, naturally – if only I could think what to give! And I need the date, of course. Something fine, something which can be inscribed upon, something – just like this.' He nearly laughed with pleasure. The more he looked at Madame Beauregard, the more he felt in his bones the rightness of the whole wonderful venture. 'What a man – ah, what a man he is!'

Madame Beauregard broke into a most dazzling smile. 'I've just had a wonderful idea. Professor Vigne-Laval must be your guest of honour. Charles has mentioned him, oh, a thousand times.'

'That's a name I recognise,' he smiled and rubbed his hands together. 'I have an idea. Let us make a surprise for your husband. We should try to keep the whole thing a secret for as long as possible.' For the glory and the honour was to be his, all his. He didn't want anybody else taking over his party.

'Now, you want me to look up the date, I suppose, you need the one on his diploma. I will come and bring it to you tomorrow, with all the names and addresses I have found.'

'Tomorrow.' He nodded. He lowered his voice conspiratorially. 'Perhaps you could come just when the pharmacy is closing, Madame, then we will have a moment to talk.' There was a very loud knocking on the door, which made them both jump.

The bleak eye of the femme de ménage fell upon them.

'Bonjour, Madame Moulins,' he said. He knew her well. Bunions, elastic stockings, ointment and plenty of it. Piles and plenty of them.

'M'sieur,' she said coldly. 'I thought you might like to know it is lunchtime and no sign of the young people.'

At once Madame Beauregard jumped up. 'Thank you, Marie. Please come with me,' she said, beckoning to Jean-Jacques. 'I really must insist on helping as far as culinary matters are concerned – the kitchen, cher Monsieur, is the province of a wife. You'll see what supplies I already have.'

He followed as she led the way past Madame Moulins who glowered on in the hallway. With modest pride, she led him into the larder. Jean-Jacques, a man starved of sensual pleasure, was fairly intoxicated by what he saw and smelt. Shelf after shelf of good things rose into the air. The ham, the cheeses, the pickles! Jar after jar of homemade condiments, of preserves and jellies. They rose up in all their shining, dark beauty. And there, with cheeks flushed a lovely rosy pink, was Madame Beauregard. She closed the door of the larder behind them.

'You see? Inhale, Monsieur,' she said in a low voice. He obeyed, staring at her. Alone in this tiny room, alone with Louise – he knew her name, of course – he sniffed the heady mixture of perfume and pâté and truffle, of ham and cloves, ginger and cardamon. She stood so close and looked at him so intently. He felt himself rock forwards and backwards, gently, on his heels. He felt slightly dizzy. Very, very gently, he rocked forwards.

'Monsieur, at last I have found something which perfectly combines my tastes and my inclinations. Perfectly.'

He gazed at her full lips, oh, full of hope. He rocked back one half a centimetre.

'Something to astonish my husband,' she went on.

Dumbly, swallowing, Jean-Jacques nodded.

'He always gets what he wants. But now it is my turn.'

There came the sound as of a sack being dragged along the floor. Madame Beauregard sighed loudly and pushed open the larder door, ushering the bewitched pharmacist out into the fresh light of day. He nearly fell over Madame Moulins who was on her knees doing something to the kitchen floor. As she moved forward with a great, shuffling, heavy groan, dragging her feet behind her as though they were a dead weight that happened to be attached to the ends of her legs, he understood the source of the noise.

'We must discuss everything, please stay for lunch,' Madame Beauregard said firmly. Dumbly, he followed her back into the dining room. 'Look, there is a place already laid. Four of us and you.'

He looked. Yes, the table was laid with five place settings.

'They are late today – we must begin without them. Sit, Monsieur,' and she was gone, returning a moment later with a steaming pot. She lifted the lid, releasing the most tantalising aroma. 'A simple potage, just some asparagus, that's all. Rabbit stew with a few herbs. Some noodles with it, very simple, just tossed in butter. A little salad, then perhaps a sliver of cheese? A morsel of tarte tatin, perhaps. Please, sit down, Monsieur.'

He spread his hands to say no – no, he couldn't. His stomach was rumbling loudly. Not a word came out. The femme de ménage was still standing glowering in the doorway. She coughed, twice. Madame Beauregard half turned and bestowed upon her domestic a most glittering smile.

'Thank you, Marie, that is enough for today. Perhaps you would like to go early?'

How dazzling, how wonderful the smile of Madame Beauregard was. The soup was yet more wonderful. The asparagus was heaven. Soon she returned. She ladled out a generous helping of the stew. Her hips moved provocatively as she tossed the salad, they rolled as the noodles received their buttery coating.

'So much, Madame, too much,' he said weakly. But the juices in his mouth were swimming in anticipation. Behind Madame's back, he saw Madame Moulins crossing the hallway clutching a large carrier bag to her ample bosoms. As he took his first mouthful, half-closing ecstatic eyes, there was an incredibly loud report, like a shotgun going off. He looked up, alarmed. Slowly, a beatific smile spread across the face of the lovely Louise.

'Don't worry. It's only Marie, Madame Moulins going home,' she said. 'She shut the door, that is all. I expect she is hurrying to catch her bus,' and she laughed. It was such a lovely, joyful sound that he had to laugh too. 'Please, Monsieur Jean-Jacques, you need a napkin,' and he felt her hand graze his knees as she laid a snowy white cloth across them.

Charles Beauregard came roaring through the woods and, just as he flipped the indicator for the left turn into the village, saw his daughter kneeling at the edge of the road and slammed on the brakes. She stood up. A green string shopping bag dangled from her hand. He reversed back to where she stood.

'Perhaps I've lost Hilary,' she said, spreading rueful hands.

'How very careless. What d'you mean, perhaps?'

'This is his, but I left him in the café,' she said in a noncommittal tone. He looked at her.

'And how long ago was that? Where did you find it?'

She shrugged. 'In the woods. Back there.'

Charles flung open the passenger seat door and without a word she got in, sitting silently while he drove to as near as he could get to La Fourchette, wove his way through the crowd, looked in the café, spoke to the waiter and, finally, telephoned Louise. With some difficulty, he negotiated a three-point turn, set off down the road again.

'Yes, he followed you. And what exactly were you doing in the woods?'

'Nothing.'

'Were you with that stupid Lardon boy? Tell me, now.'

'I gave you my word, didn't I?'

'Yes. You gave your word.' Charles stopped the car abruptly and, reaching across her, he pushed open the passenger side door. 'Go home,' he said, with suppressed fury. 'I'll find him. Tell your mother we'll be late. I will talk to you later.'

Michèle stood in the road and watched the car disappear. When it was gone, she hoisted the bag onto her shoulder. She stood for some minutes before turning and walking very slowly back into the village. Very slowly, she plodded up the hill towards home. Halfway up, while still hidden from the house, she burst into tears which would not stop. Still sobbing, she sat down and then lay and looked up at the leaves and the sky. She touched her face, which was red and shiny. Michèle, who had no need to check her appearance, did not carry a mirror in her bag. She knew how she looked and was and she waited. She would wait. Soon everything would revert to how it had been before.

Deep in the forest, Charles transcribed a second circle. When he failed to find Hilary, he decided to cover the same area, but following a slightly larger circle this time. He called out Hilary's name as he went. Next, he expanded the search zone to include the broad riding which led straight to the heart of the forest. Some instinct drew him to walk a way up it first. Perhaps it was merely the fact that the going there was so much easier. Then he saw Hilary. He was lying behind a log, very still, very white in the face. When he saw Charles, he gave a lovely smile. It occurred to Charles that the boy looked a lot like his wife.

Charles knelt down and examined him. He checked bones, pulled him straight, tested reactions. An ugly bump on his forehead.

'I feel sick,' he said, 'I knew you'd come. Can't walk on my own.'

Charles slid his arms under him and braced himself to lift him into a sitting position against a tree. Another effort, and he was up.

It was tough going. As he half staggered and half walked with his burden, Charles took deep breaths to steady himself, to set up a rhythm. In, out, one, two, he counted out loud.

Hilary's head throbbed. Blood pounded through it to its own crazy rhythm. He was in motion, he felt sick. He was on an animal. Its warmth, the mane. He was on the sea, rocking, in the hold of a ship. He was sea sick, horribly so. No wonder, the swell of the sea, throwing him from side to side, the motion was terrible. He became more and more aware that his body was swaying and throbbing.

'Michèle. Something happened to her. A man grabbed her.' Urgently he clutched at Charles's arm.

'Something happened to you. Michèle's fine, I've seen her. You banged your head hard. A miracle you didn't pass out altogether.' Charles patted Hilary's arm, unclenched the fist that was balling together the fabric of his shirt sleeve and placed Hilary's arm around his shoulders. They set off once more. 'Steady now,' he said.

Very slowly, they moved through the wood. The shafts of sun beating down through the trees were so bright that Hilary had to shut his eyes. Even from behind his lids, the sun pierced him with its dazzling lances and made him wince. Bird song trilled its torture. The wizened man in the market was warbling behind the trees. He felt the patterns the sun-dappled leaves made on him, like lace. It was all so strange. He could smell fresh bracken. He was concentrating with his whole being on walking straight and not falling over. This made his head thump. Everything was overlaid by the presence of the big man, soothing, holding him together.

His head was full of strange, incoherent thoughts, pain and pleasure mixed, relief and surprise. It felt so good to be held by Charles, so safe. His mother. Michèle. The purple baby. All in his arms. Charles had saved them all. Without him, what?

'The thing is,' Hilary said. He struggled to make it all quite clear. What was the thing? He squinted at Charles's face, received a flash of woodland brightness which made him close his eyes again. 'There was a man,' he said.

'He hit you?'

'No, no, I went into something, a tree, I don't know. Why isn't she like you?' Charles had to realise that he had to say these things. Later might be too late. He might as well say everything. Nothing to lose, all lost, the world lost for love. The deep chest swelled and receded. Was Charles laughing? Hilary thought he might cry. He quite wanted to. He had never felt more serious in his whole life.

'Be quiet,' Charles said. Hilary wasn't going to cry, no, he was made of sterner stuff, so just in case he squeezed his eyes tight shut.

They were coming out onto the road and there was the car. Charles helped him in. They were at the house and he was being carried inside and up the stairs and put to bed with painkillers inside him and a cold compress on his head. All of this happened from very far away. Hilary heard himself sleepily agreeing that he would be fine in the morning. Then he drifted away on the faint whispers of Charles and Louise conferring.

In her room, Michèle lay awake and listened for the

noises of the house. The owl's cry hooted out from the orchard. The wind was rustling up a summer storm. No sound from downstairs where, by candlelight, her parents held hands and whispered.

Hilary woke perhaps a dozen times and each time felt the tide drawing him out to sea again until at last he woke very hungry and knew that he was better. In the shower, he felt carefully at the lump on his head which was shiny and blue-green and dramatic. It hurt like hell. The towel on his head was interestingly acerbic. Putting on his shirt, he discovered how stiff his back was. His head set up a thudding counterpart to his feet, descending the stairs in gradual rallentando.

They'd had breakfast. A thermos of coffee and a basket of brioches were waiting for him. He consumed them ravenously, tearing them apart and loading the frail shells with butter and jam. Chewing hurt. Little pink rosebuds clustered winsomely in a vase on the table. For no good reason, the sight of them also hurt. Something to do with his mother, who also did arrangements like this. When he had eaten, he stayed for a long time staring at nothing. Eventually, Charles came yomping past and skidded momentarily to a halt when he spotted Hilary through the glass door.

'You all right?'

When Hilary nodded his head, a hammer inside it suddenly fell onto the front of his forehead, bouncing off to smash the cranium and then thud back again.

'Will you come out with me? Sure you can manage it?'

'Yes,' said Hilary very quietly and carefully. He didn't want to see Michèle. He followed him out. Was he so slow or was it that everything else was going so fast? Behind him, the door crashed cataclysmically. Instead of starting the car, Charles hammered the car horn impatiently. Hilary winced.

'Ah, here she is. Get a move on, can't you?' Charles bellowed out of the window at his daughter who came running up. She got in. Crash. The bang of the car door reverberated through Hilary's eggshell skull.

'Make up your mind. I have to stay in. I have to go out. In. Out,' said Michèle snappily, leaning forwards between the seats to kiss Hilary's cheek and say her 'Bonjour' to him. 'Hilary, how are you?' He didn't manage a reply. She was thrown back as the car roared away. The loud scrunch of the gravel shivered up through the framework of the Peugeot. Hilary sat in his personal hell and waited for the next thing to happen. The car stopped abruptly.

'Out, I think. You go and help your mother. Go on.' Charles sounded peremptory and there was no gainsaying that tone. The big arm reached over, banged the door shut and they were off, leaving Michèle standing there, slowly pushing her hair back off her forehead with that gesture he knew so well.

For of course Hilary turned to watch her. He had to look, despite the pain in his head, despite his certainty that she would not turn to look at him. Because knowledge of its hopelessness didn't cancel out passion. He was not going to let himself be involved, but this purely intellectual decision did not connect with his guts, which churned on regardless. And so he looked and looked, seeing, as Charles did not, that far from turning up the hill to help her mother, Michèle merely waited for them to be gone before continuing on her way.

Lunch was prepared so Louise hurried back to her work in the surgery. She knelt in front of the great box of papers, discarding some, sorting others into neat piles, slipping yet others into files, unable to prevent herself from sorting and clearing as she went. Behind the big desk and thus hidden from the patients, stood four large cardboard boxes full of unsorted papers. More paper spilled out of the files proper. At each new piece of evidence of incompetent clerking she tutted and sighed happily.

Charles followed a system of sorts. It consisted of jamming everything current into the right-hand side of the desk until this was full. At that point, the older papers were transferred to the left side, where with luck they could remain, yellowing and crumpled, for years to come. In due course, however, one of two things would occur: either Charles would need to find a particular piece of paper or an over-full drawer would jam, perhaps the one which housed something important. His matches, say, or his Swiss Army penknife. Then would come a roaring and stamping, a drumming of feet and rattling of handles. A hand would descend to hammer and bang and rip out handfuls of paper from both sides of the desk. These discards were then shoved pellmell into boxes which mingled what was current and what was long forgotten into newer and greater obscurity. Charles always claimed that he could find anything he needed within five minutes.

Another X-ray. These really did belong in the patients' files. Smoothing out the crumpled report which came with it, Louise undid the dusty green-ribboned concertina. Patients' files were haphazard affairs, not always containing medical notes, but crammed with bills for things Charles had bought from people's shops or businesses. Thus old Limousin's file had nothing on his rheumatism but a whole sheaf of papers relating to his application to convert the old barn into holiday houses. His seizures being more and more severe, his medical notes were in the right-hand side of the desk.

Ah, there was the card of the neuro-surgeon at the teaching hospital – she slipped it on top of the pile on the desk. A glass paperweight compressed the booty. Three or four pieces of paper, the top one scrawled upon a leaf torn from an exercise book with Vigne-Laval's address written in Charles's hand. She'd done well to find that. There were a couple of letters from consultants and the list she'd written out of all the eminent doctors she knew or had heard of. How pleased Monsieur Jean-Jacques would be.

Looking at her watch, Louise hurried to the kitchen to turn the oven down and down the hill she went, swinging her basket with the precious papers in it. She felt important, imbued with a sense of purpose. Jean-Jacques was hovering at the plate-glass window and, seeing her, threw the sign to closed and, ushering her inside, closed the white vertical Venetian blinds.

'They will all think we are having an assignation, Monsieur,' said Louise, laughing, and he blushed furiously from the crown of his head right down to the V of his crisp white overalls. It took the entire time that they spent talking, ridiculously enough in whispers, agreeing a date several weeks hence, passing over the list and studying it, adding the names of people the pharmacist knew – all of twenty minutes for that blush to fade. Leaving the papers with him, Louise set off on her second errand, which was to pick up some bread. Passing the Boulangerie Lardon, she averted her gaze.

Jean-Jacques watched to see the lovely Louise pass once more. Sweetly she waved. With a sigh he went up the stairs to the flat. Nothing was cooking in his kitchen. That morning's dirty breakfast dishes still lay on the table. He opened the door to the fridge and, with a grimace, closed it again.

Louise checked her watch. Charles liked his fish golden brown and piping hot, just flaking inside, but completely plain with just a sprinkling of parsley and a dash of lemon. Very simple, but it had to be just so. Setting the fish on a very low flame, she decided she'd just take five minutes to look in the attic. Up the stairs she went, humming to herself. There was a box of old papers she'd seen a year or two back.

With a conspiratorial glance left and right up and down the corridor, Nicholas tapped on the door. A cry of some kind encouraged him to enter and, as he did so, Jim turned, his face streaming with tears. Nicholas made to go out again.

'Hayfever,' Jim wheezed. 'Forgot my spray. Bloody nuisance.' He waved to him to sit. Nicholas waited for the seizure to pass, which it did, slowly and messily. Boxes of tissues lay about the place.

'How are you today, Nicholas?'

'What? Oh, fine. Well. I don't know.'

Jameson finished the job of wiping himself down and most of the desk and then sat down and looked at him.

'Silly,' Nicholas said. 'I don't know why I've come.'

'Don't you?' Jim smiled. 'Old friends should help each other, right?' This emboldened Nicholas to start the speech he had prepared.

'I think,' he said slowly, 'I think what I'd really like from you is some kind of analysis of the kind of state my wife is in – well, a diagnosis I suppose of what those symptoms represent. That should be quite simple, shouldn't it?'

'Sorry. I can't do that.'

'Jesus. Then what kind of help can you offer? What am I supposed to do? Jesus.' His hands were trembling.

'Talk to me.'

'What about? My primitive sexual fantasies? Penis envy? That I want to get back into my mother's womb, having killed my father first?' He should never have asked a friend. No, better to go to a stranger.

'If you like,' said the old man, still smiling.

*   *   *

Louise was singing. It took a mere two minutes before she pulled out a file inside which was a letter with a university crest. Then another. And another. A moment later, a piercing scream rang around the rafters. Louise threw all the papers up into the air, then scrabbled around for them again. She snatched up the first piece of paper and read it out loud: 'Regret to inform you that in these circumstances it will not be possible for you to continue as a student here.' With appalled disbelief, she read and re-read this and a number of other pieces of paper with the same crest and the same message. 'Would not readmit you to this or any other faculty' – 'lowest ever marks in a public exam' – 'failure to attend even a single lecture during the course of two semesters' – 'unusual for a student to fail each exam so unequivocally' – 'lack of application, lack of all the qualities desirable for a medical career . . .' Expelled. They had expelled him.

Spreading out the contents of the file, she examined each piece of paper. Every one spoke, not just of failure, but of a dogged determination to fail on the part of one Charles Beauregard, a student who refused to study but would not give up his right to do so.

At the very bottom of the file, she found a letter addressed 'To whom it may concern'. This was an official document which gave the date and place of issue and number of the diploma which qualified Charles Beauregard as a doctor. It was precisely what she had wanted to find. Except the date was that of his failure, the place the university that had kicked him out.

She read it four or five times, frowning, then stared at it for ages without it making any sense. She looked at the piece of paper very carefully and then held it to the light. It looked genuine enough. She held all the rejections in one hand and the certificate in the other, as if she could make them balance out in some way. Then she saw it. The crest on the certificate, at first glance identical to that on the other papers, was not. There was a horse's head on it – and the horse was winking. A forgery, a stupid joke. No, it was too much. It was so typical of Charles. His unmistakable thumbprint stamped across it.

She threw the thing down. She felt like screaming. Her chest was pounding away. The shock of it had made the blood drain from her face, she knew she had turned pale and suddenly felt terribly cold. She took a deep breath, let it out, but still her heart knocked crazily against her chest. She felt sick.

Now came rage. How could he? How dared he? How could he deceive her like this? For all these years? Not to mention the patients. Thousands of them. The man in the white coat wasn't a doctor at all. How many thousands of incidents had happened, the near misses, the non cures, the – my God, how many deaths? The implications multiplied with horrible speed. She was finished, ruined. He was a murderer – a monster. Should she have known? Their life together, everything she owned, everything she did, everything they were – the meaning had drained out of it all.

Louise sat back upon her haunches and opened her mouth, throwing her head back, ready to scream again, but only a feeble squawk came out.

'Madame! The fish is burning!' A thin but piercing cry floated up as from another world.

'Madame!' It seemed to Louise that this cry had been coming up through the house for some time, had been in her head, without her quite taking it in.

'*Madame*!' Slowly, she went downstairs. The kitchen was full of smoke, the fish had long since burnt. She needed to think. Marie stood with her head on one side, staring at the fish pan as though it was some alien creature that had flown in through the window. She had at least had the sense to take it off. Her triumphant smile creased up her stupid fat face. Louise looked at her, looked at the charred fish, through the black veil. It was all of a piece.

'It doesn't matter,' she said. Nothing mattered, not even the stupid face of Marie. The whole world had suddenly turned black.

4 ∫

Madame Ourlandes waved at Hilary who smiled back.

'In old age, Alain Ronsard remained the idealist he had been all his life,' Charles was saying. There was a faint sigh of agreement. Some people were nodding. There was a big crowd in the non-denominational crematorium, a modern concrete building which had a sweeping tick of a roof and a reverential driveway, tricked up with the symbols of religion but lacking the content. This made people uneasy. Hilary watched them. As the room filled up, people made polite remarks about how efficient the whole business was or how much more pleasant it was than they had expected. Then as they sat and waited, there was nothing to look at but the coffin, placed just where you'd expect an altar to be. It rested on a solid metal trolley, an ugly monster designed to take great weights.

'For this we can envy our friend, he who had no envy in him. To live so long and still to love mankind, that is a kind of grace. May we all come to such a state of grace in the end.'

Spreading big, deprecatory hands, Charles stepped down from the little stand, which was hardly big enough to be a pulpit but had pretensions in that direction. Music swelled up, heads bowed, people were saying prayers and Hilary, who had none, stared at the coffin instead. The whole business was bizarre. That a doctor should usurp the job of a priest at the funeral of an atheist made some sort of sense, but they had been short-changed. The fake spouting idealism insulted the dead idealist who had had such belief in mankind. Or were words so pure that it didn't matter who spoke them? He saw that the thing about Charles was that he was so often right.

He went on staring at Charles, who beckoned to him to come forward. Hilary had never seen a dead body and didn't want to start now, but he went.

A uniformed attendant opened the double doors, another came forward to take the trolley and the music got louder to cover the noise. There was a shuffling, a repositioning, people stood. The trolley was taken to the back of the building and wheeled into position facing the furnace, tilted slightly to enable the coffin to slide off and take its position on a raised dais. They watched from behind the stable door which kept onlookers at a safe distance.

Now a heavy steel plunger leapt out like a metal tongue and thrust the coffin forwards and down the slight incline. Simultaneously, the metal doors slid open letting out the roar of the furnace and a bright flicker from below. Hell-fire was glimpsed for seconds before the tongue snapped back and the doors banged shut. Gone, he was gone, irrecoverable.

The dead man's son held his hand over his eyes, then turned away. This was what lay at the end of the journey. It was perfectly mechanical, a shunt in a box, and the faces lit by that fire would be people in uniform, who hadn't known you, who couldn't have described your face. Hilary felt pity prickling round his eyes for the old man who had gone on this terrible journey alone, as all must go. He'd met Monsieur Ronsard once, in the village, and had already forgotten what he looked like.

He had forgotten the ashes. It took hours for the body to pass through the furnace and come out, sieve-sized.

Quite a few people waited for the work to be accomplished. When an attendant made a discreet sign, everyone got up. They all trooped outside into the sunshine and stood in a respectful circle on the concrete discs which, like thought bubbles, drifted together to make up an idea of a path. With a quick glance to see that they were ready, the attendant turned the base of the metal container. Calm and steady in his blue uniform, he paced and swung it to and fro with a practised hand. Like incense, the cloudy issue, finer than sand, rose into the air. It shimmered in the bright light, tiny flakes blew up and away to settle beyond on the roses and flowers. The earthly remains of a man who had lived all his life in this place as had his father and his father's father. Dust to dust indeed.

Hilary thought of the brilliance of their roses at home, which were not the equal of these. They bloomed iridescent orange and yellow, these daily recipients of human fertiliser. It was over in half a minute. Madame Ourlandes leant on her stick, apologising for the traffic jam she caused as the group of people walking to their cars down the narrow path bunched up behind her, not liking to overtake, not wanting to walk on the grass. Her hands were shaking. She crept along like a snail, her back so bent that from the rear her head almost disappeared

'I just want a minute,' she whispered, taking Hilary's hand in her bumpy claw. Every step was so precisely taken, her small weight shifted from foot to foot with infinite slowness and care. Her eyes were wise. 'I would have liked to fly like that up in the air. Do you know, my dear, that I have never flown?' She twisted her head up and laughed at him sideways and squeezed his hand. 'A country woman, all my life. I have never got away from the earth, me. Now I never shall. Please. Call him for me, Monsieur le docteur. I need him.'

People shook hands and said their farewells with that generalised sombreness of things ending. Charles spoke for a while to Madame Ourlandes then helped her into her neighbour's car.

As car doors banged, as the more timid smokers lit up and mourners called out see you there, or back at the house, he could see the upbeat reaction was starting. There was a kind of easing out, a shrugging off. On with the next thing.

Charles was gloomy, it was in the way he held his cigarette, the tilt of his head expressive of loss. 'You see? This man couldn't believe in God, but all his life he believed in human beings and what they could do. Incredible, his faith in humanity. In spite of the evidence. Me, I'm too cynical for that. And when you can't believe in God or humanity, what is left? I'll tell you. Nothing. Even Madame Ourlandes doesn't believe any more. Today I wrote a prescription that will kill her.'

Hilary looked at him. 'You can't do that.'

'She asked me – why should I not help her?'

'You can't.' Hilary clenched fists. He felt sick and angry and it flashed across his mind that Charles could not have taken the Hippocratic oath, would never have sworn to protect life. 'That's murder.'

'She suffers terribly, she wants to die.'

'She's a Catholic, she believes suicide will send her to hell—'

'So for something *you* think *she* believes in I should let her suffer? Poor Madame. Lucky for her that I am not such a hypocrite. It is for her to decide what happens to her, not for you and not for me either.'

'But what's to stop you from giving,' Hilary didn't know the phrase for what he wanted and so he invented one, les pillules de la mort – 'death pills to anyone, then?'

'Nothing.'

'But if anyone could get them from you, there's no morality in it. You have to protect human life, that's your job.'

'Please, let's not be too exalted. You have to do the best you can. Sometimes you ease pain and sometimes not. Sometimes people are in such pain that nothing helps it. And then it's not for me to judge if what they suffer is bearable or not. I am not God.'

'If you hand out death pills, you are.' He's the devil, thought Hilary.

Neither of them said much after that. Hilary went on feeling sick and anxious. In certain circumstances it might be not just conceivable but imperative to tell on Charles. The very thought of doing that made him feel like shitting in his pants.

Charles soon recovered his equanimity and by the time he dropped Hilary at the bottom of the driveway he was singing again, the hit of the season. Appropriately enough, it was a bit of advice from one man to another: 'Never-ever-ever-ever-ever tell her that you lur-urve her!'

'Sure you won't come on my rounds – see the baby you delivered?'

Mutely Hilary shook his head and stood for a long time where he had landed, staring at the gravel and at his own two feet.

Sunlight streamed into the ward, making the white coats glow with undeserved brilliance. The old man, propped up on pillows, half of him under a large cage, stared at the surgeon and held his breath. At last, Nicholas shook his head, alarming his patient who uttered a hoarse cry.

'No? Doc? Whaddayer mean, no?'

'I'm so sorry. Thinking about something else. Of course you're going home. I'll lay money on it. A fiver says you're out in, let's see, three weeks at the latest? Make that ten pounds. Nurse! You're my witness. Done.'

The old man cackled and did a jubilant high five and looked from side to side at the pleasant faces of the nurses and the junior doctors to say what a one he was, oh he was, he was. What ones they all were.

'Good, good,' said Nicholas.

Mr Coghill, pleased by so little, had had all the bones in his leg smashed by a lorry driver. This was an opportunistic moron who liked to thunder down the bus lane and whose small child had been allowed to stand, unrestrained, in the front of the cab and drink out of a can. When her dad did his bit of last-minute braking at the naturally wholly unexpected, indeed unreasonable, sight of a bus ahead of him, veering off sideways into Mr Coghill's mini, the little girl had gone spinning through the window and had bounced off two cars before picking herself up from the pavement, face shredded, arm broken but, miraculously, alive.

Not one scratch had harmed her dad, though some Coke had splashed onto him. He had experienced what he liked to term mental anguish, notably the inconvenience of his solid bulk being trapped in his cab for half an hour while rescuers tried to get out the old man. The little car had split apart like a burst paper bag. Nicholas had saved the old man's leg which had splintered through his flesh. He believed that he might walk again, eventually, on crutches. This was very unlikely, though Nicholas had no intention of telling him the truth. Medicine had made an inveterate liar of him. Besides, it was possible. Physio could do a lot but would not be able to stop the leg from hurting, always. Moron had made a cripple of him and Mr Coghill said he was lucky, Doc, wasn't he, that his dancing days were over.

The child, fortunate in being brought in very fast to one of the best plastic surgeons in Europe, might with luck eventually look something not so very far off normal, though several more operations would be required. Because of the way her nose had been flattened, she would always have breathing difficulties. The best hope was that she would merely look ugly.

And the father, unscathed and unrepentant, who had yet to visit his elder victim and was notorious in the children's wards for complaining and foul language, wept when he was told that he might lose his licence and with it his livelihood. That destroyed a man, he kept saying. He'd not failed his breath test, had he? It was the brakes what done it, not the man who never checked them. Not having a job destroyed a man. He was a victim of circumstances, that was what he was. He was immensely sorry for himself. He brought the family in to look at the kid and sympathise with him. Nicholas had had him removed from the ward when the moron had attempted to tell him these things. It was entirely possible, for the world was a cruel and remorseless place, that he might keep his job and driving habits intact. That being so, it would probably all happen again.

Smiling vaguely, finger tapping conspiratorially on nose, Nicholas strode off to the next patient followed by his customary phalanx. As usual, he paid his camp followers no attention whatsoever. He was thinking about Jim, who only that morning had asked him if he'd spoken to Amanda. After all, talking to Amanda was but the apex of the problem. Or, to be precise, her talking to him.

Jim's Cheshire cat grin stayed with Nicholas as he continued round the wards. These bedside visits involved no medical element whatsoever, for the actual business of treating these people was far too serious to be incorporated into his floor show. The point of the round was to reassure people that they were under the daily supervision of an expert and that that expert was cheerful about their prospects. Nicholas, smiling and nodding, saw that Jim's smile wasn't precisely supercilious or patronising. It held trace elements of the seen-it-all-before, though. Had he? That, of course, was also what attracted him. Increasingly he felt the urge to give in and tell Jim all his fears and hopes and dreams, yes, to cry on his shoulder like a little babby.

'Morning, my dear,' he said, looking at the old dear whose hip he'd done a week ago and using his universal appellation, for who could remember their names? It was their medical notes he needed to keep in his head. She smiled back at him and nodded. 'And how are you today?'

'Very well, Doctor, thank you.'

'Good, good, excellent. We'll have you doing a tango before the week's out. Nurse! Make a note of that, please. Put me down for the foxtrot.'

Today, the hips and knees were all friendly, all doing quite well. He tended not to listen to what the patients said unless they complained of something specific, which on the whole meant that their suffering was intense. His experience was that there were few hypochondriacs among these old folk given to British understatement. It was extraordinary, how brave people were. Naming of parts, that was what he did between wards.

Down the corridors he strode, with lyrics dancing through his head. Mrs Femur may I introduce Mrs Tibia and her charming relation Miss Patella? Miss Fibula, are you perchance connected to the little Tarsals? Everybody on their tippy-toes for the dance. Tunes bobbed up and down, acquiring words. The Scapula thinks it's humerus and the Tarsals merely numerous for we hardly dare articulate the hamate and the capitate. Yes, the drivers who are pissed, they never would be missed for I've got a little list – yes, he's got a little list.

Heading it was little Annie's dad, who should be gagged and made to spend his remaining years in some menial capacity on his knees, probably swabbing floors, in a position which would enable passing Coghills in wheel-chairs to run over his hand; arse-in-air would also allow passing doctors to give his fat bum a kick and upend the big red head into a bucketful of grey suds. Perhaps that might give the blockhead a dim notion of cause and effect. Head down, elbow-greasing, bum up and froth-ing dirt, he might just get an angle on what he was worth.

Slowly Louise walked down the drive. She was ruined. They were finished. Charles would go to prison. For how long? A very long time, evidently. A lawyer would know. There would be lawyers, all right, judges, a court, the weight of justice would crash down upon their heads and crush them to dust. She sniffed the air and smelt their dusty robes, looked at the gravel and saw the flinty look in their accusing eyes, heard their archaic language.

A catastrophe. Yet the chasm had been there all along. She had stepped across it every day of her married life and not known that it was there. She could have carried on for another twenty years and not known. She could have died without ever discovering the truth. She could that very day have been organising his retirement party to mark the end of a long and successful career. Her hands were clenched tight and it took an effort to force herself to loosen them. There were red marks where her nails had scored deep into her palms.

She stopped and shook her head in sheer disbelief, then went on, dragging her feet. The whole of her body felt rusty and locked. The first thing to do was to see Monsieur Jean-Jacques and call this fiasco of a celebration off, this mockery which had exposed her husband to her and would announce to the whole neighbourhood that he was a fraud and a criminal. Though exposure must come eventually, she would not knowingly engineer it.

For, as she crept down the hill, Louise knew that deep in some part of her being she had always expected if not this, then something like it. She was the daughter of a hairdresser from Rennes. She always would be. That she should be the doctor's wife was not fitting. It never had been. She was a fraud, just as he was. No wonder they had found each other. The journey to the point of exposure had taken her whole life and yet the surprise was not that it should have come, but that it should have come today. And the thought of the shame and humiliation of that exposure made her shudder.

Louise leant against the low stone wall to think for a little moment what she was going to say. Certainly not the truth. That would not solve the problem. Although the logical part of her understood that it was Charles who had perpetrated the actual crime, she blamed Jean-Jacques for it. Because this fool had decided to organise a celebration for the man he disliked, her life was ruined.

She felt both angry and sick. How unnecessary it all was. To sit and think up lies, in the heat. One moment the world was clean and beautiful and the next, everything was black and burnt and complicated, under a haze of smoke. And there was no going back to the clean pure time, no chance of recovering the happy person of the morning. When she thought of the trivial concerns that had seemed important then, she felt like crying. For she had been very happy and, fool that she was, she had not known it.

What would she say to Charles? It was a bit like discovering that you were married to a lunatic or murderer. Just what sort of man was he? Perhaps he had murdered people, dozens of them. To live this sort of lie each day was conceivable if it was merely a question of adopting an identity, but his deception went so much further. It took cunning. It took courage. Just what kind of mind could permit a man to live a lie that required a daily subterfuge of these dimensions? How often had he stood knowingly on the brink of disaster? It was a gigantic joke perhaps on his part, a massive piece of legerdemain, but it was the lives of others he juggled with, not his own. The more she thought about it, the more frightening it became.

Louise felt that she was walking on a cracked sheet of ice, hopping from one block to the next. The whole sheet was crazed and the cracking noise loud. Another little piece slid away under her feet, another little portion of truth and she was on the edge, staring into the icy black waters below. She feared her husband, just as much as she loved him. She had always known this without ever consciously thinking it. Fear was the blunt instrument that whetted their love.

With a trembling hand, she rapped at the plate-glass window of the pharmacy.

Jean-Jacques was returning from his errands and just coming towards the door when Louise Beauregard appeared as magically as if his wishes had grown wings and flown her to him. Her cheeks were pink and her eyes bright as if they had candles in them. 'Bonjour, Monsieur Jean-Jacques, I must talk to you,' she said. 'At once.'

'Come with me, Madame Beauregard,' and he unlocked the door and beckoned her into his inner sanctum. The dispensary was his shining temple, its hundreds of little drawers and glass-fronted shelves carried a munificence of pills and ointments and lotions. Everything the frailty of man or woman could possibly require was there, exquisitely arranged by his priest's hand. Each drawer displayed his careful lettering separating goats from sheep, not in lifeless Dewey Decimalisms, but with lovely curlicues and flourishes, with major ailments separated from minor, with alphabetically ranged brand names. Trusses and bandages, stockings and foot pads were defined and named by digit or by limb. It was his very own system and he adored it. In his ordered universe, he was creator and worshipper alike.

'People don't usually see my little cubbyhole, you know, Madame,' he said with his modest smile. 'You see here my supplies, Madame – ah, not as interesting as yours, I think. Nor so delightfully – aromatic.' There was a very particular smell, though proximity had deadened Jean-Jacques' awareness of it. It was a clean smell, combining lint and cardboard with a whiff of formaldehyde. It was faintly medical, the smell of authority.

Slowly, she spread her hands, paused, considered, made to speak again. Breathed in deeply and then out.

Jean-Jacques had had plenty of experience of things going wrong. He knew about the frail and elderly, those who sneezed or coughed or fainted, the chronic malingerers and those who came in denying all but hopelessly ill. He looked at Louise and noted symptoms. There was a pulse beating in her temple. Her hand was upon her chest which swelled and fell with strong emotion – and that hand trembled a little.

'Chère Madame,' he said, with a little self-deprecatory cough. 'I have already taken the liberty of using my lunch hour to write a number of little informal notes, to tell people of the forthcoming celebration, of the anniversary—'

'Already?' she said. 'But this is the limit!' The sharpness of her tone took him aback. She took a deep breath, supporting herself against the dispensary table.

'Why, Madame,' He shuffled his feet, 'you gave me the addresses yourself. I posted them just five minutes ago.'

'But it must be cancelled. You must stop them.'

Jean-Jacques did a little turn about his table and the presence of so many familiar things restored his nerve. He touched the ledger, admired his old-fashioned pestle; he let his hand drift across his spotless white coat lying on the back of his special chair. It was starchy crisp. He put it on and did the buttons up, one by one. His armour was impenetrable.

'Dear Madame, your charming modesty really won't stop me.' Jean-Jacques continued to smile nicely while he delivered his ultimatum. '*Nothing* will stop me. I am going to find a way to honour your husband. I assure you that the whole village insists upon it. This celebration will happen. *I* insist upon it. I won't hear another word on the subject. You see, this is not a private matter. It is in the public domain,' and even as he uttered these words he felt how well they suited his mouth. 'Now, dear Madame, you must tell me what is wrong with you. I am not a doctor, I would not dream of aspiring to it, but I know a thing or two about simple ailments and I can see you are not feeling well.'

Amanda was sitting with a book on her lap for the obligatory half-hour between clearing up dinner and the time when she could decently go to bed and she did not look up when Nicholas came, newspaper in hand, into the sitting room. He came and sat beside her, so wife shifted slightly to make room for him and reached for the TV remote control and put it beside him. There, he was settled. She found it quite convenient to sit and rest and seemingly read while actually she just thought her own thoughts and so it took a while for her to realise that Brainbox wasn't watching the news, indeed hadn't even turned the TV on. She closed her eyes, to avoid him. It was easy to block him out.

'Are you asleep, Mandy? You're smiling. Mandy? Mandy? Mandy? Mandy?'

This was irritating of him and so she pretended it wasn't happening and it wasn't until he took hold of her hand that she saw she'd have to reply. She opened her eyes to look at him. He was staring at her.

'I was nearly asleep,' she said, with wife's silly-me smile.

'Why don't you talk to me?' Stupid, you see? When any fool would know. But little dimwit wife always toed the line and so she smiled nicely and even laughed a little. 'Mandy?'

Her eyes looked at him calmly while in her head, with growing exultation, she skied down the black slope, not just well, but magnificently. At the mogul where she had fallen, she jumped. She soared into the air, she flew. Mandy, Mandy, Mandy.

'Talk to me for Christ's sake.'

'Language,' she said, just as she did to Ed and that was rather amusing and so she smiled and looked at him quite calmly. His mouth opened wide when he spoke, she could see all the black fillings. There was no need to shout and rant. She didn't see why even wife should have to put up with that and so, blocking out the noise as best she could, she sang to herself in her head. When she grew bored with having to look at him, Amanda took the remote and turned the TV on and began to watch an old film which she had seen before. Vivien Leigh in *A Streetcar Named Desire*. She watched the great star with fascination and awe, her skin as thin as the floaty chiffons she wore.

'We've seen it before,' she said. Amanda knew, of course, that Nicholas, sitting beside her with his head in his hands, was in some kind of state. There was no need for wife to do anything about that. This particular scene was, after all, very familiar. 'You see?' said Amanda. 'We've seen it all before.'

Louise was unwell and the whole house was topsy-turvy. Hilary stared at the stars and listened to the owl, which like him chose the orchard as the place to express its feelings. Tonight, it was in full cry. There was a storm coming; the air was still and humid and everything was oppressive. Through the big French window he could see Charles in the kitchen busy laying a tray with cups and making coffee. They would have coffee outside, where there might be more of a courant d'air.

Charles had made dinner for the three of them, insisting upon serving them and in the process using every dish and saucepan and plate in the place. These were all left for Madame Moulins. This, he said with a wink, meant that the morning would bring her an interesting surprise which would relieve the monotony of her life. Somewhere else in the vicinity Michèle was presumably relieving the monotony of hers. Not that he cared. It was no longer possible for him to talk to her, any more than he could talk to Charles and yet he so much wanted to – like a child he yearned to be reassured. Hilary ambled inside.

'Give me that,' he said. Gingerly, he took the pot, which was very heavy and brimming with scaldingly hot coffee.

'Don't worry, I'll bring it. Would you take Louise a tisane? For her headache? Good, good.' Charles had loaded a tray with little delicacies. He loved his wife, he was all concern. 'Tell her I'll be along in a minute.'

Hilary rapped gently on the door upstairs.

Louise lay in her bed with some kind of compress on her head. She looked pretty ropy. He put the tray down and quietly backed away.

'Don't go.'

'What can I get you?'

'Nothing. Sit here.' They were both whispering. Plaintively, Louise looked at him. When an enormous bang came, they both jumped.

Hilary hung out of the window as the storm broke and he heard the thunder rolling their way. Flashes of lightning lit the horizon. A real summer storm, you could see it rolling up and over the hill until suddenly it hit the house. The rain pattering loudly on the leaves in giant drops then thundering across the roof. Ripples of wind across the bone-dry cornfield. A roar from below as Charles gathered up his belongings and made a run for it, laughing like the devil. Hilary watched him run back out again, pick up the coffee pot, heard him curse as he burnt his fingers. In those few seconds, his shirt was completely soaked and stuck to his shoulders.

'Something terrible has happened,' said Louise.

'What?'

She shook her head and winced. 'I can't tell you. I can't tell anyone.'

'Charles?' he said. She turned her face to the wall. How literal life could get. He sat for a bit then when nothing more was said, he got up and tiptoed away. For a little moment, he hovered at the door. Her face was a white blur in the fading light.

'Will you help me, Hilary? Don't go. Are you on my side?'

'Of course I am.'

He came back and sat on the bed. She reached out and took his hand in her cold one. It was nearly dark but the room was lit by the occasional flash of lightning – which coming simultaneously with the bangs meant the storm was right above them. In these flashes they studied each other. In this light, her eyes were black. Her hand gripped his hard, tensing up with each bang. He could not read anything in her expression beyond simple fear.

It seemed to Hilary that the terrible thing that had happened to both of them was Charles – but he did not dare ask. Not by one hint dared he betray the doctor to his wife. They looked on and on at each other. This exchange of looks was so heavily freighted with meaning that he knew that she must know and yet nothing was said, nothing could be said. He waited. Then, at last, the persistent drumming on the roof began to abate and after the flash he counted to two, then five, then seven seconds before the thunder came.

The air was suddenly cool and fresh and it smelt green, of crushed leaves.

'There's going to be a party,' Louise said. Her white teeth flashed in the dark at his little exclamation of surprise, for of all possible revelations, this was the most unexpected.

'Here?'

There was a long pause. Louise stared at the ceiling. 'Of course it will be here,' she said very slowly. 'Where else? It is a party to honour Charles, you see. From the village – but of course it must be my party. I must be in charge of this. My God,' she said, sitting up suddenly. 'There is everything to arrange.'

'I'll help you,' he said.

'Will you pass me that book, please?' As if the electricity had just scored a direct hit upon her, her whole tone and manner had changed. She wanted the notepad near the telephone. At once she started scribbling and intent upon her task seemed to forget that he was there. Hilary backed away, slowly. He closed the door as quietly as he could, looking at the dark head bent, busy. How strange everything was. Coming down the stairs he passed Charles who touched his arm in his usual, confiding way and laid a finger to his lips – a finger that could have meant anything, anything at all.

Now Hilary could not help himself. He looked everywhere for Michèle, into each darkening room of the house, even the linen store, even the garage. He needed to see her. He needed her. He stood outside and let his head fall back and the warm rain poured down, making him close his eyes. When he opened his mouth he could taste the storm at the back of his throat. But the owl had stopped hooting and Michèle was not to be found.

'She was watching this old movie.' Nicholas looked at his friend. Jim didn't meet his eye at all, he just went on leaning back in his chair and very gently swivelling from side to side, never more than an inch or two in either direction, a constant motion which should have irritated but instead soothed.

'Tennessee Williams. *Streetcar Named Desire*, you know. Marlon Brando in a vest. We were just sitting on the sofa,' he said. There was a long pause. This was not the where and when of it, or even the how. He had to begin at the beginning. 'We've seen it all before.' That was what Amanda had said. He looked at Jim, who continued to study the contents of his In tray as a pleasant variation upon the lesser but no less impressive contents of Out. The desk, a handsome wooden affair, was covered with receptacles. Three jars of pens, pencils and the like, nothing uncontained. Chaos was ordered, kept at bay, was named. In and Out, yes. Nicholas began to talk very rapidly.

'You have to understand how we were, Jim, how far it's gone. I've never in my life had a friend, anybody, to talk to like Amanda. D'you know what I mean?' He thought that it had started with sex, with a complete knowing and trusting of the other person, with total honesty. His wife had been the only person in his life to whom he could say anything, anything at all. The first and last. He shut up for a bit and thought about it. He was suddenly clear-headed. How very strange it was that they had accompanied each other on this journey of life for over twenty years only to find that they were unable to speak at all.

'Professional help,' said Jim. 'That's what you need. Tell you what, here are a few names. I'll just jot them down. You have to get her to go and see somebody who can help. I mean, as a friend, I can't do what they can – I'm not a professional, am I?' He sneezed, suddenly and violently.

'God,' said Nicholas, watching him begin the business of rubbing the spray from the desk.

'You didn't really think I could do anything, did you?'

'No, of course not.'

Abandoned, Nicholas sat listening to the gentle exhalation of his own breath and the tiny scrape of Jim's pen on the paper while his solitude became a real fact in his head. He felt so sad. To be so terribly alone was sad even in his cruel world where little children could be tossed about like rag dolls, could crack their heads open and break their bones and not always be mendable.

Hilary had no time at all. He hurried and scurried and did a thousand errands for the mistress of the house. All week he scarcely caught a glimpse of Michèle. Louise had assessed what abilities her household contained. Thus Hilary became the messenger who fetched and the mule who carried, Michèle was the silver polisher, Madame Marie chief scourer and moaner, Louise the cook. The beneficiary of all this industry smiled and said a party was a wonderful idea and calculated on his fingers how long it was since they'd had one.

Charles, meanwhile, went his own sweet way. The tooting of his car setting off each day to visit patients was the signal for the delivery vans to start arriving, grinding in low gear up the hill and scattering the gravel yet further from its allotted resting place. There were deep ruts in the drive and still the vans kept coming. For there was no time to waste. The party was that very Saturday and there was no time, no time. Louise did not stop running and doing and cooking for one single instant.

This was serious food, this was the French showing off at what they did best. Her pride as a woman was at stake. And, when she wasn't preoccupied with the precise quality of sole or foie gras or the cheeses, when she wasn't off to choose between the Bordeaux or the Burgundy, they exchanged information in a cryptic manner. Hilary understood that her hand had been forced and how; he saw exactly why it was that the little pharmacist was going to get his way. What did Charles think of all this?

When the troops gathered, it was in the kitchen, the motor of the war machine. These days they also ate there, for the dining room paraded an ever-growing array of china. Whole cupboards of fine porcelain, carefully washed by Madame Moulins, drew up their ranks upon the table.

Louise would still dish up a three-course lunch. This was too important for a Frenchwoman to neglect, even in these hasty days.

'Charles – seems – so pleased with it all,' Hilary would say carefully.

'Of course. Did you think he wouldn't be?' she might reply. Hilary smiled at her. Then he dared to ask more.

'It's going to be a great celebration of him, then, with speeches and so on?'

'He's quite vain enough to enjoy that, you know.' Louise gave him a speaking look over the salad bowl – a shrug. She didn't look pale or wan any more. As the week wore on, as the supplies were delivered, not to mention the tables that would hold the groaning plenty and the chairs le tout countryside would lounge upon, Louise became more and more energetic. Each day she grew more purposeful and it seemed to Hilary that that febrile energy of hers had always needed something to feed upon and had at last found it.

Daily the pharmacist toiled up the hill with his growing guest list to discuss and his hunger alike to taste and be part of it all. He stood and sniffed at the larder door and his eyes were bright as he mentally counted and planned. He tried a little morsel of this and sneaked a fingerful of that. He went to the garage and stared at the crates of wine and, in the cellar, he inspected the tubs which were to hold the ice for the champagne. All the time his lips moved, as though he were praying.

Jean-Jacques was the bane of Madame Moulins' life. All

week she complained that 'that man' was in the way, that he brought his dusty feet onto her clean floor, that he irritated her. She would follow him up the hallway, moaning on her knees, swabbing just behind him, practically falling over him in her eagerness to remove these imaginary traces of his passage. Hilary became her new favourite and when not fetching and carrying he was treated to long accounts of her various ailments, none of which the pharmacist had managed to cure with his costly ointments and creams. Yet when Monsieur le docteur came in, dislodging small stones and ridges of earth from the giant crenellations along his boots or trailing a dripping bag of fish from the surgery to the kitchen, why then Madame Marie said not one word. She had too much respect.

At night, Hilary had time to think. He lay in the brass bed and studied the rolling line of unnaturally blue flowers across the wall and up onto the ceiling. He had it by heart, each curl of a petal grown familiar. Mostly he thought about Michèle – nothing precise, more a glancing through of memories of the day, a recording of the glimpses he had had of her. They said their good mornings and goodbyes but otherwise hardly spoke. Hilary, grown expert in the analysis of the expressions of that lovely face, believed that she was troubled by something. Perhaps it was his hope that she, like him, should not be happy. Not that he cared, oh no. Increasingly, as the week wore on, he would wonder about Charles and his extraordinary sang-froid. How it was that he could face such an event so calmly.

Hilary came to believe that something must occur to unmask him, though he was not clear whether this was something he desired or feared. He had the strongest possible sensation of something coming towards them unstoppably. He could almost see the storm coming, the wind furrowing up the corn. In the quiet dark of the night, he felt that such an outcome was right; by day, in the presence of mother and daughter, he knew this would be a catastrophe they had not deserved.

'You're a good boy,' Louise said on the Thursday night and, 'This is supposed to be a holiday, you know,' and she ruffled his hair, just as his mother did.

So Friday became the day off, the day of the fishing trip. By seven o'clock in the morning they were on the road with a basket of food and rods in the back and Charles lighting up the first fag, singing the first song. Hilary, who had hardly spent any time with him of late, felt as nervous as a lover who, fearing rejection, both longed to touch and dared not attempt it.

Before they even got near the water there was the issue of what to put on the line. Charles had a whole box of flies, which all had special names. There was le jeune Clemenceau and, more whiskery, le vieux. There was la petite pute, a voluptuous little pink dolly, and her big sister, la grande. Did Charles invent these names? Delicately, as though he was indeed touching a woman, Charles attached the flies.

The idea was to flick the rod backwards so the line snaked up behind your head and then with another deft flick it came forwards, so the fly fell lightly on the water. Or hit you on the side of the head. It looked simple and was hard, the line looked light but was heavy and it was all too easy for the novice to wallop himself on the ear. To begin with, they lay on the river bank lazily casting flies. Every now and then, in an access of energy, the naked Charles would tug on his waders and stand in the middle of the river casting his rod over the lovely clear waters, an odd enough sight without the ever-present danger – to Hilary's mind at least – of him hooking his private parts by mistake.

When he got too hot, Hilary joined him. They stood side by side in the river while he tried to master the art. The cool water was delightful against the heat of the sun on his back.

When he'd given himself a thick ear for the umpteenth time, Hilary went back to lying on the river bank and contemplating the mysteries of the universe, watching Charles as with the utmost delicacy he dropped the fly just where he wanted it. Exquisite, the brilliant little clump of feathers bobbing on the bright water, the big man so still that there was scarcely a ripple, every stone on the river bed magnified and the flash of a bird overhead a startling gash in the blue. Hilary stretched out languorously, feeling sexy in the heat, the dry warm earth alive with tiny noises and rustlings. A parade of ants carrying a single glossy leaf grouped around his giant hand, which had descended so unexpectedly, to examine the intruder and plan their next manoeuvre.

He'd fallen asleep and was startled awake by a shriek, the sun high and hot, a bug up his arse practically, Charles in the shade of the big tree that overhung the river, laughing and pulling at the line.

'The net! Quick, bring the net!'

Thrashing and crashing, Hilary snatched at the net, got into the water, stepped on something slimy, stubbed his toe and fell on his face, dropping the net altogether while Charles suddenly yelped in a different tone and caught hold of the line and Hilary simultaneously saw that he'd somehow got the line tangled round his cock and that the cause of this excitement was a huge brown fish which was getting away – it was going – gone – and then it darted away at right angles and straight into the net which Hilary had dropped. With an exultant cry he caught it up. A beauty!

He scrambled back onto the river bank and waved it about. Charles saved himself from premature emasculation and then came after him and, dropping all, embraced him. Laughing and shouting they danced about like two demented savages. It was a brown trout. A brown trout, not the usual rainbow kind; a real catch and hardly ever seen in these waters.

Were they going to take it back, show it to people?

'Never! We'll eat it, here and now,' Charles said. 'Food you have caught yourself is the most delicious in the world. I keep an old pan in the car and we have butter, and there are herbs, in the salad. You'll see. Fit for a king.' He went up to the car, carrying the fish. 'Look for some nice twigs and little branches, there you go. What's the matter?'

'Nothing.' He couldn't look while the fish was being killed.

Charles scooped up an armful of kindling from underneath the old tree. Neatly and carefully, he built a circle of flat stones and laid a fire within it. Then he laid more stones on each other until he had built a little structure to hold the pan above the flames. A bucket of water was placed in readiness. With precision he gutted the trout, turned its innards out, filled it with basil and tarragon. Rubbed a little butter onto it. Carefully he lit the little pile of wood.

'OK. Never leave a fire, not even for a second. Always have some water ready.'

'You're not worried, Charles, that people will find out about you?' Killjoy couldn't leave it, Killjoy had to know.

'Why?'

'Isn't the party a risk for you?'

'You English. The conscience of Europe. I tell you, Hilary, I can't live my life worrying about what people know and think. Je m'en fous.'

'And what if Louise knew?'

'Eh alors?'

'But if people knew – you must worry, surely, because you'd lose your house and your family and your job . . . it's against the law . . .' His voice trailed away as Charles came closer and closer until he could smell his warm smoky breath. He laid his sinewy arm round Hilary's shoulders and held him tightly against him, shoulder to shoulder.

'Do you worry that I could come up to you like this, then I might wind this line round your neck,' and he looped it round his neck and Hilary felt it resting on his flesh and then pulling slightly and he stood as still as he could and stared at the large-pored nose inches from his. Charles's voice was very, very quiet.

'Do you worry that in the next ten seconds I might strangle you and hide your body over there, in the river bank – you see the place? Nobody would ever find you. How easy it would be.' He gave the tiniest tug on the line.

Hilary nearly gagged. He stared into the eyes which stared back. He could smell the summery hot smell of sweat on Charles's skin. He stood perfectly still. Charles's arm round his shoulders did not move, the line was taut. Charles's large naked body touching his. An uncontrollable tremor ran through him, a cold blade of fear shot from his head to his feet. He could not help it; his legs trembled a little. Satisfied, the big man let go and spread his arms in an expansive gesture.

'You see? It didn't happen.'

Hilary crouched down until the trembling had ceased and then he sat there for a long moment and watched Charles go about his cooking as if nothing had happened. The fish, its skin blackened, fell off the bone, the flesh was moist and aromatic. The scent of the herbs, cooking, filled the air.

'Come, taste.' Hot fish, cold tangy salad, the crust of the bread, the faint smell of sweat, the wine, cooling in the river. All quite unreal.

'This is possibly the very best moment in the best place in the universe,' said Charles. Like a spectre at the feast, Hilary sat on the river bank. His same too-thin body, reprieved and still sitting in the sunshine as it had before, felt strange and precious. As if he had been murdered but didn't know it, he found himself turning and looking at the river bank, to see if the mound of freshly turned earth was there. His skin was simultaneously hot and icy cold. He felt the sun on it, saw the goose pimples.

Charles uncorked and poured the wine, he rolled it round his mouth and swallowed in one huge gulp and poured again. A belch of satisfaction. Hilary had a slug. Cold and dry and delicious. They drank deeply. With the wine, some of the strange feeling began to evaporate. Something was left, some aftertaste. An invisible line had been crossed.

'Your mother was like you,' Charles said after a while. 'Is this right, is this wrong? You know what matters? Nothing,' and he waved a lazy hand. He was a little drunk. 'Today I am a magician and with these hands I can make anything happen. I can catch any fish. But tomorrow I may be dead. So every day I take what I want.'

Charles curled up like a dog on the car blanket and fell asleep. Soon he snored. Watching the big fleshy face quivering, looking at those over-sized limbs, Hilary wanted to hurt him. Yet when he woke, Charles smiled at him sweetly. There was something so pleasant and amusing in the way he lay, naked and vulnerable, singing to himself, that Hilary no longer knew where attraction ended and repulsion began, spiced as both were with a thread of fear.

They overheated, they swam, they idled out the day and let it shimmer into dusk. Not until the midges began their dance over the water did they think about returning to the house. It was dark, Hilary half asleep as the car crunched up the long drive. He woke up to see Charles go from the car into the house. Through the open windows of the dining room he watched Charles pick up his wife and then put her down and kiss her, a job done thoroughly and with real ardour. She kissed him back. Hilary couldn't stop staring. I want real passion when I'm that old, he thought. Oh God, I want it now. Why couldn't he take what he wanted?

Saturday dawned as perfect as its predecessor, the faintest of mists over the orchard heralding the heat to come. Woken by the noise of an engine, Hilary looked out to see a man riding a motor mower through the orchard, scything down the long grass, and he was out there in a flash to cut shiny green swathes and pick up an apple on each turn.

By the afternoon, the long tables outside had been laid with gleaming white cloths by Hilary and Madame Moulins who, working as a team, developed a certain synchronous ability. He lifted and flicked, she caught and tucked. Along that expanse a field artillery of cutlery was arrayed and an army of plates and she, demonstrating exactly what went where, would return more than once to find that Hilary had left out something. Who could eat that much? Ah, he would see.

Then he was the plate navvy, carrying the heavy load, for apart from the mere three plates that would adorn each place setting, a new plate would be required for each course and these had to be to hand. And then there were the glasses. White wine and red wine and water and let us not forget the carafes for the water, let us not omit the crab claw crackers and the langoustine forks. When he had done the right number of places – it was sixty-two exactly – Hilary went to tell Louise that she had over-ordered. Ah, non, she said. There would be more people. There would always be some local folk who would consider it an oversight that they had not been invited and who would turn up regardless. She had catered for them. Louise stopped, looked at him, fingered her chin. It would not do to seat them quite as well as the others. She would set up another table some distance away.

'Tu verras, les gens ne se gênent pas,' she said.

So, with this in mind, Hilary laid a table for a further fourteen of the free and unembarrassed. Louise was still as fresh as anything and Hilary sweating by the time they came to the doo-dahs and decorations. Fresh flower displays had been ordered and these he now lugged on vast platters from the cool interior of the wine cellar to the garage, marginally warmer, but more accessible for the evening. The butter dishes and items to be kept cool needed, now, to be prepared and taken downstairs. Singing, she departed to do this. Beyond, in the pantry, layer upon layer of loaded platter lay. Great tubs stood at the corners of the kitchen, stacked with champagne and ice.

From the open kitchen window, her voice soared forth. Hilary couldn't think of anything nicer than that sound of a happy woman. He lay for a moment in the long grass beyond the orchard and thought about his mother and how she had sung about God not making little green apples when she was busy in the kitchen and, years ago when he was a very small boy, about inch worms measuring the marigolds. She'd shown him a little worm, humping its back and flopping, arching its small length across a leaf. Now, with his hands clasped behind his head, one foot lazily swinging, healthily tired and the whole strange but glorious evening ahead – now, he watched a small, many-footed bug scamper past and saw the macrocosm in the microcosm.

Louise had thought of everything. The grass of the orchard had been mown and raked away and re-raked. Little sparkly lights had been hung through the trees. Two hours had been allowed for everyone to retire and sleep, if they could. Laid out in a generous U shape, the subsidiary table that crucial, socially dictated distance from the others – friendly, but not too convivial – the banqueting table looked like a huge face with a slightly lopsided smile.

Later, with the blue deepening day arching down behind, with the freshly sprinkled flowers so bright and dainty, with the tablecloths caught up in elegant swags and the silver sparkling, he set out candles. Beneath the twinkling apple trees the tables were festooned with an abundance of elegant white twists fixed into those special candlesticks which Charles's grandmother had kept carefully wrapped in newspaper for decades and which Louise had discovered in the attic. Michèle had spent the whole of the previous day polishing them. When they came in from fishing she was sitting in the kitchen, scrubbing away, her hands so ingrained with the blackness of the old silver that it had seemed impossible that they would ever come clean, her smudged face concentrated into a frown.

The evening came. Hilary stood in the orchard by the tables thinking that he'd never seen anything quite as pretty as that place set up for a party with the grand silver moon brightening. Deliciously at the upstairs windows flashed come-hither glimpses, nothing in the world more enticing than lovely women, dressing. Faintly her voice asked for the green shoes. 'In your cupboard, look, my love.' The fall of upended bright hair that hung down brushing the carpet to be brushed itself suddenly swept up to fly past the window, a bird seeking to escape, naked shoulders. How his heart pounded. For fear of being noticed, staring up so, Hilary turned away.

The trumpet of Chet Baker breathed its magic out through the windows of the salon and there came Charles absurd yet elegant in a dinner jacket that was slightly too tight, carrying a bottle of champagne and two glasses. From the kitchen came the faint clatter as a dozen young men prepared to serve. Charles was scowling.

'Stupid clothes. Tonight I'm going to get drunk,' he said, filling two glasses and passing one to Hilary who, behind his back, superstitiously crossed fingers.

Jean-Jacques was hunched in the kitchen, polishing his shoes which were a little tight but so very elegant that the pain was worth it. When he could see his smile in them, he slipped them on and walked rather carefully back to the bedroom. The bow tie, a struggle, right over left. A new tie, silk, a real beauty. There. Only the jacket remained. He patted the pocket, which crackled. His speech, practised in his head each day, rewritten every night that week until it and he were both word-perfect. People would revise their opinions of him. He could almost hear the applause. Now, to fill the remaining minutes, he polished his gold dress watch. This, his finest possession, which had not worked for fifteen years, certainly looked very beautiful.

Sitting on the bed, breathing gently on the gleaming surface, his eye was drawn to his wife as she outlined her little mouth with lipstick. It occurred to Jean-Jacques that the two shining surfaces, which opened and snapped shut, had something further in common. He wondered if he would say it. Why not? People changed, things moved on, they had to. It was ever the law of the tribe that new leaders arose and came forth to supplant the old. And leaders were firm and their wives knew it.

'Héloïse?'

'Mmnh?' She was using a little brush to draw the finest of lines along the outside of her lips. Then she would brush in the colour which made them look so full and luscious. He would say it.

'You are just like my watch,' and she looked up at him. 'Beautiful to look at, but you don't work. It is exactly the same. Your insides don't work properly, but on the outside you look so perfect.'

Héloïse stared at him in the mirror. She looked startled.

'Chéri,' she said, 'What is it? Mon amour, you know I long for nothing more than a little baby. But what can I do?'

'"What can I do?"' he said in mimickry.

She didn't know what to do. So. Carefully, contemplatively even, he started to unzip the dress she had just wriggled into, first placing his watch on the dressing table for safekeeping. He exposed the strap of the brassiere, the little panties. With his eyes still on her, he bent down, untied his shoelaces, kicked off the shoes. Just as carefully, not losing the crease, he stepped out of his trousers and hung them over the occasional chair. He undid the shirt button by button. Off it came.

'Come here, chérie.'

She giggled and didn't move and so he said it again, so she would see that he meant it. He draped the shirt carefully on the coathanger, over the jacket, and removed his underpants, playfully kicking them up into the air. He extended a hand to her and she came towards him, the dress dropping to the floor. He picked it up. It was new, after all, and had cost a pretty penny. How lovely she was.

'One instant.' While he rummaged for a hanger in her cupboard, she was gone, into the bathroom, but Jean-Jacques wasn't having any of that and he darted after her and heard the door of the bathroom cabinet bang, saw her eyes wide and startled. 'Come here,' he said again and, when she didn't right away, he picked her up and, staggering a little, for tiny as she was he wasn't quite accustomed to that sort of thing, he carried her over to the bed. He put her down and kissed her, as he hadn't in years, slowly and very thoroughly. He was going to take his time about this. He was going to enjoy it, and so was she. Her face flushed. She lay quite still.

'We'll be late.'

'Yes.'

'Kiss me again, like that.'

She hummed, afterwards in the bathroom, showering at length. Jean-Jacques lay on the bed, profoundly satisfied, and watched the door open and grumbled and fussed, just the right amount. Hurry up! Time to get ready! Then, letting his shower run, he locked the door and searched her bathroom cabinet which was stuffed full of toiletries and female stuff. This was a tricky operation, for things kept falling out and had to be replaced, precisely as before. With delicate fingers he picked through it all.

It didn't take him so long to find a little case at the back of the cabinet, with the diaphragm in it which she had not had time to insert. Hidden in a big pack of cotton wool balls. Wrapped in cotton wool. He got the cap out and looked at it and plucked its rubbery texture. He showered. Then, as he towelled himself, he looked until he had found a safety pin which he used to prick a dozen tiny holes in the cap. That should do it. Carefully, he put it back so everything was precisely as he had found it. His darling, whom he would wrap in cotton wool.

'I'm sorry I said what I did. About your insides. They are beautiful.'

'I know you didn't mean it, mon amour.'

'One day we will have a baby, when the good Lord wills it.'

'It is my dearest wish,' she said.

'Good, very good, my darling,' and as they turned into the gate and up the hill and their heels crunched on the gravel, Jean-Jacques thought that it was not so very difficult to obtain his heart's desires. The trick was to go about things the right way, with lightness of touch, with elegance. He transferred the large and elaborately wrapped parcel he was carrying from his left to his right arm so he could take her hand. Little hand, so small, like a child's soft hand. He began to hum to himself.

*   *   *

The guests were all there. There had been one particular easy chair empty and Hilary felt sick whenever he looked at it, for it was the place reserved for Madame Ourlandes. But, at last, she had come, leaning on a neighbour's arm and apologising for her slow ascent of the gravel. She was resplendent in stiff blue silk that crackled when she sat. Hilary ran to get a cushion to ease her bones and as she sat he whispered in her ear that she looked beautiful. He wanted to say more, to beg her not to take the death pills, but as he hovered, trying to find the words, Louise called him away. Tonight he was the 'son of the house' and his privilege was to serve.

The phone rang on and on as Hilary passed, carrying away the empty bottles, returning with full ones. Eventually, growing sick of the noise, he picked it up.

'Oui, bonsoir?' The hubbub from the kitchen where a dozen waiters were falling over each other and shouting was now so loud that he could scarcely hear a thing. 'Pardonnez-moi? Anglais. English. Je suis anglais. Voulez-vous répéter?' At the fourth repetition he more or less got the name and, assuring the disembodied shouter that somebody would come along and collect him, went to find Louise.

The guests had all drunk a fair bit of champagne. There were a dozen or so of the uninviteds, just as Louise had predicted, who were now milling around the far table squabbling about where they were to sit. In this they were being assisted, with exaggerated care, by Charles, who was already quite drunk but didn't show it.

Moving slowly along the big table where places were marked by names, Michèle lit candles. Her simple little frock was so ravishing that you wanted to weep or sing. Slowly Hilary went along the opposite side keeping pace, just looking as, one after another, the candles glowed into life as if their sole function was to caress her intent face.

It was a perfect night, warm with the slightest of breezes. Beyond the orchard the old historic monument was about as lit up as he was. He waited as, bowing low, Monsieur Dutronc kissed his wife's hand and assisted her to her seat. Jean-Jacques in ebullient form was bouncing in and out of his chair, waving to people. Finally Hilary reached Louise.

'Some guest wants to be picked up from the station. Viande? Vivale something? Viande Lavende? He's waiting, at Tours.'

'Vigne-Laval. Oh my God,' she said.

'What? What? What is it?'

'The professor, the one Charles always talks about. I didn't think he'd come, he never replied. My God.'

'Oh, shit.' He stared at her helplessly. 'The one who taught him all he knows?'

She took hold of his two hands and looked at him pleadingly.

'I'll do something,' he said. 'Don't worry, I'll get rid of him,' and he extracted one hand and laid it on her arm and knew how the knight in shining armour felt when he got on his horse and said his piece. Louise put her two hands up and pulled his face down and kissed him on both cheeks and for an instant continued to hold his face with those cool hands and look at him with such gratitude and sympathy, such a heap of emotions, knowing that he knew that she knew and so on and etcetera. She smelt pretty damn wonderful.

'Give me the car keys.'

'Are you sure you can drive there? Have you ever driven on the right?'

'Absolument.' He felt powerful. He could do anything. Gaily, he clanged down his visor to go dragon hunting. Carefully he negotiated the drive, revving up a little, fiddling with the gears. Luckily Charles had moved the car, put it down by the gates. Right. Odd. He hadn't driven the Peugeot before, nor ever driven on the right. It was OK, it was cool. There was a fine demarcation between terror and elation and he was the dragon-slayer, on the right side of it. Learn from Charles. Why not murder the man?

Brake, indicate, find the gear lever, crunch, shit, turn left through the gates. Careful, he'd looked the wrong way. Go slowly, this was fine. The white-banded avenue of lime trees unrolled their careful stripes and then he was at the left turn leading to the crossroads, crunch, ouch, gears down, indicate, yes, this was the road.

He was climbing again, up in the cornfields, the moon brilliant and huge, the road undulating ahead so the headlamps of an occasional car, coming the other way, fired up the line of the horizon with flashes of light. He'd had one glass of champagne, enough for Dutch courage. The night smelt warm and dry. He was getting the hang of the gears. Hilary began to sing. No reason not to put his foot down a bit. He felt terrific. He was past the moated house and there were the old walled farms over there, he saw a tiny yellow dot, a light in the old wall, the blackness around it darker than that of the fields. A small animal, a rabbit or whatever stood in the road, picked out in his headlights. He slowed down. It didn't move, it stood and stared at him. He slowed, then stopped the car. It was a hare. It hunkered down again and took its time and at last hippy-hopped away into the ditch. He thought about his baby being born and life was good.

He came off the autoroute. Tours. City centre. Signs. He was going along the river, nope, that couldn't be right and so he turned off and went straight up the big shopping road, the Rue Nationale to the end where he recognised the pretty flower-power roundabout. OK, right here, and on he drove. No sign of the station. Hell, wrong again, so he did a U and came back on his tracks and crawled slowly along the Boulevard Heurteloup, looking for signs for the station. The post office. The town hall. Women looking at him. A hotel, the Printemps department store, gardens and there was the jutting hulk of the new Palais des Congrès which, more InterCity train than anything else, thrust its nosy snout into the square opposite the station. Indicate, right, there you are et Bob est ton oncle. He'd done it. He felt truly fantastic. He felt high as a kite.

Carefully, he eased the car into a parking space outside a little boulangerie. He got out of the car and stopped to have a look at the station and who was waiting there. A woman, middle-aged, only one man, an old guy with a beard and stick. Had to be him. Hilary looked around carefully, both sides of the street. Various young lovers. The old bloke had a briefcase, dark jacket, unmistakably conventional and top-drawer. Not a million miles from his dad. Prof written all over him.

There was a crowd in the square and crossing it he saw that the yoof splashing about on the beached whale of the under-lit water feature and those specimens lurching in and out of the careful grid of new, young trees were compatriots. Had to be. Best of British. It was a bunch of lager louts, half-dressed, bottoms sidling forth from little more than a pair of Union Jack shorts. They were heaving about the place, having a few drinks, nothing too terrible by the usual football standards, but rowdies all the same. They would be intimidating for a provincial who would prefer to look away and pass on the other side.

Hilary stopped near them and studied Vigne-Laval's goatee beard and the peremptory way he had of jerking his head from right to left to right. A man of opinions. Someone who didn't like to be kept waiting and who looked with particular distaste at the writhing slobbering British manhood before him.

'Hello, matie,' said one of the louts. This bloke, quite young, sported a heavy designer stubble that seemingly extended down from his skull in a dark corridor past neck and ears to broaden out into luxurious curly black hairs which covered his puny frame where it was not hidden by his Guns'n'Roses T-shirt. He looked wetly at Hilary, then put his arm round him. Fairly stunned by his badger's breath, Hilary did not resist. No sirree, he offered his friendship.

'Hello,' he said back.

'I hate France.'

'Yeah.' Badger-breath was pretty drunk and had a tattoo of daggers and hearts on his arm, very black against his pallor. The crease of his other arm had swallowed some Gothic script. There was a further tattoo on his wrist: RUDE! it said. Hilary did a few approving nods. Bloke leant blokishly forward, sharing the emanations of many previous pints. He made a stabbing gesture at his arm.

'I wuz having rouse. R-A-U-S. German. But the bloke wot done it couldn't spell, stupid fartarse. R-U-A he done before I noticed. You see where he gone over it?'

Hilary shook his head. 'Nar. Looks very good to me,' he said. The avenue of possibilities this opened up. Visit the dyslexic tattooist for Mam and Dud. Op the gonners. I love yuo.

'I hate foreigners.'

'Yeah.' An idea could not be suppressed, it rose up until it frothed irresistibly over. 'Do you want to earn a few bob?'

'Year. Yer wor?'

'D'you see that bloke over there?' Hilary said, pointing.

'Year.'

'He's a foreigner. Look at that beard. How can anyone walk the streets looking like that?' And, warming to his theme, Hilary began to whisper into a yellow, waxy ear. 'Not and expect to get away with it. What a poofter. You see the stick? Terrible.'

'Yer wor?'

'I know him. He's a real arsehole. Do you want to earn a few bob?'

'Yer wor?'

He began to lay out his plan. Laid it out again. As, slowly, understanding dawned in badger's teeny brainette, the prof took to pacing up and down and did some more looking at his watch. Loitering at the high-technology bus shelter, Hilary waited to see how the Kommandant would marshal his troops. With charming simplicity, Badger-breath rallied his fellows with a shriek. He pointed.

'See 'im? Lez gerrim. Kumon,' he yelled.

Vigne-Laval couldn't believe it. They came lurching across the road in a bobbing bundle and in one swoop they picked him up. He was borne away, protesting, over the heads of the mob, which gave him the bum's rush into the station and surged onto the platform, passing him bodily into the train that stood there. Hilary, coming up behind, watched the prof's stunned disbelief turning to helpless rage as they hustled him onto the train. He protested, the goatee rose and fell. He had no idea of why and what.

One of the lads picked up his little case and, wiping it on his bum, flicked it in. One of them began to wave. They all began to wave, twinkly sea anenome fingered. 'Byebyee, don't cryee! Byeee!'

Oh, happy synchronicity, the TGV was off. The prof snatched up his bag. Hilary watched the doors of the train close with the mob protecting it by leaning against it and pulling faces. Vigne-Laval now started thumping against the door with his entire strength and making no impression. All the passengers were staring from him to the mob. The prof ran frantically along the train to the next door, as the train slowly pulled out of the station. His baffled little face peeping out. No hope of him escaping. Hilary watched him peering out, still scarcely able to credit the idea that this bizarre thing really had happened to him, until it disappeared. The TGV didn't stop until Orléans. There was nothing more to fear.

Hilary gave them every penny he had. They were worth it.

'Yer wor, matie,' said mein Kommandant and the whole lot of them suddenly began to squabble over exactly which particular brand of liquid refreshment they'd spend it on and they were off, out of the station and across the road and streaming unstoppably into the Atac supermarket to seize more of the right stuff quickly, before it closed.

Behind him, leaning against the orange pillar where travellers validated their tickets, stood an old bloke with long strands of grey-white hair falling over his collar, wearing a Nehru jacket. With a faintly knowing look, he turned his head to watch Hilary pass. Crossing the station concourse, Hilary was aware of the man following. Outside, as he waited to cross the road, a hand touched his sleeve.

'You are English – we spoke on the telephone. So you have come for me, very nice. My name is Vigne-Laval, but you must call me Gaston,' and he held out his hand and Hilary, gobsmacked, gripped big swollen knuckles, yellow-stained.

'And your name, my friend?'

'Yes,' said Hilary, swallowing. 'Hilary, my name is.'

Gaston walked with a slight limp but was nimble and quick. He could have been anything from late fifties on. He had a sallow face that was gaunt and covered in wrinkles and creases and laughter lines, a face as lived-in as a tramp's sleeping bag. Close up, his neat-looking jacket was stained and threadbare at the collar and Hilary could smell the fags and beer on his breath. Gaston said *tu* to him, straightaway, very pally. He was disgusting.

They crossed the now empty square and got into the car. Shit, shit, shit. What was he going to do now, crash the car? Spend the evening driving the man around the countryside or what? Hilary couldn't think. Panic rose up and had to be suppressed.

'The young men at the station, friends of yours?' Hilary found no adequate reply. Gaston here didn't need much prompting, he leant over and pinched his arm, lightly. 'Ah, youth can be severe. So, my English friend, you are staying with my old pal Charles?'

'Yes,' he said. He was filled with rage. The unfairness of all this was powerful, stronger than any guilt he might have been expected to feel at propelling that other old innocent on his way to Orléans. He thought about all the appalling consequences of turning up with this bloke at the party. The motorway lay up ahead. They turned up the ramp.

'Professor, he calls me. Well, I will tell you. A long time ago, Charles and I were medical orderlies together. I, being so much older than him, taught him a great deal, I can tell you. He was so young, he didn't even have a beard. Like a girl, he was. He didn't even know how to fuck a woman properly. Sixteen he was when I met him.' Not getting a reply didn't put him off, he carried on regardless.

'But already he had a mind of his own. Now. I will tell you a story about those days that will pin back your ears, my friend. I will make you jealous of me. Me, him and four girls. One was English, long hair she had. Gee-lian. Never I forget her. What, don't you believe me? You wait.' Hilary saw the sign for Orléans, then for Paris. What if he drove him to Paris? His mind was racing, his heart beating fast. Not that he had the money for the journey. There wasn't enough petrol in the car. Think, for Christ's sake, he told himself. Think. Meanwhile, with the lunatic, this sex maniac sitting right beside him and now – please not – putting his hand right down his trousers – Jesus, was he going to pull his plonker out? Eyes on the road, he drove on.

*   *   *

Nicholas reclined on the deckchair in the middle of the lawn. It was getting late. He had always loved these midsummer evenings when like an old friend the light lingered in the sky for just a little longer than you might have hoped.

From where he sat, he could see the light in Ed's room. Amanda was up there saying goodnight. Ed never wanted to sleep in the holidays, never wanted to do anything sensible. Nicholas had done bathroom duty and said goodnight to him earlier and he had called out for his mother. Like a little boy, like a baby. For some reason this had given him a pang. She had come up, of course, as she always did, was even now kissing and tucking him up, as a good mother did. She was a very good mother to her boys. Nicholas felt any number of uneasy sensations gripping and turning at his heart, squeezing his stomach somehow, not pain but a kind of foreknowledge of pain. The body could feel limbs that had been amputated. Scratching the place where it itched was helpful, even if it was a void, so strong was the brain's ability to create an image, an aura of what had been. Pain went on for ever, even when its cause was long forgotten. Perhaps when something strong or strange was going to happen, a person might experience some kind of precursor of it. He hoped not. He sat and looked at the light until it was quite, quite dark and waited for the feeling to go away.

Inside the house, Amanda looked at Ed.

'You're bonkers, Mum,' her son said, turning over sleepily.

'What?'

'I don't mind. Dad does, though.'

'Don't be silly, Ed,' she said, smoothing down the duvet, but he merely sighed and stretched and recomposed his sleeping position.

Soon he was asleep. Amanda stood at the window of Ed's room and listened to his regular breathing and stared out at the motionless figure of Nicholas, stretched out in his deckchair in the garden. She thought with a sudden rush of anger that while she didn't particularly care what he thought or did, this buddha in a deckchair lark was something she did resent. So in due course, she went through the quiet house in a malicious frame of mind. Alongside those tasks left for her to do, she would see whether anything of his had been left unprotected.

'. . . Nurses, especially in their uniform, all nicely starched up and nothing underneath. We were a fine couple, share and share alike, say I. I was a good-looking fellow in my young days. Well, Charles was always an ugly mug, but women loved him. To see him in his married state, that will amuse me. Well, he was always a lot cleverer than me. It's no fun being on your own. Nobody to warm your back. Not that I sleep on my own so often. Now where was I? After I taught him the card tricks, one time he got me into trouble, plenty that cost me, plenty, not just money.'

Chuckling to himself, the man got a little flask out of his jacket pocket and had a slug. He'd been on the booze ever since they'd got in the car. It was the bottle he was fumbling for down there. Dirty pig.

'Yes. Look, Charles has a daughter. He lives a responsible good citizen's life.' Get the message over quick, while he was drinking, the only time he shut up. Hilary put his foot down. He'd speed past the motorway exit.

'I know it. The daughter, the wife, they are too good for me. Hey. What's this?' Gaston was dangling Hilary's watch in front of him. How had he done that? He got it back and with difficulty he put it back on, one hand steadying the wheel. The old rogue laughed and wheezed at his great joke, very amusing.

Hilary had another thought. 'D'you have any money on you?'

'Sorry, no cash.' He leant back, made a big show of turning out his pockets which were full of crap. A rusted up Swiss Army penknife – how had he achieved that? – a bottle opener, various pencils and bits of paper.

'Nothing?' And now the silly sod was holding up Hilary's wallet, he was rifling through it, chuckling away to himself. 'How did you do that? Give it back,' and with difficulty Hilary wiggled it back into the back pocket of his trousers, where he trusted it had to be safe.

'Leave the motorway here. Charles is my oldest friend. Did I tell you that? Why don't you call me tu? I say tu to you. Here! Turn here!' He snatched at the wheel, they came dangerously close to the next car – Jesus, they were going to hit it – a blare of horns. Hilary elbowed him out of the way and grabbed back the wheel and the idiot jerked at it again. They fought for control – Gaston was strong – and with a jerk and lurch, they turned off. Hilary's heart was pounding like mad. As soon as they were off the slip road, he pulled up. He felt sick.

'Never do that again. Do you hear me? You could have killed us.' His hands, on the wheel, were trembling.

The maniac fumbled in his pocket, lit two fags, passing one to Hilary which he took and threw angrily out of the window.

'Don't get so excited. You would have missed the turning. Look,' and he pointed to the road sign. 'I know, I come here before.'

'What?'

'Oh, but Madame doesn't know,' and he tapped his nose with one long yellow-stained finger. 'Madame goes away and I come, two times. But this life is not for me. Really, Charles and me, we are bachelors together. Real men. Let me see, this girl, was it nineteen seventy? Seventy-two?'

Hilary drove on. What was he supposed to do? Kill him? Yes. How? Far too rapidly, they were approaching the lime tree avenue. He braked. His passenger had wound the window on his side down and had stuck his head out of it. How about ramming it against one of the trees?

'There, you see the turning. Slow down there, take the next right. I do not think, my friend, that there is a future for you in navigation, no. Why aren't you stopping? You stop! You turn! That's it.' He reached for the wheel, Hilary elbowed him back. Again, the lunatic took the wheel, swung it round.

'I said not to do that,' Hilary roared.

They had turned into the lime tree avenue.

'What was I saying? This girl was called Madeleine and she had an incredible body and an incredible flat. Tits like melons. We are talking in the centre of Paris, mon pote, in those days a place like that cost, ouf, let me see . . .'

The problem was this guy's unerring sense of direction, which worked in inverse ratio to his conversational sense. Oh shit, Hilary thought. Gaston again stuck his big stupid head out of the window.

'Look, my friend, I am trying to help you. Yes! I know this one. Nearly there.'

Bloody wonderful, this was.

'Here, OK? You turn, just there. RIGHT, take a RIGHT.' He hung onto Hilary's arm like a weasel, all sinew and tug, shouting, 'Turn! Turn! Turn!'

'All right, lay off, leave me alone.' Hilary tried to shake him off. He was like a rat. Grimly, Hilary clung to the wheel and drove past the house. At the crossroads, where he had to stop, Gaston opened the door, hopped out and loped off back the way they'd come. At this Hilary lost his cool. He roared after him.

'You're not a doctor! What are you? What is this?'

'Me? Don't be so stupid,' he shouted back at Hilary. 'What d'you think I am, you little shit?'

Hilary let his head rest upon the wheel. He thought,

that's it, I'm finished. In the rearview mirror, he saw the mad old fart moving rapidly along the dark hedgerows, his jacket a paler blur. Hilary reversed at speed, hoping nobody was coming the other way. The bugger was even quicker. Leaving the car at the foot of the hill, for the whole driveway was blocked with cars, moaning to himself, Hilary ran after him. Gaston had a surprising turn of speed.

They came up past the house with Gaston clucking and panting. He stopped to get his breath and Hilary grabbed him. Last-ditch stuff, this. They wrestled for a moment in what Gasbag clearly took to be a playful manner and then he broke loose and loped round the trees and into the orchard shouting, 'Charles, j'arrive!'

Now things were beyond any control. Up stood Charles and he opened his arms and let out a great gurgling cry. They embraced. They swayed and turned together. They kissed, four cheeks, they slapped each other on the back, the works. Charles was drunk.

Louise rose and Gaston took her hand and kissed it. Then he and Charles went arm in arm round the table. Tenderly, Charles held onto him.

Hilary and Louise stood there, banjaxed. 'I'm so very sorry. I couldn't – didn't – he wouldn't – he's un maniaque.' Laughing, re-arranging chairs, Charles busily fixed things so his old pal could sit opposite him. Gaston crossed arms, stuck out a paw to each of his neighbours and fell upon the food and drink. Charles leant forward over the table and filled up his glass; the man emptied it in one vast gulp, tilting his head back like a hound and letting the wine run down his throat. Charles laughed and filled it again.

'Jesus,' said Hilary. He watched with horrible fascination. In his dad's hospital, he had seen old tramps eat like that, with a mouth full and a forkful ready and one hand busy on the bread and the other curled protectively round the glass, because somebody might snatch the food away. Gaston's gob was kept full as he chewed busily and rapidly but also kept a bulging eye on the main chance which, in this instance, was his neighbour, Héloïse's swelling décolletée.

All around there was a general easing of waistbands and wiping of mouths, a laying down of napkins and raising up of glasses, a fumbling for cigarettes. A mountain range rose next to the kitchen door, as plates were cleared from the table to join their fellows in the pre-ordained spot, each peak rising as happy testimony to the powers of knife and fork. Hilary carried another pile of plates over and set it down.

Gaston had now hoovered up so much and so fast that it seemed incredible that he hadn't yet thrown up. The more he filled his belly, the more confiding and pally he became. Behind his chair, Hilary hovered and looked at the white hand of Héloïse who was fingering her blonde curls.

'What tricks I taught him. He has good hands, you see, big but very, very careful – skilled. Now you, you I think, let me see – ah, you could be taught, oh, many things,' and his hand slid up her arm and towards her bosom and she, giggling, pulled it away though not, by Hilary's reckoning, quite as quickly as she could have done. He caught a glimpse of the pharmacist turning in time to clock this. His face turned a deep red colour.

'I love you, mon vieux,' yelled Gaston to Charles.

'Moi aussi, je t'aime.' Tears welled up in Gaston's eyes. They clasped hands across the table. Charles again filled their glasses. By Hilary's reckoning, Charles should by now be extremely drunk, but you wouldn't know it, the hand was steady, he looked normal. Another bellow came from the riff-raff. Hilary moved reluctantly towards them.

'. . . try this. You'll see. Not as fine as the langoustine we had for Martine's birthday but not bad either . . .' At the uncouth end the uninviteds were cleaning up various platters of odds and sods which had been left near them for precisely that purpose. They had finely honed culinary senses and were particular about their sauces and condiments. One big buck with a cheeky face had even had the gall to suggest to Hilary that next time Madame might like to get her baguettes somewhere different, laughing at his own wit. Boulangerie Lardon, that was the place. Hilary shouldered their cast-offs, as requested.

'. . . Never saw a nurse with a nicer arse and what fabulous tits . . .' The return journey past Gaston, audible at some distance. Hilary looked at Louise. She no longer seemed upset. She looked fine, sitting nearly opposite quite calmly and looking from face to face as if measuring them up for something. He went over to her. Waves of noise were coming off the table and rolling through the trees and the branches swayed with it, the silvery-green leaves twinkled and the little lights trembled.

Close up, he realised that she was after all in some sort of state; she was gritting her teeth so hard that the whole of her jaw was locked and a muscle in her cheek twitched. He poured her some water, put the glass in her hand. She gulped it down.

Gaston winked at Hilary and then, as if that wasn't enough, stagily raised a finger and laid it along one side of his nose. This, which should have been reassuring, had the opposite effect. He followed this with a slow, deliberate wink at Héloïse which did him no good whatsoever with her husband who looked as though for two pins he'd poke him in the eye. Charles, sitting opposite, winked back.

'Eh! Mon pote!' roared Gaston, 'Think of the ones we did for – in our day!' They both roared with laughter.

Jean-Jacques's emotions were in conflict. He felt as though he was the victim of something, a shipwreck perhaps, being tossed about from one side to another. But the dinner was a success, excellent. They were on the home stretch with two-thirds of this long and copious meal in his belly. He watched as the guest of honour, this vulgar, nasty man, this professor, again pawed his wife. This concentrated his mind upon his loathing – yes, it was that strong – of the medical profession.

He loathed the way the long greasy hair curled over the collar, the bleary eye, the mouth that never stopped, whether chewing or talking. Every pore of his body disliked this man, this insult to humanity. The wine rose to his head in an angry surge. Jean-Jacques looked again in the direction of Madame Beauregard who nodded at him and gestured that he should rise. Charles Beauregard was not a bad man, no. The other. *He* was a bad man. The pharmacist felt a new and pure sensation, a small tenderness towards his old enemy whom he was about to honour.

He stood, cleared his throat, swallowed. The lank and silvery head of this professor fellow swivelled to look at him. Again, he swallowed and cleared his throat. He opened his mouth. Then he closed it again.

For this was not what he really wanted to do. He wanted to make his mark more literally. What would satisfy him would be to take that fellow and hit him, not so hard that he was permanently damaged, but enough to mark him. The man was a shit. And Jean-Jacques Albert was no speechifyer.

Everybody was looking at him. This made him feel powerful which in turn made him feel more real than he usually did. His toes, in the too-tight shoes, tingled slightly. He would suffer for it tomorrow, but that day had not yet come. It was still today and his heart was beating rapidly, so much so that it seemed to have swelled beyond its normal size. Feeling in his pocket, he drew out his carefully prepared papers and waved them at the other guests, smiling. He felt a dropping away, the absence of a weight on his body. The speech fell onto the grass and the pharmacist spoke from his heart.

'What a party!' he heard himself say. 'Isn't this something, ladies and gentlemen? I'm not making a speech – you needn't worry. We're here to raise our glasses and celebrate twenty years of our good doctor here. Let us drink to twenty more – and to Madame his wife! A good doctor, a wonderful wife, and as you see a most wonderful cook! Ladies and gentlemen, to the doctor! And to Madame!'

As glasses and voices were raised, Jean-Jacques leant down and under cover of the general hubbub shot a remark over Héloïse.

'Touch her one more time and I'll plaster you across the table.'

Professor Vigne-Laval stared at his glass as if he hadn't understood what he'd been told and then, swivelling slowly, he returned his bloodshot gaze to Héloïse.

'Quel magnifique châssis,' he said breathily.

Yes, he would hit him. This knowledge sang louder and louder through Jean-Jacques. The tingling spread round his whole body, as though his flow of blood was invigorated by the very thought. His right hand began to bunch itself into a fist as though he had no control over it, to unbunch and bunch again. He saw the doctor looking at him, saw on Charles Beauregard's face a kind smile. Yes, he smiled at him in sympathy and in understanding, oh, the sweetness of it swept over Jean-Jacques. Let this oaf drink and wink and nod. The pharmacist, who could have been burdened through the years with an idiot like this one, realised that he was a lucky man. The doctor was laughing. With the utmost pleasure, Jean-Jacques laughed back at him.

Charles rose and held up one hand. At once the noise died down.

'Friends,' he said loudly, 'you're all friends tonight, every one of you. I'll drink to that,' and round the table the glasses were lifted and drained. Jean-Jacques stayed on his feet, his fist still in its state of expectancy. 'Twenty years we've been here and tonight I'll tell you the truth. I'm no doctor, I never was.' Charles Beauregard's voice boomed out and, getting the joke, Jean-Jacques laughed out loud, he even leant forwards and banged on the table though his Héloïse shot him a disapproving glance. There was a little ripple of laughter round the table.

'Listen, all of you,' the doctor said. 'I never qualified to treat you. All I've got is what you see here.' He held up two empty hands. 'That's all.'

'No! You've got more than that, my friend.' The idiot beside Jean-Jacques had the effrontery to get up on his hind legs and start braying like the donkey he was. Vigne-Laval was visibly swaying and, face on, Jean-Jacques was repelled by his pungent breath.

'Shut up! I know nothing, do you understand? *I know nothing at all.*' Loud as the doctor shouted, the other voice was yet more powerful.

'*He's a fucker, ladies and gentlemen,*' bellowed the professor. 'Let us not forget,' slurring his words and shrieking so loudly that nothing else could be heard, 'his wife! Never forget the love of a woman! I drink to woman, to wine, and to women everywhere!' He laughed coarsely and wiped away the flecks of spittle from his mouth with a sleeve. 'Women, unforgettable, beautiful, lovely, I love them all. They have been my university and I have a PhD in pussy.' At this point Héloïse started tugging at his jacket, hissing at him to sit down. And at this moment, with utter astonishment, Jean-Jacques saw that in his hand the professor held his own beautiful, precious gold pocket watch.

'Give that back,' he said, tugging at his sleeve. Vigne-Laval ignored him, leering across the table at Louise Beauregard. Jean-Jacques pulled back his arm and with a feeling of the most intense jubilation let him have it. With an upward jerk he slammed Vigne-Laval in the chin as hard as he possibly could. The professor, who was too drunk to see it coming, reeled back and fell heavily onto Héloïse.

For the second before his hand began to hurt like hell, before Héloïse screamed and the fool fell over and everything became messy – for that split second Jean-Jacques felt wonderful. Yes, he felt as good as he'd ever felt, about anything, ever. He felt pretty good afterwards, too, but that first connection, that crunch of bone against tissue, counted as one of the very best moments in his whole life.

Hilary, who had been holding his breath, let out a huge exhalation and dashed round the table, getting there just as Héloïse stood up and pushed away Gaston who now crumpled to the ground. He did this very neatly, knees buckling, head down between them as though he was practising for an airline disaster. Jean-Jacques was hopping about, nursing his hand. Gaston started muttering and thrashing with his feet in spasms. Hilary strained to get him up. He was much heavier than he had expected. Charles came up and between them they lifted him. From somewhere a shout rang out.

'Let the doctor deal with him! He can raise the dead, and the dead drunk!'

They staggered towards the house with Gaston mumbling and cursing and doing that classic drunk's thing of twisting his feet round and tripping himself up. The pharmacist came dancing along behind them. Charles was carrying most of the weight and with a good deal of fumbling they got Gaston into the study and onto the couch.

'I didn't think I hit him so hard,' said Jean-Jacques, exulting.

Outside, a wave of music burst forth. The dancing had begun. 'Good,' said the pharmacist, 'Good,' and with a swagger he turned and went to the door. He flexed his hand once or twice. 'So. For my part, I am going to dance,' and he went.

Gaston leant back on the couch and his mouth dropped open. Hilary looked at him. The man was white-faced, his skin looked slack and shone with a sheen of sweat. Charles, by contrast, seemed sober. His mood had suddenly suffered an abrupt change and he waved to Hilary to go.

'Go.'

Hilary backed away and waited just along the corridor, intensely curious to hear what might happen between these two.

'Toi,' he heard Charles say. 'Tu es une ordure.' He was angry and his voice was different, a calm, smooth voice which gave Hilary a ripple of goosepimples.

Charles closed the door with a quiet click. There came a noise, which might have been the sound of a clap or smack, it was hard to tell. Hilary waited nervously but now he could hear nothing, for the music outside was getting louder. He felt all at once how badly he needed to dance with Michèle, how overdue some pleasure was. The cooler air outside was refreshing and in search of Michèle Hilary went past the tables where coffee was being served, where people were getting stuck into liqueurs. No matter what had been before and no matter what came of it or didn't, he was owed this: to hold her in his arms once, to let his cheek rest against hers, to breathe in the whole delicious smell of her. It wouldn't harm her, would it, to let him have this small pleasure, which meant so much? It wouldn't have harmed her to kiss him once properly, so he'd remember it. But he could not find her anywhere.

Hilary sat in a kind of stupor under the apple tree and watched the dancers, the drinkers, the surge and pattern of it all. Later, Charles emerged and Hilary saw him help Madame Ourlandes down the drive to the car – for she was the first to go. Hilary would have liked to say goodbye to her and now it was too late. Some force was pressing down upon him. Because of it, he stayed where he was under the apple tree and watched. He watched his host dance with his wife, he watched people applaud. Finally, with a disagreeable effort, he thought he had better see if Gaston was all right.

The couch in the study was empty; the man was gone. Hilary went from room to room and did not find him. He was not in any of the bedrooms or anywhere in the house. He looked in each bathroom, each cupboard and store, looked in the garage where there was noise and found a gang of waiters smoking and drinking, playing cards. As one, they turned their faces to him and just stared, so there was nothing to do but turn and go away. Not there, not anywhere.

Now Hilary went up and down the driveway looking in all the cars and, finally, walked along the perimeter of the garden. Then he traversed it up and down and did this twice. He did not find him. It was impossible that that man could have walked from there unaided, in his condition. Impossible. And only one car had departed with Madame Ourlandes in it driven by her neighbour. So he had not left. Hilary would have seen him. Again he walked around and now he looked for a mound of new earth but this, too, was not to be found, though the finding of it would not have been a surprise. Yet as he thought of how it would be to stumble upon turned earth, even to smell the tangy odour of it, he felt sick and his heart pounded with a horrible anticipation. The cars were beginning to leave and he stood, pale apparition, between the trees and counted them out.

At four in the morning there were still two couples dancing under the trees and a last half-dozen hardy souls sitting and quaffing Armagnac at the table. A halo of aromatic cigar smoke hung in the trees and the dawn was just signalling its intention of appearing soon.

Jean-Jacques had been sitting for hours supporting Héloïse, who slept with her head in his lap. He was nearly asleep himself. Now, he jerked upright.

'Time to go, my darling,' he said. With a little difficulty, he leant forward and his foot touched something. He hooked it out from under the table, a big box wrapped up in shiny paper. He edged it towards Charles with his foot. 'To think I nearly forgot. This is for you.'

Charles opened it and drew forth a shiny, new, big black doctor's bag. There was a collective sigh of recognition. Inside, it was full to the brim with packets of cigarettes. The mayor, who sat beside them, began to cackle. With slow pleasure, Charles drew off the cellophane, lit up.

'I like it,' Dutronc said. 'I like it. Eh, Monsieur? Not bad, eh? There's a sense of humour, eh? There's a bit of fun.' His wife nodded her assent as Jean-Jacques beckoned to Charles.

'My friend,' and now he began to whisper. 'You have your special gift – you know. Will you pass your hands across my wife? Down below – you know?'

Charles looked at him.

With another furtive glance at his sleeping wife, the pharmacist gestured from his chest downwards across his abdomen in a sweeping gesture. 'Please. There are things no medicine can do,' and he made a cradling gesture with his arms and rocked his imaginary baby to and fro.

Very carefully Charles pressed his hands against Héloïse, smoothing her down from just below the waist to the knees, passing his hands across her belly in curving movements. She smiled and muttered something in her sleep and turned a little. Charles did it again. Jean-Jacques watched intently. Dutronc, a little embarrassed, looked the other way. With one hand smoothing his wife's cheek, Jean-Jacques put the other in his pocket and felt for his watch. Carefully, he drew it out, held it to his ear and listened to its ticking. A smile spread across his face.

Everybody stood and now it really was over, the last people straggling down the hill.

'Remember,' Charles said, spreading out his arms to embrace Dutronc and then Jean-Jacques. 'Remember what I've told you, that I know nothing at all.' Nodding and smiling, they agreed. Whatever you say, Monsieur le docteur.

Hilary remained outside as Charles went into the house and he watched for the bathroom light and the bedroom one to come on and go off again. Now he was alone but for the last two lads taking down the trestle tables.

He sat on under the trees. His heart was beating in a dull thudding motion which told him how tired he must be. He had long abandoned all hope of Michèle, who must have gone to bed hours ago. The magic was going out of the place. A grey-blue shimmer over the horizon showed where another hot day was coming. Somebody turned off the lights in the trees. There were shouts of goodbye from the last two young men, the crunch of their feet on the gravel, leaving. The sound of the owl hooting on the far side of the orchard. The last night. He began to think of things ending and his going and now he began to feel stranger than ever. The new day had come. He would be leaving for home in a matter of hours.

He wandered slowly through the orchard to the far side. A final tour of the place. Michèle's window dark.

He was walking backwards and looking upwards at her window when something tripped him and he fell over. It took a second to understand it was something warm and soft. A body – oh God. He had found the body of Gaston Vigne–Laval. Oh Jesus. A leg. He touched it and it was still warm. A moaning sound. He sprang away. A face half hidden in the bushes. He went closer, closer – with a shock of recognition, he saw that he was staring into Michèle's face. A horrible moment when he thought she was dead and his heart lurched and he felt sick, for her eyes were open. He went closer – too close.

Michèle was spread-eagled on her back half naked, her dress pulled up to her waist. A dark-haired man was fucking her, groaning, so intent he didn't even realise Hilary was there. Michèle, who did, continued to watch him, quite expressionless. White buttocks pumping up and down, up and down, the man had pulled his trousers down to his knees. He wore a white shirt and round his neck on a cord, slung over his back so it wouldn't get in the way, was a warbler from the market, just like the one that Hilary had bought for Ed.

Hilary leant forward, took hold of it and tugged and felt the sudden pull of the cord at the man's neck. He tugged again. The man might die, he might kill him, for he was starting to make a terrible strangled noise. He was struggling to get off her, up, away. Hilary pulled once more. It was right, what he was doing felt right. He pulled the cord tighter still. He pulled with all his strength so the man would die. So this was what he had learnt here. But they had to know why.

'Pute,' Hilary said and then he repeated it, louder. The word for prostitute. With his head thrumming with a terrific agony of excitement, he pulled at the warbler in sharp tugs, again, again, and the pumping intensified, and then the warbler came loose and he had it in his hand. Freed, the man collapsed sideways, panting and groaning and gurgling for breath. Perhaps it was merely that he had climaxed. When Hilary saw his face, he knew him. The big guy at the uninviteds' table, the son of the boulanger – the man of the woods.

Hilary turned and walked away and as he did so he found that he was blowing on the warbler. The cry of an owl came out. Dear God Almighty. He blew again and again.

He was the owl in the orchard. He was the owl. He was the owl.

Tears began quite unexpectedly to stream down his face. He took the thing out of his mouth and threw it away and then he was running, faster and faster. He felt like screaming though he was also so stunned by the surprise, so shocked, that when he opened his mouth nothing at all came out, though some little insects came in and he stopped, spat them out and then he retched.

Hilary had the aisle seat. As the TGV pulled out of Saint-Pierre-des-Corps he leant back to have an hour's sleep before Paris. Couldn't, though he tried. There was the same pixie face in the mirror, the same bit of luggage shoved under the seat, the same leather jacket. Things bore the same appearance as before. Blood beat round his head in slow waves.

Madame Ourlandes had been found dead in her bed. Poor soul, Louise had said, poor old soul. It was a release from suffering. She had been gentle with him, had driven him to the station and seen him off quietly.

Secrets were strange things, they both filled you up and left you empty. They hooked and held you, like a fish on a line. You couldn't get away, you might have to live with the barb through your cheek for the rest of your life.

Hilary stared out of the window at the smooth green indifference of the fields. It was possible to live with intense desire that could never be satisfied. He knew these cravings were illogical. Sense and reason would soon intervene. He looked out of the window and waited for them to do their stuff. Michèle was a tart, forget her. But what he felt wasn't so much to do with her but himself, a kind of shock of recognition that he was just going to have to carry on with all these acute sensations surging around. Knowing Gaston was an old lag didn't stop the anxiety. Knowing Michèle was a tart did nothing to assuage his pain. He could remember the crisp sound that Madame Ourlandes' blue silk had made when she sat. The night had been so very beautiful, hadn't it? Meanwhile, other people couldn't be expected to know what bothered him or even that anything did, nor could they be told. It was shocking, that this could all be so personal. And now he saw that the only victim he could be perfectly sure of was himself.

This was a shock. How long would it take for this to fade? The shock would become something calmer as it turned to memory. Wouldn't it? His heart thumped away. How long would it take? Because he could still see how she had looked, lying there, the picture was exact. How long? Think about something else. After all, there was a moral issue, wasn't there? An angle. Watching the lush landscape zoom past, the little copses and mini woods, the gentle roll of the slopes up and down, he tried to find it. He could examine a number of issues. Firstly, there was the question of whether the conflict or difference wasn't as much to do with nationality as anything else. For he saw some kind of moral conflict, didn't he, he didn't just feel gutted on a personal level, there was a whole other business there to do with how a sixteen-year-old girl was expected to behave. He thought, too, about Charles, who had not said goodbye to him. Was that the right way to behave? Was that correct? But whatever else he had done, Charles had always told the truth. A strange thing to say of the fraud who so liberally handed out the death pills. Then he thought about Gaston. Always, though, it came back to the same thing, the cord round the neck, always that, back to it again and again, the back and the buttocks up and down and the cord and her face and the body and the cord and her face. He would never forget it, never, never.

Michèle. Oh, Michèle, how could she? She had broken his heart. His whole chest hurt as if he'd been kicked. He folded his hands across it to keep everything more or less in place and stared out at his reflection and felt the deep ache of it, felt a searing pain which burnt everything, even the insides of his eyes which wanted to cry but of course didn't. He would never cry again.

5

Michèle Beauregard was sunbathing. She could not remain still for more than a few moments at a time and now, sitting up, she loosened her hair, permitted it to flow down over her shoulders charmingly, and with a series of little shakes of the head and stretching movements eased herself over until she was supine. A moment later, she removed the skimpy little bikini top and lay down again. The earth, which had held its breath for excitement at this manoeuvre, once more let it out. The air was thick with the exhalation of atoms colliding as they, too, jostled for position.

Nicholas, twitching at his curtain, absorbed that her breasts were, excitingly, degrees paler than the rest of her. On the lush green of his well-watered grass, in the bright sun, her flesh was altogether paler than indoors. The glint of a thin gold chain on her ankle. Rosebuds, tips, delicate things, silken. He was too far away to see if there might be the faint mottling of the towel or the crease of a blade of grass imprinted on her leg. From his dry throat came an involuntary groan.

From the landing, he passed with stealth into Ed's room and there he rummaged. Months since he'd been in here. There, perhaps in his son's collection of weapons or maybe on his bookshelf. Drawer after drawer displayed his son's lack of taste, his consistency in that alone. Hilary had come home from France and mooched about for the last fortnight and in all that time had said nothing about Michèle. Incredible. Was the boy blind? Were both his sons daft?

Nicholas had bought the binoculars for his son's ninth birthday. A tight red rage was building at the remembered cost. Look at this rubbish he's accumulated, ridiculous waste of money, a boy his age, plastic trash and look at the state of this room, they must be here – look at this *mess*. While each drawer was rammed back with anger, the deep inner part of him was reverberating with its own ragings. Bonkers, it screamed, off yer bleedin' rocker, leave it out, mate – a coarser version of the same faux demotic he used on his rounds. Alien forces had moved in three days ago, the day of her arrival. They had found Nicholas and taken him over and they gave him no rest, they ran him up and down the stairs and in and out and all the time said hurry, hurry, hurry. Gerra move on, you bloody nitwit. Carpe diem, quam minimum credula postero. Michèle teased him with brevity in all forms. Michèle was staying with them for a mere two weeks.

Nicholas was sick. The sickness lay in his garden, the worm in the bud. Oh rose, thou art. Layer after layer of it, unreasoning, mad, impossible desire. Beyond each furl and curl another one, tight, below, fresh-minted.

He pulled at the last drawer, much too hard, and it jammed then jerked out and littered its cargo of rubbish, its old Beano annuals and plastic bits and half-done kits, all over his shoes. The trash stash. A little tin of paint in gun-metal grey rolled quietly away. He kicked it, hard. A thin grey smear laid itself out across the carpet and mocked him. A tiny oil slick dripped from the lid.

High on the roof of the handsome Queen Anne house there was a flash and a glint of binoculars in the hands of Edward, Ed the daring, Ed the bold – though he was wobbling a trifle insecurely on his dizzy perch. To get up there involved climbing out through the attic window, then over an overhanging bit, then edging up the roof tiles. He'd taken off his sandals and socks, so with bare feet he had a better grip. Sweaty, the soles, just a bit. He wasn't scared any more. The binoculars were a middling pair, not brilliant, but the lenses were OK. Carefully, breathing rather heavily through his mouth, Ed adjusted the focus and blinked as Michèle leapt out at him. He contemplated the faint golden down that lay along her arms and then followed the arm up and down and examined her armpits for a good long bit. He wasn't fussy, he wanted to see everything and he didn't know when he'd get such a good chance again.

Ed was experiencing a golden age. He was on holiday. A beautiful French girl who liked taking her clothes off was staying in the house. She did not seem to mind him staring at her. She never wore a bra. She had allowed him several puffs of a cigarette. She winked at him now and then. Neither of his parents was paying him the slightest bit of attention. His mother was always busy cooking and stuff, and apart from the odd session shelling peas, she left him alone. He was going away to camp, but that wasn't for a bit yet. His unfettered leisure stretched out deliciously.

The only black spot was the presence of his brother. Eight years separated them and had ever done so with great effectiveness. Hilary belonged to the country of the grown-ups, with the added bonus of indifference, exclusion from the wonderland of his room being an acceptable price to pay. But since he'd got back from France, and particularly since Michèle had arrived, Hilary was very funny peculiar. He'd never paid any attention to his brother in the past, beyond a certain amount of cuffing and cursing. Of late, more than once, Hilary had tried to talk to Ed when it wasn't at all necessary. Asking him how he felt, strange things like that. Ed could see him now as he sauntered up the lane. He looked at the hangdog way Hilary was coming along and hastily withdrew a little, ducking his head down as far as he could.

Ambling along, Hilary caught the glint of the binoculars and turned to look over the hedge. What a demon Ed was.

'Edd-wardd! You'll kill yourself, you dork. Come on down! Hey! Ed!' The boy on the roof retreated and put his head down further as though, ostrich fashion, that made him invisible. What a bloody fool Ed was. Pathetic little pre-pubescent.

There she lay, a slumbering beauty. No. She saw him too, for one eye, nearly closed, opened wider. She turned on her side, tossed her hair. Hilary stared down at his tennis shoes. Carefully, he continued his self-appointed task of walking between the tracks. The sun beat lazily on his head. The road which in winter could turn into a mudslip was now ridged with parallel prominences separated by the width of a caterpillar tyre. He walked between them, feeling the hard earth through his soles, fingering the cow parsley. He reached out and tugged at the odd greenish blackberry. He didn't go in through the gate. No, he would go round to the back.

So he kept his head down and did not see a blurred white oval of a face rise behind opal glass at the house. Nicholas Lennox had found the means to his end. The eminent surgeon had achieved his desired sight line by means of the wicker laundry basket, the cork-topped bathroom stool being too low, the crouch turning into a kneeling position. Down the knees went onto the wickerwork. Swinging open the window, he achieved the dream of an unimpeded view. Being on this glorious hot Sunday dressed for tennis, his knees were bare. He should have put a towel on the basket. Never mind. No time to lose. When in due course he went down for lunch, Amanda would notice the latticework pattern imprinted on his knees and would think in a distant way that perhaps he had hurt himself. Which was quite true.

'Mum?'

'Just give me a hand with the basket, will you. Thank you, darling, lovely day for it.' Amanda wiped her hand on her pinnie and took a breather, staring out through the open kitchen window at that one particular spot, peculiarly prominent, on which Michèle had chosen to recline and where, sitting up, she was lighting yet another cigarette. This nymph made the veins on the backs of Amanda's hands stand out. She exacerbated both the sagging skin around her throat and a certain ache inside it. Amanda wondered, vaguely, if she should take up smoking herself. She looked at her hands which seemed such a strange colour against the wedding ring. A dark reddish colour on the knuckles, almost as if they'd been injured. Perhaps if she took it off. She tugged and, when it wouldn't, started to massage hand cream into the red knuckles.

'Mum? Cup of tea?'

'What a star you are. Madame B's brought out your feminine side. Ummh?' Amanda sat at the table and looked at her son, whose beauty was intensified by his shorts, his semi-nakedness, his tan. She had always admired his looks, so very different from hers in every respect, most crucially in the way they went on improving with age. Even as a baby he had been elegant.

'Did you talk to her a lot, honey? She didn't look terribly chatty . . . Not like your Mum, I suppose, terribly elegant, that's what I thought. I mean. Not that I got a glimpse. You tell me.' There she was, looking at him again, waiting for his reply.

'Earl Grey?' said Hilary. 'Louise is, um, well she's not what I'd call chatty, not in the normal way.'

His mother listened to what he said about France with a stillness and attention that was, frankly, scary. Not terrifying as her silence had been – no, this was quite different. She no longer cried in silence, tears dripping from her cheeks unheeded making little damp channels down her dress. He said to himself that that stage was over. She was on to the next bit and now everything was concealed. Not from him of course, just from the others. But this business of him knowing made it impossible to tell her anything, had any telling been possible in the first place. Which it wasn't. Yet she would keep on asking. Ironic, really, when he so badly wanted to tell her everything and ask her advice.

So Hilary smiled vaguely and poured water on a tea bag and thought that it was wonderful, how she could stand in her kitchen, a rock, frumpily dressed in the summer uniform of her class – a print frock which revealed freckly arms and sagged rather but was a favourite. Then there were the ancient sandals, the hair pulled back in a pony tail because the heat wave went on and on – and none of it mattered to her. She didn't give a stuff about her appearance. All around were baskets overflowing with her produce, with sprigs of mint and strawberries and peas from the garden. Endearing, that was what it all was. Good for her.

'Give me the peas,' said Hilary, splitting them and running his nail down and eating half as he went. 'Food's her thing. The only time I saw Louise really passionate was to do with the size of the oysters and how they weren't fine claires number whatsits, you know. So you could never know what she might've been like when she was young.'

'She was beautiful. Like Michèle. You can see it.'

Hilary watched his mother as she stared into some alien landscape in her mind while gulping down the tea. She was always busy cooking, peeling, doing. She slaved over the hot Aga, day in, day out. Today there would be the classic

English roast lamb, pink inside, new and roast potatoes, gravy, two veg and salad, homemade apple pie, cream. With a bottle or two of claret. The best food in the world, really. Try doing that for a hundred odd people. Hilary uncorked the claret and put the bottles to stand. Tea break was sacred.

There were long silences. He was aware of a certain amount of marital stress here, quite apart from the Charles business. It was as if there was some primeval slime or bubbling stew in her which went on and on all the time, a kind of biological life force that just was. Creative and all that, but not so as you'd see. But every now and then the slime surged and threw up an idea, like a bubble rising slowly through mud. Then it would pop and there would be nothing to show you that anything had happened, but the idea would be there, in the air.

'Charles hasn't changed. I did think that – not that you'd know. Well. I mean, how could you, darling. But you can see – some people have a kind of strength that's just in them.'

'Strength, weakness – they're like two halves of the same coin,' he said. Dimbat.

'Tell me more about France. You've hardly said.'

'Oh, France. Well, you're right about Louise being elegant. A real stunner, she is. Amazing cook. She makes this great apple tart. Almost as good as you, Mum. But she's not half as pretty as you, Mum, not a quarter. You know, it's all, like, make-up and labels. And food is everything, it's their religion.'

She nodded. 'It's impossible for a woman to spend time on herself, when there's so much to do in the house and garden, Hilary,' and she looked as though she was going to cry. 'Hands like these – well, you can't stop it. It's just part of the aging process.' She blinked quite rapidly.

That was the thing which drove him bonkers. Hilary

watched her with amazed affection. Did every remark have to relate to her? Wasn't it possible for a woman to take a compliment to another not as an insult to herself? Gender differences came down to this. Women never let themselves out of the beam of the critical spotlight, whereas men never took anything to apply to them. She sipped her tea and went on looking wobbly. No sense. Here was a woman who, told by the weathermen that there was a fifty per cent chance of rain on Friday and a fifty per cent chance on Saturday, would cancel her picnic because there was a total certainty of rain. He felt suddenly terribly fond of her for caring, just as fond as he'd been two secs ago for not, and went up and kissed her on the cheek.

'Mum. Please. You look gorgeous,' he said. The hand was really awfully red, around the knuckle especially. Perhaps she'd burnt it on something.

Amanda dished up lunch. They all ate plenty, Ed nose down in the trough and shovelling it in in concentrated feeding mode, then coming up for air.

'But it all gets mixed up in your tummy, doesn't it? So what's the big deal?' Ed was just trying to understand, you could see that. His eyes like saucers with mock amazement, his face all screwed up with the effort of it.

'No, no we serve separate the légumes. Not with meat. Separate the salad. Then some cheeses. Traditional, you know. Everyone in France do this.' She shrugged polished, bare shoulders.

'So you can never have gravy on your earth apples. Get it? Earth apples. Mum, pommes de terre, get it? Mum? Michèle's taught me lots of French. Dad? Do you know what gravy is in French? Le gravy?'

'Hilary's the expert,' said Nicholas, who'd got up to carve more meat and was offering the plate round, oozing charm.

She looked at it. A thin pink fluid, in runnels, beyond the valley of the spikes.

'Mum?'

Would he have been like this, if he'd been Charles's son? Odd, to imagine a non-English Ed, a solemn little boy who would never mash up his roast potatoes and make a well in the centre for gravy. Which he always ate from the outside in.

'Mum?'

'No, Edward, she doesn't know the word. They don't have gravy in France like we do,' said Hilary.

'No gravy? Pas de gravy, Michèle? C'est impossible. Pas de gravy, quel disaster. I'm not going to France then. Pas de mint sauce, Michèle?'

Michèle smiled and shook her head. 'What is the sauce à la menthe?' Her eyebrows flew up, for she was amazed by everything – the failure to peel all the potatoes, the way all the vegetables went on one plate with the meat, a highly uncouth practice to French eyes, the way that Nicholas dissected his meat, finding Latin names for sinews and knobbly bits which he liked to hold up to public inspection in a way she clearly found hilarious. And he was funny, his rubbery face pulled into expressions of utmost astonishment. Expertly, he forked a piece of meat onto his own plate. Smilingly, he took a little blob of mint sauce, put it on the girl's plate. Ed roared with laughter at her face as she tried it. She made a little moue, dead charming, of course.

Nobody noticed Amanda's face when Nicholas did his Latin party piece for perhaps the thousandth time in her married life. Nobody took their eyes off Michèle for a second, while Amanda cleared, helped intermittently by Hilary, and washed up and made coffee which, regrettably, she allowed to boil and which, like everything she did, was not quite good enough for her husband. She put the stuff on a tray and took it outside and the others sauntered out through the French windows onto the terrace and there she served it, smiling pleasantly. Then she went back in.

They sat on outside and had coffee and the afternoon was glorious and Michèle hoiked up the floaty pretty dress she'd put on to have lunch in and let her gorgeous legs tan a little more. Such skin she had, like a child's, which she of course was, just. Though in her soul that girl was ancient as Amanda had never been and still wasn't. That girl had lived her previous lives to the full.

'Hil, honey, take out some chocolates. Sweetie day, after all,' She passed them through the window. Ed with pillage noises of a Viking nature fell upon the box.

The mistress of the house sat in the kitchen with the door open and put her feet up because they ached, easing them out of the sandals and onto a chair and looking at the knobbly bones and the little veins, from childbirth, which Louise probably didn't have. Little dark lines, wispy, ugly, there. Nor those yellowy ugly heels which she particularly hated herself.

Her three men clustered round Michèle. They sought words for hazelnut and for cream fondant, which was French, wasn't it, and Nicholas led the laughter and fun in a manner which made it clear that only a bad sport would take his remarks seriously. Ho ho. And now and then a shout would come – buck up, Amanda! Come and enjoy the day, darling! Only a spoilsport would stay indoors and do cooking and clearing up on such a glorious day. Wife wasn't interested in the day, though, was she? The glories were hers anyway, wherever she was.

Wife got on with it. She made beds, loaded and unloaded the washing machine, went shopping with the ubiquitous basket in the charming local town. Wife got on with it. She organised more food, more meals, everything with a smile, always slightly harried, driving young Edward off to summer camp, back down the motorway. Get a nice bunch of flowers, cut the stems, dissolve the white stuff you got these days in warm water, arrange the flowers, fold the washing, see the place behind the machine where the powder fell, clean it, Betty bloody Boardman too old now, too stiff, and couldn't reach. Swab with the cloth, wipe down the cord, rewind the twisted bit of the kettle. Never had been any good, cleaning ladies difficult, this one very much so. Thanks, Mrs B, see you on Monday!

Saturday afternoon and wife sank with a sigh into the hands of the hairdresser, Georgie of the little-boy name and slightly wizened looks, who while an expert on appearances considered himself beyond all criticism. Wanted to say, just once, look, dear, we all know it's a fake tan and the trousers are so tacky. No, you couldn't, grateful that he came to the house. Look, Georgie, whatever made you think that anyone cared whose hair you'd done? On a Saturday, special customer, grumbled a bit, big tip required she knew, how kind of him to come. Amanda's eyes closed, she was far, far away.

Nicholas was playing tennis with something more than his usual competitiveness. He threw the ball a little to one side, caught it and started again. The serve thwacked away well, skimmed just over the net, Hilary scooped it up but returned it weakly, allowing his father to smash it back this time unreturnably. They were very alike in build and height but Nicholas felt bulky and old when he looked at his son. Hair, thinning on top, this year he had sunburn on the top of his head which had painfully brought home the truth of the matter. The business with the angling mirrors in the bathroom, compulsive, to look and then feel – what? Rage, at himself? Michèle ambled by and sat on a low wall.

'Come and play, Michèle, take this boy to the cleaners.' She shook her head. Nicholas was sweating. 'Ball girl then?'

Out of his mouth came casual nonsense which did not alleviate a painful series of double faults. Without ever looking in her direction and without even trying, Hilary now began to wipe him out. Hit inadvertently on one sensitised knee by one of his son's slam-banging ace serves, he leapt into the air and jumped about the court like a wounded frog. How high the boy threw the ball, how high. He squinted at it.

'Forty love.' Hilary served and hit a fourth ace. 'Five–one, same end.'

Nicholas was sweating profusely, he swigged at the bottle of water and choked a bit on it. He felt the heat of the sun on his bald patch, felt in his breathy gasp for air as his boy gave him the runaround that he was old and dead and buried and his brain was gone. Why else would the husk run around so, sweating and hustling and trying so hard? Why? She sat there and she knew bloody why.

Georgie expertly parted her hair with the comb and examined the roots as nobody since Miss Leeming had done, for nits, years back. Satisfied, he nodded, combed it through so the foul-smelling paste penetrated a squidge further towards the tips.

'Colour's taken really nicely,' he said. 'Lovely. Five more minutes.' He always congratulated himself fulsomely on whatever he did.

She gave no sign of life as the time passed, nor when he rinsed her hair twice and smoothed in the conditioner. It dripped a little on her neck. She pretended that his hands, which were adept but impersonal and which quite often hurt when he massaged her scalp, really belonged to Charles. Curious, then, that when he pulled her hair it was she who said ouch – sorry. He never apologised. Never said a thing even if the hairdo was grim. Lovely, he said. Suits you. Her fault, for putting up with it. Charles would never hurt a fly. She thought what it might be like, to be in his hands in this bathroom. She took a long time about that one.

'Sit up, Mrs L,' said Georgie.

'I've not had a proper orgasm in fifteen years,' Amanda replied. Her eyes were fixed on the white tiles with the rich blue pattern which she had chosen herself and, come to think of it, never liked. It was a speciality of hers, then. Georgie lifted his head and stared where she looked, at the pattern, whence no elucidation came. The hair, bunched up, had taken on the colour and sheen of an alien metal.

'I'd leave him tomorrow if I thought that Charles wanted me. Today. Charles has more sex in his little finger than Nicholas has in his whole body.' Her unseeing eyes closed again. The hairdresser, lost for words, stared at the little lines around the eyes and rinsed that final time and adjusted the temperature.

'Water's a shade too hot, Mrs Lennox?' Georgie said in tones more than usually deferential.

'It's not just sex,' she said. 'You have to understand I'm talking about simple humanity.'

There was a rough rubbing, a towel drying, then Georgie smoothed new towels – hers, naturally, to spoil and launder – round her, the whole with great care and she smiled at him, for he wasn't normally so gentle. The purse of his lips told that he would have said something, if only he had had some faint idea of what might be appropriate. Amanda's smile grew broader in the mirror.

'Well done, Georgie,' she said. It was the first time, even for a second, that she had felt that she had the upper hand.

As it dried, the alien colour changed into something which, without ever being natural or even pleasant, did approximate to the sort of thing some humans might have chosen to have on their head. Georgie pulled and smoothed and eased the dryer up and down and was careful, very. Amanda wondered why it was that these hairdressers, who spoke so much of condition and texture, who swore by this spray and that cream, who sold you things right left and centre, always chose to have their dark poodle hair streaked with yellow straw?

That was it, then, and the purse clicked and she gave him a fiver which was far too much but he expected it and was satisfied, she saw it in his face. Mean little eyes he had, like a poodle's.

Wife sallied forth on Monday, hair newly minted, to chair the meeting of the Ladies' Committee of the Cricket Club. She hated Georgie for doing this to her and yet accepted that this was how things were and that he would do the same again, a matter of weeks hence. She would smile and thank him, just as at the club she smiled and nodded and did her impersonation of a woman with an agenda which could be written down.

'Are you sure, dear Amanda, that you can do all those lovely puddings as well as the flowers?'

'Of course, really, I mean I'd mind a lot if you asked anyone else.'

Ho, a little polite laugh and wife smiled particularly brightly at that. It was pleasing to her that she could make them think that this was what she cared about. Puddings and pie and make them all cry. At home, she would pick redcurrants and blackcurrants, basket after basket, until her hands were stained red. The violent red mulch which she would sweeten and serve up to them until they were sick on it.

Wife was the chairperson of the Ladies' Committee of the Cricket Club and it fell to her to organise the annual dinner dance, which the entire village believed to be the social event of the year. It had taken years for her turn to come, years in which – and it was astonishing to think of this – she had continued in the face of all the evidence to believe that such institutions had some importance. Wife spoke at length about prices she had paid for things and smiled in that particular way which caused those present to congratulate her, whether they understood the cost of things or not. She could make things up and they would not notice or, if they did, care. Charles Beauregard would be arriving with his wife in a week's time and, as she did not hesitate to inform Mrs Dobbs, the treasurer's wife, he would be coming to, if not at, this event. Following which she laughed quite a long time. Mrs Dobbs laughed with her and then fell silent. Later, Mrs Dobbs told her husband.

'I'd call it a really filthy laugh if I didn't know that Mrs Lennox is so obviously a lady. Such lovely puddings she makes too,' Mrs Dobbs sighed, meaning in a vague way what she truly felt, which was that it was all a real shame.

'That French girl staying,' Mr Dobbs said. 'I've seen her. In the village. Wearing very short shorts and backless T-shirts. You know. I wouldn't like to even think of our daughter seen going around like that.'

His wife smiled and said, 'Quite right and it's just that sort of thing I'm thinking of, if you know what I mean. Poor Mrs Lennox.' They always agreed with each other and there was no need for anyone to remind anyone that poor Janice with her thunder thighs could never have got away with a mini skirt, let alone a pair of shorts.

Unconscious of such pity, Amanda sat behind into the sweet afternoon and, humming to herself, piled up the chairs and locked the committee room and was satisfied. It was wonderful to walk down the lane and feel the slight wind ruffle up the helmet she wore and take the lacquer out of it and the day was hers, for there was no Ed now for two weeks, and Hilary and Michèle had gone up to town with Nicholas to watch an operation. Dimly, fingering blades of grass and feeling the ruts of the track through the soles of her feet, she remembered that long ago she too had wanted to go and watch and that the moment had never come. There had always been some more pressing thing to do. Now, when she was completely free, there was nothing that interested her less. Why, she thought, she had forgotten so many things and how good that was, for her brain was still far too full and she wanted to strip the trivia out of it as, now, she stripped seeds from the husks of wild corn that grew in the hedgerows.

Hilary and Michèle looked down at Nicholas, who could not help knowing that he was the very archetype of an Englishman. He wore his green overalls and boots with aplomb, with a smile and a twinkle. In everything he did he breathed good humour. He blindly chose instruments with a patiently outstretched hand, dropped them if the nurse offered something that was not right and touched nothing if not with the utmost delicacy and concentration. Thus, he parted flesh, an act that could never be anything other than indelicate, with a gesture that was almost surreally light of touch and jocular. The irony of knowing and yet doing informed every breath he took. In Mr Lennox's operations, the atmosphere was ever light-hearted, even entertaining, for the surgeon was a well-known wag. The surgeon never let anyone down and especially not himself.

When he came into the operating theatre there was a wonderfully expectant pause. Eyes met in anticipation. There was no point being a character if you didn't enter into the whole thing wholeheartedly and give the performance every time. So he stood there in parody of himself and waited. Then, over the loudpeakers came a roar of Gilbert and Sullivan comic operetta and he joined in the choruses in a loud, nasal hum, let the odd refrain burst forth, gave the whole operation the tempo of the song. He knew all the words. He was counted on for that.

It was a new operation and there was a long waiting list for it and later Michèle would shake hands with an old woman who would hold her little hand tight and explain that it was a claw before, that she'd not been able to do that for years and the surgeon was a miracle worker, oh he was. Michèle smiled and looked away and didn't necessarily understand a word. From the other side of the ward, Nicholas felt that touch of her soft palm.

'You're a pretty little thing,' the old lady said. She stared at Nicholas adoringly. She held up her hand again and waved it about, seeking the great man's attention and admiration. Because of Michèle, he pretended not to notice.

Nicholas moved on to continue his performance elsewhere. It was a performance which brooked no added element, the whole was set and rigid, there was no interpretation in it. He excelled in the mechanical repetition of what seemed to have worked before. The operation and its aftermath, both sterile and both perfectly successful. Concave and convex, the perfect fit of two hollow vessels.

All morning Hilary had not been able to stop himself from feeling a grudging admiration of his old man alongside a full range of irritations and even rage at his grotesque mannerisms. The way his father talked to his admiring circle of students about the technology of the operation, which was what mattered, hardly glancing at the old woman's face, just giving her his standard cheery how-are-you-my-dear-fine-very-good line. The old fart, the old faker, the silly sod. The very stance of him, the very stripe of the grey suit, the very polish of a brogue sawed and grated at Hilary. The old dear wanted to talk to him and what did he care? All that and then there was the plus factor which tipped the scales, there was what he actually said. Crap from beginning to end. He was a bloody faker, he was unreal.

'Your father – he talks to his patients,' he said. Michèle looked at him, said nothing. So Hilary went back to the old dear and he hovered at her bedside and expressed his sympathy and regret and tried to say something personal.

'Do you need anything? I mean, can I get you anything?'

'You a student, dear?' she said. 'Just a mo, shush a minute, I'm trying to hear Mr Lennox,' and she flapped at him, meanwhile craning over his shoulder to see the great man doing his rounds, to hear the unintelligible banter.

'No, I'm his son,' he said, annoyed, whereupon she looked at him and saw his face and the resemblance, presumably, and seized his hand and shouted, not once, but several times.

'Oh look at this here! Lovely boy! Lovely! Lovely boy, Mr Lennox, lucky he took after his mum!' and by this means obtained her desire, which was that the surgeon should look at her and smile.

This day was different. It was screwed to a high pitch, tight and tense with expectation though Nicholas was not sure why until they were on the train and on the way home. Then, in front of everyone and while the train rocked and hummed and showed him all the usual places, Michèle leant over and put her elegant little hand on his knee with utter casualness.

'I love the English country, the looking,' she said. The corners of her mouth turned up in a wicked little smile. 'You like too, yes?'

Hilary read his book.

Nicholas felt his very bones dissolve with an acute mingling of pain and lust. 'Very nice.'

The hand remained on his knee. Sweat prickled everywhere. The warmth penetrated up and down, deep into his soul. She was just a little girl, she couldn't know what she was doing, she could not mean it. The hand burned through the thin fabric of his trousers, burned its imprint onto his flesh.

'So you think in France we don't have, no? Not so nice? You have to try, I think. Then maybe you like.'

'Yes. Indeed. Love to,' he said and swallowed. Oh Jesus. Wouldn't he like.

She looked straight at him with those clever eyes of hers and smiled out of her velvet face at him. Unmistakable the message of the hand, which now squeezed gently – yet she couldn't, could she? How and *when*? And his mind leapt ahead to think about that one and then came back again. She took back her hand. He composed a liturgy in his head of the little bones that made up her hand – bone by elegant bone he analysed and sang through her whole body, Gilbert and Sullivan or rather Lord High Executioner style, in his head, to the rhythm of the wheels. All the time she leant forward in the seat and looked at his face and he tried to stop his eyes from staring down the cleft between the lovely breasts, from sliding over the nipples which seemed, oh yes, to smile at him.

And Hilary finished his chapter and closed the book and put it down on the seat beside him and they all looked out of the window, for they were there. Polite as ever, Nicholas opened the door, held it, closed it afterwards with that sepulchral bang which went right through his head. That was it, but it wasn't.

Walking up the lane afterwards, she lagged behind.

'Nicholas? You know, I like the English gentleman, oh, very much,' in her lilting voice. She took his hand and held it to her breast. He stopped dead, for one long instant, held his breath. Looked at the way his son walked on ahead. Closed his eyes for an instant, just was, just was. Felt the air warm in his mouth.

'Don't you like me?' she said. 'I like you. Don't you want

me?' This, in deep, warm tones. He nodded, dumb, dizzy, desiring.

Hilary ambled on kicking at the long grasses and the evening smelt dizzyingly sweet. Nicholas could not say a word. His hand, on her breast. Smiling, she took it away. This moment of anticipation made Nicholas breathless and, to be sure, the presence of his son was an added savour to it – the fact that his wife was a few yards away and could indeed have seen him from the bathroom window, had she been there, had she chosen to look. Nothing in the world could stop this moment, nor its inevitable corollary. His hand, which had touched her breast, which lay down his side and retained the shape in its palm.

Nicholas knew what was coming. He had nothing to say. It was in the head of that beautiful girl, what would happen, if she so chose, for he was whatever she might make of him. Her plaything, or so he hoped. Anything, just to touch. Just to be able to look at her, naked, that would be a great deal. To touch – oh please, to touch.

Nicholas had a wife. Sometimes people asked about her, patients for example. He had a stock response. He would say that he was a lucky fellow. He had a pretty, kind, lovely wife whom he adored, who was a wonderful mother and, last but not least, a great cook. He had said as much that very morning out of the blue to his barber, who smiled and wondered what he was up to. It was very strange and told Nicholas just how new he was to this game, that it should have taken him the whole day to realise that for himself. As if he hadn't known it, from the way he was hiding from Jim. How's the wife? Fine – better! Fine! He had already dismissed her and now he knew why. All this passed through his head in the short walk between one life ending, with that touch, and the beginnings of the next life.

It was a waiting game. He sat on alone in the kitchen, with his bundle of *Times* crossword puzzles which he solved in tens – for when a person was quite good at doing them, that person needed to save them up, just as he did with chess puzzles which he liked to lay out on the kitchen table a dozen at a time and get through in twenty minutes with closed eyes. His eyes were closed just as if he was busy in his head, but the moves could not be planned with quite such ease. It was a question of when, not if, and the tension of it was exquisite, oh, the finest, purest drawn thread of lovely anguished pain. He could still feel her hand on his knee. His hand on her breast.

So she reeled him in.

On Wednesday he mowed the lawn and tugged at her with each stripe, backwards and forwards willing her until, at last, she walked out from the kitchen in the lovely early evening with her long bare legs and a glass of lemonade. She sat on the old grey bench and watched him finish the job and then all casual ease she walked back to the shed with him and he emptied out the cuttings and put the machine away and wiped its oily surfaces. Look, she said. Grass stains on her bare feet. There, beside the weathered wall between the compost heap and the shed she leant forward and ran her hands down his back and up under his shirt and pushed herself up against him and guided his hand under her skirt and one finger touched the elastic of her panties. One finger. He thought he would explode. Before he could kiss her she skipped away.

The fine afternoon came when Hilary went out with his mother to the club and without even a smile, indeed with a very grave look, Michèle came over to Nicholas. She reached out and took him by the hand.

'Come. Now. You come please.'

She smiled as he stood and took off her shirt and showed him what he knew, which was that she wore nothing underneath. And as they went up the stairs, she disrobed and so in the doorway of his bedroom – for she led him to no other place – she was already naked and he was rewarded with an erection so large that it took a little moment to undo the zip, that task made yet more delightfully difficult by her insistence upon freeing him herself. His head was completely empty of anything else. That was the thing that was most amazing, the silence of his head which was never like this but which now held only the moment, the now and the urgency of need. He said not a word, nothing, there was nothing to say.

So it came about that that fine afternoon Hilary and his mother walked slowly back together from the cricket club up the lane, swishing at the cow parsley, silently but not because of any particular anticipation or unrest, each thinking their own thoughts. They were home earlier than planned and Amanda, thinking just quickly to brush her hair – for she took each opportunity to inspect herself, ever in hope, thinking to detect some improvement in some sphere – went to her room. She opened the bedroom door. She was touching her hair, shaking her head, she did not at first look at the bed, prominent though it was, because it had not occurred to her that there could be anything to see.

Hilary who had noticed Michèle's shirt upon the floor of the sitting room came swiftly up the stairs and round the landing to see what his mother saw and they stood and the pair of them watched Nicholas's back, dark with hair and with brown marks on the shoulders, Nicholas's white buttocks pumping between the brown legs agape and raised up of the girl, her hair tumbling loose and her face raised up, contorted with an expression which could not be read, her eyes open and staring over the man's shoulder. What a noise he made, he grunted and groaned and panted – and something must have alerted him to a presence, some change in the composition of the light, some current of air, for all at once the noise took on a different quality. The sound of an animal – Hilary thought of the owl and the whistle and his father was no different from the son of the boulanger.

Hilary shut the door. 'Right. Let's make a cup of tea, Mum,' he said with huge, with astonishing savoir-faire, putting his arms round her – for he'd seen it all before, hadn't he? He'd seen it all before. Just this view, dear God, he'd seen, just this, and Amanda paused a second – waited, and Hilary looked at her face. Flesh of my flesh, he thought, and she was no different to him in waiting, as he had waited, for the end of it. Yes, he had seen it all before. Waiting for it to be done. And when it was over, he went downstairs and put a tea bag in a mug and made tea, just as she liked it.

Unstoppably, unforgivably, above all noisily with groans that mingled the extremes of pleasure with existential angst, behind the door, Nicholas climaxed. He lay for a long moment face down on the girl, listening to the thudding of his heart and its counterpart, the footsteps not hurried, not hard, just soberly going down the stairs – and still he could not quite believe it. This had happened to him. Surely this had not happened to them. To him, to him? Had this really happened to him, to him?

'It was them?' he said to Michèle who, as soon as he was done, was busily wriggling her way out from underneath him. She walked away into the bathroom and began running a bath and started swabbing between her legs with toilet paper and called out to him – and this act, of all the least erotic he had ever seen, had a kind of deft purposefulness that was truly ugly.

'It was them,' she said, calmly and without any particular reaction or even any interest. She did not even look in his direction. It was them – it had happened to him. Any idea he had had of tenderness, of love even, any idea of anything died. She had not kissed him, not once. He hadn't noticed, before.

For Nicholas, who was so very far from being versed in affairs of the heart or of any other organ, had not imagined this. That they would lie together, yes, that the excitement would be unbearably drawn out, yes, that there would be words spoken – something – but not this. So matter-of-fact. 'Yes, it was them.' How banal, how sad it all was, that such intensity gave rise to this, to nothing, to something less than nothing.

He lay on the bed and watched through the open bathroom door as Michèle bathed, washing herself with thoroughness, not in haste but not slowly either, giving the act its due as he had received his due. He was too tired to move, certainly too tired to go anywhere. He thought that he might sleep for a thousand years.

She came out and picked up her clothes and he looked at her, naked, and then dressing without any self-consciousness. He felt no desire. He had so much wanted to just look at her and admire and now he had his moment and could look as much as he chose and that was it. There was no explaining. Unthinkable, the transition, from major to minor. She went away without saying another word and closed the door, firmly but quietly behind her. A deep lassitude fell over him, like a blanket of darkness.

He turned over onto his back and let his heavy body press with its full weight against the uxorial counterpane. He heard Michèle's faint footsteps go down the stairs and, incredibly, into the kitchen – on and through. No voices. Normally, with the windows open, he would hear something. He levered his head from the pillow and looked. It was a mighty effort, for gravity doubled and redoubled itself every second.

Michèle Beauregard lay in the garden, sunbathing topless; she lay in her usual place and stretched herself out as she had so often before. She could not remain still for more than a few moments at a time and so an instant after lying down she sat up and went through the series of little shakes of the head and stretching movements, and eased herself over until she was supine. The sun glinted on her hair as she spread it out.

Nicholas could not bear to watch. His head was so very heavy. He fell back onto the bed and lay inert for a long, long time. He drifted into sleep and out again and let the thing pass over him and woke, then, in the dusky late evening and with a shamed, sudden eagerness showered for a long time and tried to make himself clean. He found no thoughts in his head at all, nothing but the same listlessness and heaviness and waiting.

Afterwards, not being able to gauge which offence was worse, he still lay on the bed, for surely to appear downstairs was unthinkable and, for the others, would be unbearable. In due course, there were footsteps. Amanda came upstairs and into the bedroom and in her usual manner undressed and brushed her hair and then went into the bathroom. There was the usual assembly of noises. The bathroom cupboard opened and closed and opened again. If he had lifted his head, which was no longer possible, he might have been able to see her go through her face-cleaning routine, which involved a white cream, then a pink lotion, then another white cream. She always stared at herself with intensity while applying a further, more yellowy cream to the tender area underneath her eyes. Last of all she would do her teeth. He listened to the familiar noise and finally the spit and rinse and she came and got into bed, all as usual.

'Goodnight,' she said. She turned over, plumped her pillow, let her head drop onto it – everything so normal, so deeply familiar that suddenly tears stood in his eyes.

'Oh, Amanda, Mandy, darling oh please,' he said, with a quiver in his voice.

There was a long silence.

'I have to sleep. Goodnight.' She turned over. Her tone was completely neutral.

The long weekend passed, the heatwave continued, everything continued as if it was just the same and Amanda said nothing to him. Hilary said nothing. Nicholas, wandering mournfully around his beautiful house and gardens and looking at his son and his wife, wondering if he had lost everything through his insane stupidity, was held in a torture of suspense by their silence. He could not stand to look at Michèle who was demurely picking currants for summer pudding. It was wrong to blame her for what had occurred when it was surely all his fault. However, he did attribute some measure of wilfulness to her. It was impossible to understand what had impelled this girl to do what she had done. Finally, because there had to be a reason and he could not flatter himself that it was desire, it crossed his mind Michèle had done this because of his son. Or – and this was a further turn of the screw – perhaps she had also fucked Hilary on this one-off, get it over with basis. Why had he never asked? He couldn't ask now.

In the garden, avoiding the spot where she lay, he marched up and down the stripes of the lawn. The grass grew lush and longer and so it would go on. He did not get the motor mower out. That side of things was done. It was all over. Let the forces of disorder prevail. He wanted it to run wild, he wanted it to be unchecked. Fiercely he imagined himself wading through knee-high bracken.

Saturday night came and after dinner the house was very quiet. Nicholas telephoned various friends and even, for the first time in years, met one of them in a pub for a Sunday lunchtime drink, finding out to his surprise that he could not confide in a bloke. It was early, the big mahogany bar of the Dog was nearly empty and it smelt of stale beer and polish and he supped his pint and spoke of the weather and wondered, as old Brian must have wondered too, just what they were doing there.

Sunday came and went and the long empty day held its usual pattern and food was eaten and drink drunk and the long shadows came across the garden and had no meaning. Monday came and he went to work and the day was as other days and there was no sense in it.

That night, Nicholas went home as ever, stretching out his legs in the first-class compartment, staring out at the yellow fields and the lovely summer's evening with a face of despair. He was terrified, but ready to listen – ready to hear. He was ready.

Amanda said nothing. Now, this was not the same silence as before. The wall was there, it had been there for some time, but it was of a different composition. Nicholas understood perfectly well that there were different shades and textures of white and black. His wife had acquired a different texture. She did not speak to him, not because she particularly meant to punish him but rather with the air of a busy woman who had many things on her mind and could not speak for good reasons. They sat together in silence. So it was all decided, all decided, all done and finished. That was what he thought.

Hilary avoided his father in a far more knowing manner and his eyes slipped past when they met. Hilary evidently hated him.

Nicholas saw that his life was unbearable and that it was without meaning. Then with a terrible jolt which took his breath away and made him feel for an instant that he had been seared inside, came the second recognition. Of course. This was precisely how his wife had felt. The silence and the tears. So something had happened to change matters for her. The only thing the poor, vain fool could think of was that it must be due to him. Now that it was too late he remembered that she had always been the only person he had ever really talked to in his whole life. The only one he'd always trusted and depended upon. The ironies of his position unfolded like Chinese boxes, each one containing a new and yet more intricately patterned one inside. Nicholas too cried, not like Amanda, but noisily, gulping and sobbing and wiping his nose on the back of his hand, snot runnelled, like a child.

It was the day when the Beauregards were due and wife had entered into a state of almost pure abstraction, in which everything was done which had to be. She swam through the air with slow movements of her arms and legs. Wife knew that responses were expected of her which she could not supply. Nicholas, for instance, with his hangdog miserable air was waiting for something. The French girl, for instance, should have received some sort of reprimand and she would keep looking at her hostess as if she expected her to say something. Really, it was absurd. Wife saw it all, but there was nothing at all which she could think to say to either of them.

Charles was on his way. It became a matter of hours, then of minutes. Amanda in this final, crystal moment of clarity could see that there was something different in the way that Michèle looked at Hilary and that this new thing was hurtful to him. The girl had taken to making little remarks which seemed to ask for a response. Someone who did not know her might have taken these for a sign of friendliness. Amanda, knowing better, felt deeply for her son. Shock was written all over him, in the coldness of that studied neutrality, the way in which he got through the day speaking all the necessary words, never once referring to what had occurred. Of course there would be some reaction and she would not rule out a potentially violent response of her own, but not just yet when there were forty, thirty, only twenty minutes to go. Couldn't he just realise that this was how things had to be? She could not be a mother now. It was cruel and harsh of Michèle to behave like this, and Amanda felt her newly active presence going through the house. This went on with intensity while wife performed the ritual dance of dinner and then with careful mannered ease sat to polish her silver candlesticks and waited and counted the minutes.

An hour and twenty minutes beyond the latest possible time, the car turned up the drive. There were voluble exclamations to do with timekeeping and ferries missed and caught and husbands and driving on the wrong side. Noisily, the Beauregards spilled out onto the gravel. Michèle came to be kissed and admired.

Charles lightly kissed Amanda on both cheeks and grasped her hands in his large, warm ones. He carried a big suitcase into the house. They walked together. Nicholas took the other one and politely listened to the voluble Louise who had much to say about the sandwiches on sale on the ferry and her husband's timekeeping and whose complaints and observations made her seem alive in a rather simple way that was now very remote from him.

Amanda with a pounding heart led Charles into the kitchen. This was where she lived. He closed the door behind them and looked at her. So many things she had forgotten, to do with texture and shape and the multi-coloured strands of his hair which were the colour of thick honey and the way the hollows of his neck moved when he spoke. The stubble on his cheeks, which she wanted to touch.

When Charles looked at Amanda, it was as though black and white was turning into Technicolour. He kissed her with thoroughness, heedless of anyone else, for they could hear that in the hallway Michèle was chattering on to her mother while Louise for her part tried to talk to Hilary and Nicholas kept saying something. Lapped by all of these sounds Amanda tasted the incredible sweetness of the man. She lay against his chest and his warm breath fell upon her hair and she felt the sensation of being alive course up and down her, simultaneously making her knees turn soft and her face burn, as though it would burst from so much sensation. They came together with such extreme naturalness. The extraordinary taste of him, which she could not get enough of, was causing some sort of chemical reaction inside her mouth. As wine should, excellent wine, the taste of the kiss grew and became rich and deep.

The evening would grow and bloom and Amanda blossomed, a slow-motion film speeded up until she hardly recognised herself. She was changing with startling speed. She understood that she was becoming much more vivacious, a kind of approximation of the woman he remembered, or rather her remembered approximation of the same. The taste of him was in her mouth. That and the unhurried grace with which he moved and spoke and the overpowering knowledge of all that was to come filled her up with intensity. This, then, was joy. So simple, so very strong.

While Amanda lived, so vividly, with Charles, wife became more opaque, dense or rather condensed into an abstraction of herself. This had to be. The wifeness was now so thick and heavy that, like heavy water, it could never be got rid of. The very molecules of which wife was composed might implode upon themselves at any moment. Meltdown would come, it was unavoidable. Amanda saw it all with dispassionate interest. Wife could barely speak, she went through the usual motions and people smiled and nodded and ate and said things through the thick green glass.

Every year the cricket club dinner was preceded by a one-day match between the Lennox's club and the neighbouring village's team, always the cause of much passion locally. The Lennox's side, ever hopeful, had never yet beaten the opposition village, which had the great luck of being home to a good county cricketer, Sandy Wicks. This match was seen as the climax of the season, despite all the cricket that would be played after it, for the grand dinner at which the home team entertained the visiting team was seen as a matter of great local pride and the only event in the year at which all local people sat and ate and drank together.

Nicholas was talking to Charles. He was trying to explain the composition of the team which included him and his son and which was once again doomed to failure. Charles did not understand why their team did not hire a better captain.

'The honour of the village,' Nicholas said, and, 'It's an amateur game.'

'You want to win, you get the best player, no? The other people have a good one. For you it is important to win, yes? So? You take the good player.'

Nicholas wanted very much to convince him and altogether felt that he wanted him on his side. He had only the faintest, dimmest memory of the French doctor from all those years ago. He had been much slimmer, younger, naturally. It seemed to him incredible that his wife had ever recognised him at the airport. Mind, the whole foreign exchange business was incredible, not least his own part in it.

Hilary's dreams at this time were exceptionally vivid. Not dreams exactly but something nearer to nightmares, for he woke sweating and with deep creases on his face where he had burrowed into the pillow and it had fought back. It was a shock to find himself in his own bed and not back in France and before he opened his eyes he expected each time to see the flowery tendrils of the wallpaper which he had so often followed along the ceiling and across the wall to the place of deliverance at the window.

He dreamt that he was delivering the baby. Charles was not there and he was the master of proceedings. He was in the kitchen, searching for the knife and failing to find it. Drawer after drawer was opened and he knew that someone had hidden the thin knife, the one he needed, hidden it where no stranger would ever find it. At last, he sharpened a wholly unsuitable knife, a serrated bread knife, on the old grindstone. When he turned the wheel, it groaned, as his father had groaned. The knife became blunt, not sharp. The teeth of the knife were moving along the blade, back and forth. They jittered and spun round. The young wife was screaming upstairs.

There was always a giddy moment, in the dream, when he thought he had looked away for an instant too long and in that terrible second the blade had done its work, had cut off all the fingers of one hand. It was a kind of delirium within the dream and he would have to remind himself that it was not possible and yet he would always look at his hand and then at the floor, one quick glance, to be quite sure that no fingers lay there. Then he held the knife with both hands like a dagger, pointing away from him. The teeth of the blade sang their own strange song.

Up the stairs he stole, to the room with the smoky light and the terrified woman in the bed and the yellow smile of the farmer. But there was no Charles there. He was alone, he would have to deliver the baby, and as the woman screamed once more he looked at the knife and knew that with this knife he would surely kill her. Then, lifting his head to say something and calm her, because he needed badly to calm himself, he realised that the woman on the bed was not the farmer's wife at all. It was Madame Ourlandes. She looked at him. Her stomach was swollen, pregnant, but her eyes were very old. The mouth, open to scream, closed. She fell silent. She knew that she would die. They both knew that he was going to kill her. Always, now, he refused the dream with violence and made himself wake.

Each time he found his teeth were chattering with dread and he had to calm himself by saying his mantra. It's all all right, it's fine, don't be silly. It's all right, it's over, it's only a dream. Over and over, except that it wasn't . Often, unable to sleep afterwards, he would replay the birth in his head to make it be all right, but always it came back to Michèle's open legs. Always, his discovery of her being fucked in the orchard, then back to the scene of her being fucked by his father. He did not just let himself see it all, he made it all happen, replaying, rewinding. He thought that this stratagem would eventually make it all bearable, oh, but it took so long.

On one of these nights, Hilary awoke with an idea in his head which would not go away. In the dream, he had the nylon fishing line round the head of the man fucking Michèle in the orchard but as he pulled it tighter and tighter, he heard the hooting of the owl right behind him and realised that it was his father he was strangling. This woke him abruptly. Perhaps he did want to kill him.

He turned on the little lamp, stared about the room grimly. It was three in the morning. He still had an exact picture of Michèle looking at him over the head of the man from the boulangerie and then, with the same look, over his father's bent, desperate back. The two were connected in more than the obvious respect. She looked at him and there was a message in her eyes. Hilary sat up in bed. She looked at him and saw him. She had planned it. She had come to England and had chosen to seduce his father as revenge upon him. It was strange and horrible. But she continued to look at him with triumph.

The day of the match dawned as hot as its predecessors. Father and son dressed in their white gear in their respective bedrooms, alone in the house. The French couple strolled along the lanes and up to the club, with Michèle mooching along behind. Amanda was already in the club house, organising tea and cucumber sandwiches and slicing up seed cake. This day of endless activity had started for her at five in the morning and would go on till the small hours, yet she was calm and even happy.

In silence, Hilary and Nicholas walked to the match. At the last corner of the lane, his father held out his hand to shake.

'Good luck, then,' he said.

Hilary nodded but would not accept his father's hand.

'Come off it. Don't be so fucking sanctimonious,' said Nicholas.

'I've not said a *fucking* word.' Hilary pushed him in the chest quite hard. A moment later, Nicholas pushed back. Hilary jabbed at his face and missed, just. Nicholas jeered at him.

'You bastard.'

'Go on, go on, give it a try, you little shit.'

Nicholas, who would have been pleased to relieve tension in any way possible and would happily have been hit by his son if that made anything better for him, or for that matter for anyone, noticed that up ahead Michèle had stopped and was waiting. Did she want them to come to blows? His boy looked at her, desisting from the fight, which he was clearly spoiling for, with a curious, clouded face. Grief blurred his features. Rapidly, he went on past her. Nicholas now saw the odd, the expectant way the girl looked at Hilary who would not look at her, staring instead at his feet.

'Oh fucking fuckhead,' said Nicholas. He stood there in the lane, clenching and unclenching his fists. He saw it now. Quite separately from what he'd done to his wife, he'd fucked the girl his son was in love with. He felt like crying, terrible self-pity prickled behind his eyelids.

He didn't of course, no, he did his crying in private. Oh hell. With face half turned away, Michèle stood there. Tears brimmed up and began to fall silently down her cheeks. This was completely unexpected. He stared at her. That she had emotions was not something he'd exactly realised before.

Mr Dobbs passed with a cheery wave. 'What a day for it! Hot enough for you?'

'Yes,' said Nicholas.

There was a big crowd, for practically every inhabitant of both villages had turned out. They always did. Amanda in a sleeveless linen dress was slaving over tea urns in the big marquee erected next to the club house, where the evening's dance would also take place. Over the course of the past few hours, every dip and fall under her feet had become familiar. The urns hummed and buzzed with their own particular excitement.

At the open flap of the tent stood Charles who was not looking at the cricket. He was watching her admiringly. Before she turned and saw him there, she could feel it, felt all along one side of her body a kind of tingling awareness of his presence.

Over on the cricket field, Michèle was lying down on her towel quite far away and to one side of the pitch. She wriggled out of her skirt and T-shirt to reveal the skimpy bikini on her faultless body.

Before too long a couple of the local yokels were gawping at the French beauty from a couple of dozen yards away. Hilary, at outfield, felt suddenly acutely conscious of her and of their admiration of her. But then, everything was making him nervous today.

Teatime was nearly upon them. Amanda, who had gone to sit behind the marquee to have a rest in the shade, saw Charles appear, once more demonstrating his unerring instinct when it came to finding her.

'Hello.'

'Hello, you.'

He smiled and sat down on the grass beside her. It was very peaceful here, between the guy ropes. He was there, it was enough. She didn't need to say anything. Because of other people, she used every bit of energy in her body to stop her hand from reaching out to touch him. She very badly wanted to touch him, but not now. It would wait, the touching would be all the sweeter for it.

'You are so beautiful,' he said, quietly. 'Always the same. Today I am so happy.'

'And me'. She closed her eyes and could have cried with it.

He was looking at her, she felt his look warm on her face.

'I never forget you, never.'

'No,' she said.

Amanda could hear the rhythmic regular thwack of the ball, together with the faint buzzing of applause and soothing comment. The sun was quite exceptionally hot, the smell of grass delicious, the whites in the distance dazzling. A huge fat bumble bee paused in its progress to look at them and then carried on. And, curiously, this was all quite astonishingly real, in a way all recent events had not been, in a way that nothing had been real for years now. She felt each breath of her body, each pore, each beat of her heart telling her that she was alive and that life was good and sweet.

Out on the pitch, the visiting team was making short work of the defenders. The score was up on the board. Somebody from the village called out something to her in passing and with a little effort she stood to see. It was the last of fifty overs. She rocked a little on the dry grass, feeling under her elbow the place where Charles's warm hand had rested as he helped her up. He stood next to her and the sleeve of his shirt just touched her arm. She was intensely happy.

Sandy Wicks was now batting. There was a mighty crack of leather on willow which made Amanda look up. He hit a ball which caught Nicholas neatly on the kneecap and he doubled up. She saw him rolling over and over in the distance some way beyond Hilary. The sun glinted on the batsman's spectacles, he waved victory.

The score was 230 in fifty overs for six wickets. The Lennox's side were never going to match that and the buzz in the tea tent was already faintly disappointed, apologetic.

Inside the tent it was hot, though all the flaps had been pinned back. Pitchers of lemonade stood ready, homemade, and the supply of cups of tea went on and on. There was no end to the thirst, she poured and poured.

A plume of smoke curled up from Charles's cigarette as he sat and watched Amanda. He was looking at her arm. She looked down and saw the way the shaft of sun coming in made the tiny hairs on her arm glint gold. In the distance, Louise was lying out on the pitch next to Michèle, the pair of them making a ravishing distraction for the yokels, who had doubled in number. Looking back, seeing the way Charles still looked at her arm, Amanda felt herself blushing deeply. It was the sexiest thing in the world. There she stood, next to the tea urns, in all the heat.

'What a scorcher, Mrs Lennox!' Wife smiled vaguely at whoever had said that. Dobbs. She stood on, for she could not have moved for anyone, for anything. Very slowly, Charles reached out his hand and began, very gently, to stroke Amanda's arm. Paralysed with pleasure, she stood there. Nobody noticed. Just the soft part of the upper arm, where the flesh was most tender.

'I am sorry,' said Charles, meaning something else entirely.

'Of course.' She closed her eyes and smiled back at him,

closed her eyes in bliss, because she could not help it. 'The sun is very hot,' she said.

All the helpers were busy, there were hundreds of people in the tent, cups of tea to be done, and nobody noticed Mrs Lennox standing between the urns with the absurd smile on her face.

Over on the pitch, the local lad who was sitting closest to Michèle was talking intently. All the time his eyes flicked up and down her, for sheer animal amazement. He had told her that his name was John four times. Still she called him 'you'.

'So now they make the runs, they win perhaps?'

'No, no, you see they can't possibly win now. You'd need a miracle to win.'

'But they have the same time as the other people?'

He shook his head, patiently, started again to explain it.

'Why should they not win? You don't explain right, you.'

'Well, for a start, they never do.'

'Never? Look. I say this time they win.'

Louise stood up and wandered towards the tent. She soon came across Nicholas sitting on his own behind the tea tent with his head in his hands, not looking at anyone. He had rolled up one trouser leg and with a little moan was inspecting the wounded knee. He was a strange person but she thought him kind. His eyes smiled.

The second innings began. Hilary was in to bat and almost at once the other batsman was caught out. A desultory clapping greeted him as he walked back to the pavilion. The village had lost heart. Wicks, bowling, was cheerfully dismissing one batsman after the next as, very slowly, the local side built up its score. Hilary batted on.

Soon enough they had reached the last over, with Hilary still batting and Sandy Wicks still bowling. He raised his floppy sunhat, wiped his forehead with a rolled up end of a sleeve. The spectacles needed to be wiped. All this was done with the deliberation and that very English self-deprecation which was his hallmark. In a little moment now they would win. It wasn't county cricket but Wicks was a crowd-pleaser. Foregone conclusion, this was. There was enough of a showman in him to want to eke it out a little.

'Nearly had it,' said John, the young man sitting beside Michèle. 'See? He's a gonner.'

'No,' she said fiercely, looking at Hilary, who stood in the ready position, holding the bat. 'You know nothing, you.'

'Don't be silly, I was nearly on the team, wasn't I,' but she wasn't listening.

Michèle rose to her feet. With the first ball, the bowler got the last but one batsman out and now it was the turn of the last man. Nicholas strode onto the pitch with only the faintest hint of a limp. Behind him, looking anxious, was Louise. Slowly, she walked over to the main part of the crowd which had laid itself out on rugs and deckchairs all along the edge.

In the tea tent at this particular moment, Amanda was slowly stacking saucers on a tray. Charles came up behind her, reached round her for the heavy tray, just for one second cradled her back in his arms. Amanda's eyes closed as she sank into him, fitting together like spoons just for one instant. Nobody noticed a thing.

Out on the field, Nicholas made one run. Now Hilary was in to bat, the score four behind at 225. Wicks bowled a beauty and there was no score on the third ball. Getting ready to make his run for the fourth ball, Wicks fleetingly lost his concentration, becoming aware of a distractingly gorgeous girl – naked? No, in a bikini – crossing his field of vision and it was a little while before he recovered his concentration. He bowled hard and cleanly and it was all

Hilary could do just to give it a touch with the bat. He was sweating like a pig.

No score.

It was the fifth ball of the last over and Hilary was steadying his bat. Michèle walked behind the sight screens. Just as she disappeared behind them, she removed the top half of her bikini and let it swing from one naughty finger. From her bikini bottoms, she drew a little tube.

Sandy Wicks prepared to bowl. There, straight in front of him, stood Michèle, looking at him, wearing only the skimpy bottom half of her bikini. In this position, only the bowler could see her. Slowly as he walked back, then faster, as he made his run, with immaculate timing and with undoubted erotic intent she began with both hands to rub cream into her wonderful bosoms, paying particular attention to the nipples.

The ball left Wicks's nerveless hands and, as it did so, it curved as though drawn to Hilary's bat. As he swung to hit it, Michèle slowly and suggestively rotated her pelvis and threw her head back. She did it faster, faster, one hand moved down towards the bikini bottom and then slipped inside it.

Hilary hit the ball as hard as he possibly could. Wicks was transfixed. He remained where he was, standing stock still and precisely in the path of the ball as, with unerring accuracy and huge velocity, it hit him between the eyes, neatly shearing his spectacles in two. He and they dropped, a roar went up from the crowd.

Spectators now started running over to help Wicks up. He was groping in the grass for his glasses as Michèle hooked up her bikini top. He managed to mend them, just, using a wodge of sticking plaster which one of the fielders had in his pocket. He put the glasses on. He was seeing double. He shook his head and blinked.

Over near the marquee, hope ran through the crowd

and people began to sit up in their deckchairs. Some were even standing up to watch the match. Wicks steadied himself, for he was reeling slightly, and prepared to bowl the last ball of the match. He wasn't feeling quite right.

Hilary hit the ball with a mighty crack and started to run. Nicholas, also running, watched the ball wobble and bounce and jump its way right to the very edge of the field, and the young outfielder was running and he threw the ball back and Wicks, running backwards with his hand outstretched, saw one ball, then two and then three. A multiplicity of balls came at him and he tried to get hold of one of them and missed the catch. The ball bounced on towards the other side of the field and our men were still running. It was a five. Incredibly, they had won.

Around the pitch there was a hubbub. People were cheering and rushing up and down and there was a ripple of applause starting up. Young John Hardeman looked at Michèle who, ignoring him, now stood to put her T-shirt back on. For a moment, the head was gone. The blonde hair was pulled through the neck of the T-shirt and shaken out, smoothed. The head was back and it smiled broadly, the mouth curved up and when she smiled, she was staggering. The thing was, she wasn't smiling at him. He turned his head and followed her line of vision. She seemed to be smiling at the Lennox lad, but he wasn't looking at anyone. Unreal. Life was so bloody unfair. He thought of his girl friend, Angela, who was very nice and that, but not like this. Not like this.

Hilary saw but did not look at Michèle and instead he ducked his head, modestly. He walked slowly back towards the pavilion. Disbelief and pleasure and sun all joined up. The sight of people clapping, the smells and sounds of the day. A little avenue parted, of people clapping up ahead.

Nicholas made his way across the pitch behind his son and as he did so something inside him gathered momentum. He started to run and to shout. Whooping loudly, he threw his cap in the air, caught it, threw it up again, rushed up and in a totally unEnglish way caught up with and embraced his son.

'You're bloody marvellous,' he said.

Hilary smiled back. He didn't want to, but there was no negotiating a position with his traitorous face. What was he going to do, pretend he wasn't pleased? He hit Nicholas in a sort of playful way on one arm. It was a blow, but without heat. His dad smiled in a curious way. He got it. Hilary hit him again, a little harder, but smiling, still. Father and son walked back together. Something was eased through this, somehow, or was beginning to ease.

'Enough?' said his father, raising mock coward's arms.

'Yeah.' Hilary felt all right. Actually, he felt as good as he had for ages.

In the tent, Amanda busied herself and rapidly prepared an ice pack which Sandy Wicks gingerly placed on his bruised head. Then she went back over to the tea urns.

Lying flat on his back with eyes half closed, feeling like hell, Wicks could not help watching with great interest the way that Mrs Lennox stood completely still, staring deep into the eyes of a big shambling bear of a man who stood beside her and very slowly and hypnotically went on stroking her arm. His head pounded. Perhaps it was a mirage, as the girl had been, or then again not. The girl had been so beautiful. She was worth it, sort of. Almost. If he'd had the strength, he'd have gone looking for her. Meanwhile he looked at what was there. Knew the husband. Funny, this business with the wife. Pretty woman, she was. Funny, that she didn't seem to care who looked.

Mrs Lennox and the man split into two and then four then six and it was a long moment before they reassembled into the right number of arms and legs.

6 ♪

The day cooled as the sun dipped behind the huge oak tree and threw its shade over the pitch where the score would stand triumphant over lesser matches for respectful weeks to come. The field was empty, as was the pitch. Only Amanda was there, absent-mindedly jingling the keys to the club house and staring aimlessly at a courting couple lost in an embrace. The crowd was down at the White Hart. The pub spilled them out of every window and door and still they came. Total strangers, thrusting through, caught some of the glory of it and were buoyant by the time they got to the bar. Winners and losers sank their pints and toasted each other. It was a fine sight, the men in their white flannels and the long day still smiling at them, the shadows lengthening against the mellow stone.

On the green the local lads and lasses sipped at their halves and eyed each other. Half a dozen tough leather lads on motorbikes rode slowly through the village, much admired in secret but sneered at in public. It was a famous night. The whole countryside was wound up and ready. Tonight, a hundred sets of parents would go out, releasing their houses and gardens for youth to spring upon its moment. All tumbledown merry, a dozen romances would start and two finish. Three virginities would be lost, two babies conceived, one marriage broken and another saved.

From house to house, warm Sussex water which had once bubbled through chalk now gurgled perfumed anti-clockwise down pipes. The ladies bathed. Louise rose from her bath and Michèle slipped into hers. Milly Dobbs puffed powder on her nose and cleavage and Betty Boardman tripped on a pebble as she hurried up the lane, ten minutes late. The sandals were to blame. These were the height of glamour, gold and high-heeled with Roman thongs which clung to her ankles and dug into her round countrywoman's calves. She had known that they were stupid. If you did them up loosely, they fell down. Betty equally cursed the chafing tightness of her girdle which left red weals round her waist and thighs. It was the new one, fancy, lacy and a little too tight. What night, if not this one, to christen what was new and special? In the name of beauty for miles around innumerable curlers unsprang in victory rolls. Betty's feet were in torment and by the end of the evening her toes would be red raw, ten uncooked sausages squeezing through a net. Yet, if she had to choose between comfort and beauty, Betty still took beauty every time.

In the pub, Old Spice clinked against Coty. They hurrayed Hilary. Strangers shook his hand and lined up more pints than any hero could manage. Nicholas bought a round and was bought several by people he barely knew. He gave a pint to Charles, who picked up Hilary and hugged him in the public bar, kissing him on both cheeks. The village roared and thundered its childlike joy.

In the rose garden behind the White Hart, a local lad and former reserve on the team, John Hardeman, gave the heave-ho to his childhood sweetheart, who loved him as nobody ever would again, for the sake of Michèle who had already forgotten that he existed. He said that he needed to be free. This betrayal was so urgent and necessary that it caused him not one pang. The French girl had smiled at him and all else was eclipsed. Upon the bowling green, Charles challenged Mr Dobbs to a game of boules and Dobbs, who was on his fourth short, kissed Charles on both cheeks. At his bathroom mirror, Sandy Wicks inspected his shiner through part-closed eyes and then shut his eyes, all the better to think about the mirage girl. The glory hour was on them.

In the marquee, where the heat of the day still hung, Amanda smoothed the little wrinkles in tablecloths and arranged pink bud roses on each table. By the time they sat down to eat, the buds would have opened. Her roses, gathered in the last hour, brought in at the last minute. A number of silver-plated rose bowls had been borrowed for the evening and she wished now that she had polished them.

Betty Boardman, so butter-fingered, had broken two glasses – tripping, jolting a table, down they fell. Those heels of hers, absurd. Could be worse, could be worse. Amanda felt happy. The band on their narrow dais were making a mess, with their electric leads winding off all over the place, but they were nice young men. Morris dancing they said they did, at a pinch, smiling at her disbelieving face. Oh yes, they did, nothing was too foolish. Whatever people wanted. It was a living. The bread rolls were either too soft and doughy white or poppy-seed-sprinkled and too hard. Never mind. One on each plate. Betty, she said, you do it. Thinking, of course, that they at least could not be broken. Betty set about doling them out using tongs, dropped one and with a sideways glance and a grunt, bent to recover it and quickly blew off the dust, popping it back with her fingers. By the third table it was fingers only.

The room looked very pretty. Hitherto undreamt of heights of sophistication had been reached. The village had never had a do like this, nor so much to celebrate. Her luck, the evening turning out so well, such weather and a famous victory. Her luck was that she would dance with Charles. He would hold her in his arms. She stood still for a moment and let her arms hang at her side and her skin remembered how he had touched her, in this place.

'Stress incontinence, that's what she said. That new doctor. She give me the name for it.' Betty Boardman started down her last row. 'Never heard of it meself, before Dr Cross said. Lovely dress, Mrs Ell. Belle of the ball, you'll be.'

'You could have rubber pants,' said nasty Amanda, thinking yes, she could, but it was very sharp of her and it was as well that just then the throbbing of the acoustic guitar drowned her words.

'What was that? Sorry, Mrs Ell? Butter pats?' Remorseless, Betty was, and for that alone, plus the remainder of her sins, wife appreciated and Amanda disliked her. Not that Betty ever seemed to realise.

Amanda worked her way along the long VIP table which was six eight-person ones pushed together in a giant U shape, folding the napkins. The team plus their wives, the president who sat next to the treasurer and their ladies. Ladies, it always said on the invitation, and the stupid word summed up how they thought of themselves and what she thought of them. The central places for the captains of both teams, naturally. For them the special centrepiece, with sprays of flowers projecting from her own silver bowl. It looked very pretty. The VIPs had the good damask napkins. Why not? Her finest, starched, ironed by Betty. Creases in the corners. Should have done it herself. Sod the napkins. Still, as she folded, she sang.

'Most women get it, after babies. Stands to reason. You know,' and Betty lowered her voice, though there was nobody else there to hear, 'sometimes, when you sneeze. Or laugh. Suddenly, you know.' Betty and her bitter butter, remorseless, had caught up. Amanda's old affection for her had been worn so thin by it. She needed oiling, smoothing out. Perhaps she needed a man. Curious thought. Betty had a lascivious cleft between her front teeth between which two miniature gummy dewlaps hung. Betty had a man, not that he did her much good. Boardman lived down to his name, thick as two short planks. Never did a decent day's work in his life. That was what he was famous for.

'Primrose oil,' Amanda said. It was a cure-all. Why, since all Betty's complaints were unmentionable, had that never stopped her from speaking about them? Why were unmentionables so patently the reverse? She was old, past pensionable age. Naturally, Amanda had never suggested such a thing. The only possible outcome would have been that Betty would have received a pension from her while ceasing to do any work at all.

'The thing is, Betty, you don't need a pension. What you need is a man,' Amanda said, wandering on and out of the tent to look for the lark. She was sure she had heard a lark. The sky called her, it was the richest, deepest blue streaked with gold.

Betty stared after Mrs Ell. She had probably misheard. Wax in her ears, needed syringing again. Dr Cross would do it. Tartar on her teeth, built up fast. A little bump on her foot one day, a bloody great corn the next. Nails which grew like wildfire. A blooming human dynamo, she was. Betty loved Mrs Ell, kindness itself and unfailingly good to her, as her own son George was not. Her husband Alf was an old husk of a man, useless at everything, always had been. You could say he was consistent, mind. Blue dress she wore, new, electric blue they called it. Bright against the tent. Betty decided that probably it was the Change. That explained primrose oil, didn't it? Needing a man, well, who didn't? Vitamin E Mrs Ell took, on her bedside cabinet it stood, new make-up and undies, she'd noticed, couldn't help it. From that lovely shop in Brighton, such a price in there, gorgeous things they had. Poor Mrs Ell. The Change on its own was enough to make you wish you'd never been born.

But Amanda, outside, heard a lark, saw the shimmering day fall through the trees, felt the warm earth through thin-soled shoes. The earth rotated through the black universe so that night should come for her alone. The very stars were up there, waiting behind the thin blue air, preparing to come forth for her personal delight.

She looked back through the tent flaps and saw that it was good. The tables were all done and the plates out, everything ready to serve. Chilled soup first, then the salmon. All ready in the club house by the time the men left the pub and walked back to the house through the lanes. The dog roses were in flower. Brambles and hedgerows had been newly cut and the green smell was heady and strong.

Nicholas did his rubber face as he tied his bow tie in the children's bathroom. Big grimace of a smile. He was whistling in a thoughtful sort of a way. His jacket hung on a hook on the door. He felt cramped in here. But his bedroom was full of dresses. Some kind of female explosion had taken place in it, a scattering of underwear and stockings, frills which he hadn't known his wife possessed. The things all looked new. Was that possible? Keep out, the room said. Keep away. Which was more than she had said to him of late. She said it with her face, with her rapid steps hurrying about, with her back. Busy. Amanda was very busy, with guests and the dinner and so on, and he remembered about the speech. It was traditional that the chairwoman of the Ladies' Committee who organised the dinner spoke a few words and then there was a toast to her. He stopped tying the bow and thought about it. How the hell was Mandy going to make a speech?

Banished from his usual domain, Hilary had ended up

dressing in Ed's room. The Eric Cantona posters on the wall laughed at him. Tied the bow tie a second and a third time and still didn't get it quite right. Needed one on an elastic, like Ed's. For tuppence he'd have worn that and his Spiderman outfit. What was it like, then, to be nine? Deeply self-centred as he was, Ed was nevertheless a prey to all kinds of strange ideas and fears. Couldn't stand to be seen naked, terrified of a woman seeing him without his clothes on. Wouldn't play football, claiming it hurt your brain, but loved rugger. Said he was afraid of the sound of the flute but mad about birds. Wouldn't sleep in a room in which the waste paper basket had anything in it. Neurotic, that was what he was, which was to do with the boy and not his age. As a baby Ed had been what he already was, an eccentric of the first order.

Hilary looked at himself in the mirror. He felt a bloody fool and, hey presto, now he looked like one. He opened the door, paused in the corridor. Somebody humming. Louise, was it? Funny thing, he thought. Something else. He used to think about sex. All the time, really. Not that that had gone, no, he was as interested in leg-over as the next man, but over the summer his horizons had expanded. Goal posts had shifted. Sex and neurosis. Love and death. He intoned the words in a deep, husky voice. Winning was good for you, it made you feel better. His heart was broken, but that didn't mean that all life ceased. Just that it had no meaning.

It was Michèle singing. A small, sweet voice. Cheerful, then, was she? Ha. He had never heard her sing or even hum before. He leant against the wall and listened with closed eyes and felt that this was as intimate with her as he had ever been. As he might ever get. He let the sound trickle through his head and sweep over his sore, sad heart.

There in the garden was a plume of smoke. Hilary went out. Charles was wearing the same too-tight evening clothes he remembered from before. It gave him a curious little moment when he saw him like this, with his cigarette and his glass, all as it had been but in the wrong place. This version of Charles went with the orchard and that huge moon. The big man put his arm round him and hugged him. Hilary felt the old warmth, felt the old familiar tug, the dance. Magnetic whatsit. Charles had got a bottle of wine from somewhere.

'Your maman gave it to me. What a woman, eh? Drink?'

'Sure. Doesn't it remind you of your party?'

'Maybe. No. It smells different here. England is full of flowers. English roses, like Amanda. Look at this,' and he waved a hand at a whole hedge of them. Yes, marvellous, wonderful, amazing. 'Your mother does the garden, no? Everywhere she makes beautiful.'

'About that night, about your party,' Hilary said, 'I never knew – I mean, you never said what happened to your friend. Vigne-Laval. You know, the professor.'

'Professor, yes. Ha. Like I am a doctor. Funny, huh, that he came?'

'Yes.'

'He came, he went. Such people, you know, come and go. Un clochard.'

'Vagabond?'

'Yes. Man of the streets, you mean? No real home, no place. You know what it is, Eelaree? I remember him better, so very different. When we was both so young. He was not like that. Sometimes it is better that way, when you remember. Better than seeing. You know, he is not a real person at all. Not having any value to anyone. That is his problem. But when I thought I knew, really he was always like that. Then I felt angry with him and with me for not seeing it before. But maybe mostly because we were young once and now not. You. You live it. You know?' The big man smiled and shrugged and sighed.

'Youth's not all it's cracked up to be,' said Hilary. 'What happened to him then?'

'I think maybe he just became more of himself. And now he is too strong. Too concentrated.'

'No, look. I mean, did you say anything to him?' He was bottling out here, and he knew it. It was hard to ask the question he really had in mind. Unsurprisingly.

'What do you mean?'

'He talked to me about girls, you know. In the car, when I went to pick him up. How they were all mad about him and so on. This fuck and that fuck.'

'I can imagine.'

'Tits like melons,' said Hilary. He screwed up his forehead and remembered. The wiry forearm on the wheel, the infallible sense of direction.

'The professor of pussy.' Ironic, Charles's tone.

'Yes.' He swigged his glass down. Slowly, they walked back towards the house. That same smell Charles had, of Gitanes and warmth and him and some kind of lemony perfume.

'I know. Sure, he was a pig. Sixteen I was when we met. He was twenty. I loved him. He told me everything I wanted to know about everything. Treated me like a man. Introduced me to his friends, taught me how to drink, how to talk to women. How to screw them. I loved him for it. Everything that was worth knowing. So I always loved him but later I stopped liking him, because he was such a pig. Dirt, I don't see why a person has to live like an animal. His teeth, nails, everything, like an animal. Une ordure. Then I was angry, you know, to see him again in this state and remember what I rather would have forgotten. So. Now we go to see your maman?'

'She's up at the club. Wait, you didn't say . . .'

'What? Why are you looking so worried? Don't do your face like that.'

'Look, never mind. I mean, what happened? I didn't find out what happened. I mean, that's what I wanted to know. He'd gone, you know, after that bit of a punch-up.' Hilary jabbed the air with one fist, to show. Charles looked thoughtful. 'You know. We put him in the house – you remember, don't you?'

But Charles was shaking his head. 'I don't remember, exactly,' he said. 'He came. He went. Come. I am anxious to go and see your maman. What she has made for us for tonight. What a woman, you know? Exceptional. Look at this garden. Everything.'

'My father does the garden,' said Hilary, rather foolishly, screwing up his courage, saying now or never, now or never, over and over in his head. Charles scared him.

They looked at the garden. Hilary noticed that the grass was very long. His fanatical father, king of the pinstriped lawn, was letting it run, quite literally, to seed. He felt too much rage at his dad to wonder how he was thinking, but it did occur to him now, just briefly, that the old shit was suffering and was punishing himself. That he should express this in dandelions and meadowgrass was strange but not unsuitable.

'You know, it's idiotic and everything,' Hilary said, ten paces on and a bit breathlessly and quickly, 'but for a minute I thought you might've done him in. You know. Killed him.' He drew a line across his throat and smiled and moved a step away as Charles moved a step nearer and grabbed him with one arm.

'For being un clochard?' Charles held him clamped with one arm. Now he squeezed his shoulder, tight. Hilary breathed in and out rapidly, looking up and seeing, strangely, Michèle's face at his bedroom window. She was leaning out and watching them. This made him do something and he jerked away from her father.

'Yes.'

Charles inhaled, let out a warm rush of air, laughed. Gitanes smell and lemony warm, he wasn't going to kill him.

'Silly, huh?'

'No. You think like me. Good boy. That is what I think he deserves. Nothing. You see, people who give nothing deserve nothing. What is his pig-life worth? Un rien.'

Louise blotted her lipstick, twice, and was ready. Charles had zipped her into her beautiful white silk dress. She had done her face, put up her hair. Now, she went in to Michèle's room to see if her daughter needed help. She was conscious of the faint rustling sound. She wore thin silk stockings. She didn't like bare legs, even in the summer, for evening wear. Not elegant. Her shoes were an extravagance and very beautiful. She looked down at them admiringly.

The bed was full of dresses. Discards. Michèle was rather soberly dressed in a demure frock which set off her flaming beauty. She was leaning on the cill, looking out of the window. Down below, Hilary and Charles were walking in the garden. Louise went to look and followed the blue line of her husband's smoke through the topiary.

'You look beautiful.'

'Thank you. You too.'

'Nothing compared to my daughter.'

The two of them stood at the window and looked down. Louise felt the same old tug between love and fear. Charles so tall and big, the grumbling deep laugh, the charming boy beside him. Always something held in reserve, something not quite right. Apart from her husband, her daughter was the only other person who could inspire such ambiguous feelings. Yet she loved them both. She could not quite love them as she wanted to for those reasons, for knowing too much. Yet perhaps if they had been more straightforward, more ordinary, she who hated herself for that might never have loved them at all.

'Chérie? You are coming down?'

A shake of the head.

'Madame has gone on already. It is her special dinner. You know.'

'Maman?'

Louise looked at her daughter, whose beauty was so extraordinary. 'Mmh?'

'Did you ever do something stupid with Papa – you know, to mess it up with you and him? So he didn't like you any more?'

Louise paused. It was such a long time since she'd been honoured with her daughter's confidence. Not through the whole of the boulangerie boy affair. She wanted to say something that would please Michèle and bring her close. The silence was heavy between them and she tried to think how to fill it. But even in the brief pause before she replied, in one second of her not being quick enough, her daughter's mood turned.

'Don't tell me anything. Not you. Not you – I expect you always did everything exactly comme il faut.' She turned away. The bitter note in her voice prompted Louise's anger. How wilful she was.

'I think I did. Always. As you say, just what I thought was right. You like the other approach, don't you? You know, it didn't make any difference in the end. What do you want me to say? I'm not like you. You can't cut against the grain. Your papa – well, he is the other kind, the kind who does as he feels, right or wrong. Me, I always worry about being right. And in the end it makes no difference. To what happens. Believe me. The strong take what they want. They are the winners in the end. So don't complain. The weak, they can complain.'

In silence, they went down together.

So the little party walked up the lane to the club, Charles walking alongside Nicholas in front. Hilary thought that neither of them seemed to know what to say to each other. Both were slightly tipsy. So was he, for that matter. One glass and he was anyone's.

Behind them came the two women, Louise and Michèle, both so pretty, arm in arm, but they too were silent. Last of all Hilary who dreaded the whole business and had got out of accompanying the walk by going back to lock up. He loitered in the lane. Two elegant women, so like each other in figure and height, so different in every particular. The lane was quite full of people. Silk dresses, high heels, laughter.

The marquee flew its flags, the buzz of English polite conversation was punctuated with the sound of popping corks. How warm it was, they all said, thirstily drinking all they could. The village was dry-throated as much from its need to celebrate as from the much-discussed heat-retaining properties of canvas. Keeps the heat in, bit of a breeze, wait till later, yes, yes, yes. They bored him and perhaps even themselves.

Service came courtesy of Betty and Flora and Flora's three big sons. Every place had its bowl of chilled soup with a swirl of cream and mint, its bread roll. Wine was being poured, water jugs were full. Hilary lived it all through a dream-like state. It seemed to him that the evening was overlaid with the noises of France and himself carrying the plates backwards and forwards and it was curious that he wouldn't be doing it tonight, though he had volunteered. His mother had said she did not need him. He smiled at her, even waved, but she didn't seem to see him.

She sat at the main table and her eye floated from side to side and saw everything and nothing. Hilary could see that what she mostly looked at was Charles. Now the Frenchman, catching her eye, raised a glass to her and they toasted each other, silently, across three tables, and nobody seemed to see or care but him. His father did nothing. Not a bloody thing. Just sat there. Hilary gave him a hard look. Not a muscle moved.

Jack O'Brien, the president, rose to his feet and coughed and laughed and held up his glass until they had all hushed. They opened with a toast: 'The winners – and the losers!' he cried. They all held up the single glass of champagne, which was all the budget allowed.

Hilary swigged his down sharpish. 'The losers!' That was his party. Get drunk, that was the thing. Fizzy, a bit too warm. The blob next to him wandered away, so he sank his drink, quickly. He was two tables away from his parents who were at the main table, three from the Beauregards who were on the honorary table. Nicely placed to view them all. How delicately, when it came, Louise filleted her fish. Hilary drank what there was.

Compliments flew on the salmon and its mousse, on the new potatoes and on the mint peas, always so delicious, so English, and afterwards there were strawberries and cream and summer pudding which clever Amanda had made for everyone. Marvellous, your mother, they said, and 'Dee-licious!' Old Betty was bringing in trays of stuff, going out with pudding plates, coming in with decanters of port. A large Stilton cheese stood proudly to one side.

The dinner was said to be the best ever. Belts were undone. Speeches began. Hilary feeling only slightly drunk went outside. To have a slash.

Sandy Wicks looked slightly ill and felt more so.

Dobbs was conscious of his wife's cheeks aflame, as they always were when she was in public and excited. Apple round and red they were, not that she could help it, poor thing, though he always felt the same twinge, something between annoyance and embarrassment for her. She was a woman who could not stand to be wrong or at fault in any way. Funny, then, that her own body so often betrayed her.

O'Brien stood and waited for them to fall silent. When they didn't, he spoke up. 'Gentlemen, ladies, members, guests,' he said and smiled his rather foolish smile. 'It's been a wonderful match and a wonderful dinner and I'm not going to spoil it by going on now, but just to raise a glass to Mrs Lennox, the chairwoman of the Ladies' Committee, who's given us all such a fine spread. And not to mention her two men, two members of the victorious team and our winning batsman!' He looked around and beamed. 'Ladies and gentlemen, Mrs Lennox and young Hilary!'

Over in the corner, Betty Boardman put down her pile of pudding plates as Mrs Ell rose. She wouldn't have missed this for anything. People were clapping and pounding their feet. The new corset now hurt like crazy. She thought about the other, old, soft one. It had a tear in it, a kind rent, which made it very comfy. Still, fat stomach, not pretty, was it? Oh, so long since she'd had a figure. Bit of a stitch too. Still, she didn't like to sit down and stood throughout instead, staring fixedly at Mrs Ell and nodding and smiling in case she looked over, and meanwhile sipping at a little celebratory glass of port she'd kept ready, over to one side.

Amanda knew exactly what she was going to say. From her vantage point she saw it all. Among the faces turning to look at her was the guarded one of Michèle. Nicholas's betrayal had given Amanda her carte blanche. But she would never bring herself to tell Michèle that the person she had really hurt was herself. The daughter was wilful and stubborn, she was a creature of passions like her father. She would have to learn that when you lived that way a price had to be paid. People were clapping and she surveyed them. For her and Charles, there was no going back, no remaking of the past; for them there was the present moment and its glories. She caught his eye and smiled.

Nicholas was in agony as his wife rose. All through the eating he had felt acutely aware of the coming speech. He had been unable to stop staring at her, it was so long since he had studied her, but she did not once return his gaze. Part of his face was almost numb with not being looked at, cold and ignored. As he deserved, but still his heart raced with anxiety for her.

She stood and looked perfectly calm. Not a flutter. And now, with the aplomb of a seasoned speaker, Mandy waited for the noise to die down. She looked around, smilingly, held a glass up. For her, they fell silent. In that moment, Hilary came in.

'Ladies and gentlemen, members of the club and of course members of the teams, let us pause for a minute and raise our glasses to the unsung heroes and heroines of tonight.'

Mandy spoke fluently. She was bright as fire, radiant in her dress of brilliant blue. Nicholas understood that she was transported out of herself by all that had occurred. She turned her head and for an instant stared at her husband, just as if she was indeed aware of the high degree of attention which he, unusually, was paying her. Attention unequalled in years. He looked at his wife and thought that she was like somebody else, somebody very familiar but whom he had forgotten. It was a funny feeling. As though she wasn't his wife at all. As though he was seeing her for the first time. And he remembered how beautiful she had been, her hair long and blonde, and how when he first saw the laughing girl among the crowd he had felt that strong taste he got sometimes, of the thing being perfect and wonderful and true to itself. Three or four times he'd felt that. His wife, really, and the children – the same when the children were born, each perfect, each so different. The strongest feeling in the world, he could almost taste it thickly in his mouth.

'Not the players, they get their applause. No, my toast is all the people backstage. Those who put up with so much – the wives who are forced to see and to hear such a lot about activities they may find, well, disgusting, those who stand and wait, those who serve their lordships, those whose job it is just to open doors,' and she turned and looked at him now and people laughed. Nicholas felt as though he was turned to stone. His tongue was suddenly fat and thick in his mouth, swollen up. As if he was having an allergic reaction. His blood pounded slowly and heavily round his head. His fingers had gone numb.

'My husband knows what I mean. Well, we the ladies of the team. Women, I'd rather call them. Oh, so many things we women put up with. I don't just mean the domestic service. My husband now, there's a man of action for you. Marvellous action as we've all seen today on the pitch. But he is one who does know about the very special view of things you can get from my angle. I mean the rear view – well, you know, don't you, Nicholas?'

He smiled and nodded and laughed, turned his head from side to side in order to meet the looks of idiotic people who looked at him and winked and smiled and raised glasses. In celebration of what? It was nightmarish, as though they knew what she meant inside those words she was saying about him, though of course they couldn't. Two tables away, Hilary sat with his head in his hands.

'Ladies and gentlemen, tonight is special for everyone and particularly for me. It's my chance to speak up, I suppose. My moment to say what I really think. And that is because of the actions of two people in particular who are here tonight. Two people who have done so much. They both know who they are. Stand up, please,' and heads swivelled across the room and Nicholas felt his heart pounding. 'My toast tonight, ladies and gentlemen – to Betty Boardman and Flora Jones!'

Betty, who listened hard and nodded a lot and yet did not expect this, sank abruptly onto a chair while Flora, more intelligent, quickly scuttled out of the tent without knowing what she was doing or where she was going. Thus outside, sprawled between two guy ropes, she heard the low murmur and the applause for her name. There was a good deal of it, dying down, then almost at once a burble of conversation which was almost as loud as people set to the port, the wine and cheese, the whole overlaid by the low rumblings of the guitars being plugged in. Then Flora knew that it was safe to go back in.

Nicholas was safe, too. He knew that he was alive, just. She was letting him off, sort of. He saw how, politely, the French couple applauded the applause. He saw his son raise his face and look at him with a curious expression. Nicholas saw the old Amanda, the woman he'd married, meet his eye, hers sparkling with wit and sharp intelligence and glee at having said what she had. He stood up and went towards her.

Amanda was already on her feet and walking away from him. Nicholas saw the intimate manner in which bloody Charles smiled at her and lifted his glass and toasted her. Then she said something to the Frenchman and he got up. They stood in the middle of the dance floor as the band twanged up, the first couple there. They began to dance.

Purposefully, Nicholas moved over three or four seats. He sat again. There was a bottle of brandy there, one he recognised for it had come from his house. It stood just beside the floral arrangement and right in front of Sandy Wicks. He took his glass with him.

'Sandy? Mind if I?'

'Not at all, help yourself. Wonderful woman, your wife.'

'Wonderful.'

'Still seeing funnily, you know. Two of her. You know, that ball I got. Two of her.' He chortled. 'One for you and one for me, eh?' Sandy laughed at his joke and blinked a lot. He had an enormous and perfectly circular bruise between his eyes which was a kind of greeny-purple colour. Lucky not to have broken his nose, from the look of it. His glasses accordingly were being worn somewhat lower down his nose than usual. Over the top of them he peered short-sightedly round the room.

'Looking for someone?' said Nicholas.

'Oh no. No, not at all,' said Sandy, continuing to look. Now he spotted the glorious girl, who was better than he remembered. He wondered if he'd get the courage up to do anything about her. A drink, for Dutch courage.

Nicholas poured a liberal helping for himself and his companion in suffering and let the liquid roll smoothly round his mouth. He would sit there and he would wait. Nothing else for him to do. Dance floor was filling up. Dobbs was there, dancing with his missus. Her face was a funny colour, bright purply red. Heart and lungs working too hard. All the people dancing were middle-aged. He watched his wife dance with the Frenchman and saw how he held her in a kind of embrace, wrapping his arms round her, and how she seemed to enjoy that. The brandy had a faintly anaesthetising effect, thank God.

Nothing to do but wait. Something in her face told him that everything had been decided, as far as she was concerned. She never looked once in his direction. Clear enough message there. He sipped at the brandy and waited for it to still the unhappy knockings of his heart.

Hilary watched Michèle. She too was very silent. He'd not said a word to anyone yet, nor did he feel the need. He was aware of his father, his mother, of her, her parents. When anyone from his lot moved, some sensor registered it. A whole set of vibes came from his mother dancing with Charles. They bounced off his father's face. He had no desire to look himself.

He was conscious that from time to time Michèle glanced at him, but he did not respond. He was aware of each glance brushing his face, like a flicker of flame running down it. Still he stayed where he was. Various local yokels came up to her and were given the brush-off. She stayed where she was and sat and watched Hilary. He thought that she looked very demure in her dress. He had not seen her like that before.

He kept an eye on John Hardeman, who'd have been reserve on the team if he'd not broken his leg earlier in the season. He'd been sitting next to the Beauregards all the way through the match. John had a very stupid look on him, he was staring at Michèle as though he'd like to eat her up. In due course – and the whole daft progress was wholly foreseeable, from his loiterings over near Betty, from his idle pausing and gazing at the band, to his sudden purposeful but seemingly unpremeditated start across the room – John went over to Michèle and asked for a dance. She shook her head. He looked at her for a moment in complete disbelief. Inside, Hilary smiled grimly. Silly sod. Could've told you.

Hilary looked around, no Angela. John was a fixture with Angela from the post office, had been for yonks. Hilary stared dispassionately over at the poor sap. He was pleading with her, practically on his knees. Pathetic. Poor Angela. Michèle lit a cigarette and, with those impatient gestures which were so familiar to him, blew out the smoke. Again, she turned to look at Hilary. Again, he failed to respond.

Now the acoustic guitar was thrumming and the four young men were right into the old favourites. These thrashes would always culminate in a number of them – 'Brown Sugar', 'Jumping Jack Flash', 'Knights in White Satin' – but there'd be other stuff in the meanwhile, the crowd-pleasers prior to the big numbers. His parents, who always claimed this era as though it were some kind of personal achievement of theirs, would be dead chuffed. Hilary ignored the music and sat on and with sardonic pleasure watched John Hardeman get his, lumps and all.

As Charles danced with Amanda, she felt a kind of shuddery feeling through her whole body which she could not resist. She felt herself blush from her toes to the crown of her bright blonde hair. She had forgotten what it felt like to be intimate with another human being. Long ago, they had held each other like this. All those years ago when she was young and free they had spoken to each other as lovers did, who cared about each thought and each emotion the other might feel.

'Mon amour,' said Charles and his breath was warm in her hair and this alone made her intensely happy. Over his shoulder, dreamily, she was aware of Nicholas sitting with his drink and his stupid expression, poleaxed, very satisfactorily so. It was curious, to think that both these men were truly there. She had thought so much of Charles that she was not sure that he was real, for all the warm breath and the weight of the arm which held her. Tonight Amanda had a second chance. She frowned a little. Still she could not think why it was that she had chosen Nicholas over this man. She remembered that Charles had given her an ultimatum.

Charles tutted at her. With one finger, he smoothed the wrinkle in her brow and smiled at her with such a delicious, naughty face that she could have laughed out loud for sheer delight. She felt consumed from the feet up by the most intense lust for him, the urgent need to touch and taste him immediately.

'Where can we go?' she said into his hair.

'Now?'

'Now.'

He looked around the room. Louise had gone up to the main table and was holding out one hand to Nicholas who, with the rictus she knew too well and the air of a condemned man, rose to his feet. Smiling, the elegant Frenchwoman pulled him onto the dance floor. He stumbled a little near the edge.

Charles looked back at her with a broad speculative smile.

'Here?'

He shrugged. She began to push at him, very gently but firmly, steering him to the far edge of the dance floor and away from his wife, her husband and the band. Once there she swivelled him round and looked over his shoulder. She felt weak with longing.

She surveyed the room. The noise was now intense. The band were doing their utmost, the strobe lights were on and at least three-quarters of those present were dancing. The remaining ones were getting stuck into the drink. General clamour and clatter and from one second to the next people disappeared in slow motion under the flashing lights.

'Here,' she said and nodded at the table. The cloth hung low. 'You go from there.' She pointed.

The lady president and chairwoman of the annual dance dropped to her knees at one end of the long U-shaped table. The Frenchman entered the space from the other. She did not know if anybody had seen them. It did not matter if they had. From their separate directions, they crawled under the tables towards each other, towards a meeting in the middle. The noise was intense. The strobe flashed. The long white tablecloth hung low. She felt the juddering of the feet, so near, pounding the ground and it jolted up her knees. As she went she pulled up her dress, so she could move more freely. She left her shoes somewhere near the entrance place.

The darkness beneath their white tent concealed them but was nevertheless bright enough for them to see each other. He did not smile. He looked at her with such intensity that she felt that she could have fainted. Carefully, they arranged themselves. It would be possible to lie, yes. Feet, those of Sandy Wicks, were safely a few feet away. Charles knelt before her, keeping his head low as he must and they kissed, the delicious taste of him flooding through her. She felt his hand reaching to unzip the dress and it was with joy that she felt it fall away from her. He smiled. Now, languorously, carefully, they lay side by side, he clothed, she naked, and looking intently at her he began to stroke her, beginning with her ear lobes and working with slow patience down.

Amanda felt all the delight and unreality of this, the coldness of the ground, the intense pleasure of her own nakedness allied to the incredible intelligence of his touch. Here were hands which seemed to have studied her pleasure. All this was so powerful that she could have fainted. Her imagination, so powerful a force, was doubly intensified by its collision with real pleasure. The strangeness of the time and place intensified it yet further, as did its illicit nature, as did the noise which allowed her to groan faintly, unstoppably as he pleasured her and yet not be heard. With slow, practised movements, he stroked and stroked. Her skin felt incandescent with pleasure. She was vibrating, like a spinning top, and she heard the humming sound he made, the sound of purring. The world could end, but not until this sweet pleasure had finished. She began to climax almost immediately, and as he felt this his mouth fastened upon hers and she was flooded with piercing sweetness.

She was a comet in outer space, she was a streak of flame through blackness of overwhelming intensity. As the first shuddering subsided, as he continued to stroke her, she begged him to enter her but he shook his head.

'First I make you come again,' he whispered.

To feel all this, a woman had to be Amanda. No young person could have this experience. The whole quivering rawness of acute sensation which went with youth had been overlaid by layer upon layer of conscious memory. So everything that happened was informed by something else. His warm breath, his touch like this, the tablecloth and its pattern belonged to her, her reward for having lived her forty years, their patterns ironed into her and possessed by her and as inimitable as the whorls of his fingertips. The flickering ecstacy of his tongue, remembered and now. Her acute consciousness of everything, above and below, even to the shape of the field upon which the tent stood in which all this could happen, even to the shape of the moon in the night sky. The waiting and wanting which made today so intense. All this came as a blinding revelation of interconnectedness of which these sweet deep feelings sweeping through her from head to foot were only one part. She alone, here and now and with this man, could feel such sweet sure intensity of pleasure doubled and redoubled almost to pain. The whole giddy universe was created for her at this minute of that day and all the connections were hers alone.

She cried out, she could not stop it, her body shuddered violently with blissful sensation.

At this moment precisely things stopped being unreal. She was here, now, this was the reality of her life. Wife and Amanda abruptly fused. It was no game. What was happening was real and serious as much as it was physically extraordinary – and she knew it.

*   *   *

The table heaved and the centrepiece jumped. Sandy bent down, lifted the cloth. He looked through the legs of the rough trestle table. He blinked.

He saw the ecstatic face of Amanda Lennox, eyes tightly closed, blurring into double vision then back again. He blinked, pulled back. Then looked again. She lay naked and with her back arching, spread-eagled on the floor under the next table. Her large breasts were exposed, they seemed to be fighting their way up. Partly on top of her, with his face buried in her loins, was a bare-chested man who was not her husband. Her husband was there, glum-faced and no wonder, dancing over in the corner. Mrs Lennox's hands were clutched in this bloke's hair. It seemed to be his attempt to remove his trousers which had caused the commotion. Yes, there he went. He was about to manage it. She moaned and thrashed about. Fine. All clear then.

Sandy dropped the cloth once more and stared at the jug of water which, yes, was trembling. Though this could have been from the vibrations of the noise. Which was considerable. As he knew from his thundering head. The table jerked and then was still. Right, he thought. He didn't exactly want to look again.

Sandy stayed quite still, sitting in solitary splendour at the table where he had been indulging in a cigar and brandy. Practically everyone else in the room was dancing. He had been feeling sick for some time, too sick to go, or stay either. He felt queasy as hell. His smoke and drink were not a good cure though he had not been able to resist either. The sick feeling heaved up in a tidal wave and left a nasty taste in his mouth before subsiding. This caused him just for an instant to lay his head upon the table. For some reason, the thrumming noise, wherever it was coming from, entering his ear from this piece of wood, found some other resonance and only then did it occur to him how powerfully erotic that scene had been. But he felt so very sick.

With a trembling hand, he poured himself a glass of water and had a drink. He got out a handkerchief to wipe his glowing brow and winced. As he did so, his glasses, which were still held together with sticking plaster, fell neatly apart. He moaned to himself, mended them, just sticking the ends into the wodge, put the glasses on, carefully tweaked the sides of the frames, which were very wonky. At once, the glasses came apart again and fell off. He cursed some more. Put them in his pocket.

Sandy had had enough. The room split from double to quadruple vision. The tidal wave rose and fell again, a bit quicker this time. He began to think that he might be about to throw up. Years and years since he'd done that. He got up and, sighing deeply and shaking his head in disbelief, he slowly made his way out of the tent. Fresh air. That was what he needed. Mrs Lennox, eh. Well. His erotic fantasies would henceforth involve tablecloths, a degree of voyeurism and the lovely breasts of Mrs Lennox. Oh, but how his head hurt.

Coming out of the tent, Sandy saw his dream girl, the girl of the pitch. Pity. As he blinked she swam in and out of focus. He was probably concussed.

They lay for a long time quietly. With his healing hands, Charles was stroking her face and hair and throat. Her eyes never left his face, she had a beatific smile. Eventually, without urgency, they dressed, helping each other.

Amanda emerged quietly, discreetly, and as far as she knew unseen. In the cricket pavilion loo mirror she looked the same, but felt quite different. Charles's touch had done something to her. She felt it all over her, like a second skin.

Staring into the mirror, she thought about him. The smell

of him on her. There had been a morning long ago when she had gone on duty, the white coat fresh but she herself rumpled from his bed. From his hands, as now. So this was it. She closed her eyes and leant against the door and waited for the picture to return.

Why had she married Nicholas? That night, she had still been on duty after a twelve-hour shift and Charles had come into casualty looking for her. White coat and stethoscope and she'd laughed. He didn't have the right, not that that ever stopped him. He took what he wanted. That piratical side was what made him so alluring.

She was a junior doctor on the ward. He was a visiting student, he should not have been there. He had his wilful ways, his arrogance, his spirit of devilry. But she had told him off for the imposture. She remembered that he had laughed and stuck his tongue out at her.

A tramp had just been brought in off the streets, a desperate creature with feet in an appalling state, dead drunk, a middle-aged man with lank dirty hair and a face covered in bruises where he'd fallen. Blood oozed from a nasty cut on his head. Suspected fracture of the arm, she'd touched it and he'd winced. He didn't want to undress. Years, probably, since he'd taken his clothes off. Boots, half off, with a terrible stench coming from them. Ingrowing toenails, scurvy, filth, emaciated, liver disease for sure, with the meths bottles he had, one in each pocket. He'd fought the nurse to keep those, one in each hand. A lot of his body was covered with bruises. He'd fought to keep his clothes on, had scratched her face.

He'd stunk. She'd wrinkled up her nose, not meaning to, and he'd got huffy with her and then obscene. He'd used obscene gestures. Tried to put his hand up her skirt. She had been roughly pulled at by him, his breath was rank and unspeakably foetid and so she'd drawn the curtain, told him she'd fetch another doctor to help. Told the junior nurse outside with the basin to deal with somebody else. Leave him be, she'd said. Because he would maul her too. He was mad, drunk, you name it.

Charles had gone into the cubicle then. She'd seen it from the corner of one eye as she was leaving. He'd been angry. Hadn't liked the way the man spoke to her. Seeing that, she'd gone back. 'You shouldn't be here. Go and wait somewhere.'

Charles had sat down beside the neat little trolley on which the stinking human relict lay, glowering at him.

'You don't speak like that to a lady,' he had said.

She'd hovered in the curtains. He'd waved a hand to her to go away. 'I will stay with him,' he'd said.

'Fuck the lady,' said the tramp, laughing. He had terrible eyes, dark and bloodshot and was completely mad. He'd blown his nose with his fingers, onto the floor. Disgusting. He'd laughed at her face. 'Come here,' he said to her and, 'Nice bit of skirt.'

'Go. Go on.' Charles had flapped a hand at her. 'You need a consultant, yes? Go and get one and then you can get off.'

So she had gone. She'd wanted to get a senior doctor to look at the arm. Everything always took longer than you thought and it had taken time to find a doctor to come. There'd been more obviously urgent cases in casualty that night. There was a child, badly burnt, a nightie had gone up in flames.

When she got back with her clipboard, with her papers ready and with a senior doctor in tow and still busily apologising for troubling him, the tramp was dead. She knew something was wrong. From outside, even before she drew the curtains, she had smelt the acrid smell of his vomit. He'd lain there, so very still. Choked to death on his own vomit, the coroner had recorded. There he'd lain, on his own. All alone inside the cubicle.

Charles had told her that he'd got bored, he'd gone home to wait for her. But Amanda had known, had felt in her gut and belly, without ever being able to be sure of course, that Charles had struck him. One well-placed blow to the gut would do it and what was one more bruise among so many? She had felt with cold dread that it was on her behalf. That her French boy friend had killed the old man to avenge the insult.

She'd said nothing to anyone. What could she do? Accuse him? Tell people her boy friend had dressed up in a white coat and stethoscope to kill an old man? Unthinkable. But she knew, then, what to do. She had married good, decent, safe Nicholas and she had given up medicine since one of them had to look after the baby. She had let him deal with the dirty stuff. She had been too scared to deal with it herself. So. So that was why.

Slowly, she went back across the field. The noise was intense. The band was playing up a storm, people were going mad. The tent looked beautiful, all lit up in the darkness like a giant inflatable that had come to rest. She went in through the back, past the table full of her china, the place full of her and her house, her flowers and her tablecloths. She looked at it all. Then one by one across the faces until she found Charles. Cupped hands, lighting a cigarette. Such big strong hands, like the rest of him. So strange, that the healing, in his hands, was still so powerful a force. Good and bad alike were there, two sides of the same thing.

He didn't see her. He went outside through the main entrance for his smoke. Amanda began with increasing urgency to look for her husband.

Nicholas was sitting on the ground near the oak tree, not doing anything really, just waiting. As she rounded the edge of the tent she saw others about. Michèle was also nearby. Charles said something to her and behind them a couple kissed. The band finished. Silence fell and there was a whooping yelling storm of applause. Then the sound of voices. Somebody shouted ha ha twice, very loudly.

When she was nearly at the tree, the band struck up one of those ridiculous Roger de Coverly-style country dances which obliged the participants to meet and part and sweep around with a fol-de-rol and so on. Amanda stopped and bowed to her husband. He stood up. Very courtly. She looked at his face. Nicholas by moonlight was pale and his nose left a shadow like a crater, a hole in his face. They looked at each other.

'You're arrogant,' she said. 'Opinionated and often offensive. You don't take much notice of people at all, for all that caring profession stuff. I think the worst thing you do is to pretend you don't notice things. Sexually, you're selfish. Morally, well not quite bankrupt, that's what they say about politicians, but bloody low in the scale. In the red, that's for sure. You've lost the sense of right and wrong in some deep way. I mean, not because of that girl, but anyway. Perhaps it's middle age or the male menopause, people say that stuff, but I don't think so. I think it's self-indulgence. Cut off, cold, miserable.' She paused and looked at him. He nodded.

'You know better, that's the worst bit. If you were stupid or insensitive one would, well, understand. All that point-scoring. Like a child.'

'Yes,' he said. Nicholas studied his wife intensively. He felt like a child, just wanting to sit with her, feel her warmth, hold her hand maybe. He wondered if she'd let him hold her hand.

'Do you know that I've just fucked Charles? On the floor, just over there?'

'Oh,' said Nicholas. 'Is he the one you want?'

She cocked her head, looked at him, did not reply. 'No,'

she said at last. 'I think it's you. You were the better man always. That's why I chose you.'

'Oh,' he said.

There was a very long pause. They both sat down and leant against the oak tree. 'Can I hold your hand?' he said, after a good long moment. In the distance, they could see Charles. They both followed the arc of his cigarette as he flicked it into the air.

In the marquee, Charles cut in on the fellow making up to his wife and took Louise in his arms. She was so lovely, his wife, she understood him so very well. She smiled at him so very sweetly.

'You've been so long. He was standing on my foot. A medical emergency, was it?'

'Perhaps.'

'You always rescue me.'

'No, you me.'

'Anyway. Together, that is all I care about,' and she thought it was true and how strange, that so many different things could be true all at once. They danced on wonderfully, perfectly synchronised. They had always had that ability, from the first moment. People looked and they would remember, afterwards, and remark upon them and say what a strong, indeed striking, couple they made.

Hilary pressed out the smouldering cigarette some dope had left just near the canvas. Yuk. Michèle was out here. There was a kind of trace of her in the air, the Gauloise, the perfume, whatever. Maybe he was just over-sensitised or something. Anyway. He looked around. There she stood, just round the corner, the flare of a match cupped in her hands, the light warming her face. For heaven's sake. He wandered round the tent in the opposite direction.

He kicked at the guy ropes, made the canvas shudder,

thought that there were things he should be thinking about and wasn't. Like his parents. For the first time in his whole existence he felt sorry for Ed, so indulged, so weird, such a pain, but the one who was going to bear the brunt of their bust-up while he was safely away. From the back of the tent, where Betty laboured with coffee cups, he got a glimpse of the activities within. A lot of smooching was going on. He saw Charles and Louise in a slow embrace. Le slow, as we call it. No sign of his parents though. As if.

Coming round the other side, he heard the peevish tones of John Hardeman once again trying his luck. Michèle was bored with the lad. She dismissed him. 'Go home. Go away. Go on. I don't need you.'

The local boy, dumbfounded, tricked, astonished, grew angry at such venom. 'What did I do?'

'You're the wrong one,' she said.

'Don't you like me? You cow. You liked me this afternoon, didn't you?'

'No, I don't like you. Go away. I never like you.'

'You little slut.'

'Go away!' She was shouting.

Hilary's heart was beating fast. What did she think she was doing, standing there? It was her own lookout. Not his business. He was going to do what he did for himself alone. To please himself. Oh yes, very likely, and he jumped the guy rope and rounded the corner with fists up and ready, Mr Confrontation. Yo!

But John was walking away, hunched up, hands in pockets.

Michèle looked at him, blew out a smoke ring. Unsurprised, just as if she was waiting for him. Waiting, who knows, for what. They looked at each other. She pulled on the cigarette with a deliberate air.

'What took you so long?' she said rather pugnaciously.

Waiting for him. So. His heart began to beat a little faster.

Inside the tent, the hokey cokey started up with a roar and a bellow. But outside the long-awaited breeze blew. The night was fine and calm and everything was as it was before and nothing could ever be the same.

'I don't like smoke,' he said. 'I hate it.'

'I will give it up.'

'All right. Go on.'

Michèle threw the cigarette away onto the grass, its arc bright, and then bent forward as Hilary did and the two of them practically knocked their heads together, thinking to stub it out. The country girl. She was a country girl, after all. His heart was beating like an express. Incredible thumpings and poundings which went right up into his throat.

'Anything else you want?' she said.

'Yeah. Who's the right one?' he said. Mr Hard-to-get.

She wasn't having that. She tugged at him and pulled his arms round her waist. Fine. This far he would go. She pulled again, so they stood as close as possible. She laid her head against his shoulder with a sigh and closed her eyes. He looked at that curve of cheek, the way the mouth turned up. The blue vein of her eyelids which fluttered, slightly.

He closed his eyes too and without trying particularly hard, their mouths met. The strong taste of tobacco mingled with something incredibly sweet and powerful. Like honey. Like wine. Whatever. She hugged him so tight, he felt breathless. They stood there for about a thousand years and embraced, came up for air, did it again.

The air was sweet and slow. From within the tent, they heard the thudding, rumbling roar as the hokey cokey reached its ludicrous finale.

For the first time, he was holding her in his arms. Slowly they began to dance in the little space between the guy ropes. Well, move around. More of a lean than a dance. His prick, on full aching alert, let them both know just how interested he was. What was he to do? She pleased him, as she always had.

He kissed her again. She tasted incredible. Astonishing, really. She knew it, she opened her eyes and looked at him; he looked back. Hilary felt mesmerised. They stared at each other's faces, mouths, he watched as her eyes closed voluptuously, saw the way the long lashes lay above the delicate curve of her cheek. There had never been a girl like this. Never would be. He smiled.

'Funny, huh?' She'd opened one eye and squinted at him.

'Maybe.'

Gradually the faintest flicker of a smile grew on her face. Hilary laughed. They both started to laugh. A gurgly, real thing, this laugh, with the head thrown back to expose that kissable throat. A wonderful sound. Pure pleasure. But he wasn't going to say anything. Nope.

Over her shoulder he saw a strange sight. His parents, wandering away down the lane. Hand in hand. For Christ's sake. Hand in hand. He'd have said something to her, but she didn't care. She was giving him that look. She was wanting his full attention and, fair dos, this she could have. He took her face in both hands. Her eyes were closed, waiting for a kiss. She smelt incredible. Whatever it was in the perfume line, however much it cost, it was worth it.

'Please, do it again.' The eyes opened. 'What is it?'

'You have to say something to me,' he said. 'Or I won't kiss you.'

'I never say things. Please? You mean please?'

He shook his head and stood and waited until her eyes looked away and were abashed and then looked back again.

'You are – oh, I don't know,' she said, in a small squeaky voice. 'I can't say things.'

He waited.

'You are – impossible.'

'No.' He shook his head.

He was silent for a long, long time, just standing with her in his arms and waiting as the whole world did, for a word. In this moment there was no breeze, the hare on the hill sat with its paw up, alert, the stars paused in their orbits. His breath in and out the only movement in the universe.

'Bon. I see. *I* am impossible. Now you kiss me?'

The grass grew up through the soles of his shoes and the seasons changed and the tent could fold upon itself and all crumble away. But he was a rock, a fortress, a hard man.

'You want more?'

'Oh yes, much more.'

'Oh. Oh Hilary. I am so sorry, so very sorry, so sorry, very.' A warm tear, just one, trickled out of one eye and lay on her cheek. It was salty, delicious. It was surrender. Her breath was so warm, so sweet against the sour, he wanted to cling to the moment, but already the stars were in motion and the hare had thumped its alert and the world turned on its axis towards the new, the coming day.

The warm summer's night laid itself out over the hedgerows and fields. The sound of the music grew ever fainter and fainter as they walked away, hand in hand. The smell of the dog roses in the lane. Three babies made. A marriage broken and another saved. A love story beginning.

Halfway down the lane Nicholas stopped and made a ridiculous fumbling lunge at her, something which had not happened in twenty years, no more. Amanda started to laugh. Then he kissed her. Not bad.

She felt a kind of deep laughter inside, a rich full feeling, a laugh waiting too far down to rise up. It would come out later. The main thing was that it was there. It lay there like a deep grinding feeling within her. Giant tectonic plates being pushed. Continents which had been separated, meeting. Silly, she thought. But in her head, she was already singing the new tune.

Children of Chance
ELIZABETH PEWSEY

In the sultry heat of an uncommonly hot English summer, young Prue Pagan heads north to take up a holiday job at Mountjoy Castle. Newly released from the confines of her convent school, she tastes the pleasures – and dangers – of her new position with innocent abandon. At nearby Midwinter Hall, Prue's more worldly friend Cleo is also working for the summer, in the employ of a famous cellist. While Prue is stalked by Lord Mountjoy's irascible heir, Cleo pursues her own quarry in typically uninhibited fashion. Nothing is quite what it seems, however, and many secrets lie hidden between castle, hall and village. By the time the summer is out so are most of the secrets, and Prue is not the only one wiser in the ways of the world.

'A deliciously wicked tale of the shedding of innocence'
Company

The Lost Child
ANNE ATKINS

'They have been asking me to talk about Poppy for several years now. Of course, I've always said no. Not just for the obvious reasons, either; not just for the reasons to do with Poppy herself, and my relationship with her. But all the others too. After all, it's a story about all of us. What will my parents make of it? And the rest of my family? We never talk about what happened that summer.

Caz is a successful author of children's books. She is at a watershed, both personally and professionally: she has bought a new house, met a new man, and is planning a new book. But this book will be very different from anything she's written before.

Because there is something Caz must face before she can wholeheartedly embrace the future; something in the past which still haunts her. And as she remembers that summer, the summer when everything changed, she finds herself confronting the child she once was in order to understand the woman she has become. Could it have been different? Was there, after all, anything she could have done . . .?

'The perceptions of childhood are excellent, and the central issue is presented in an original way.'
Daily Telegraph

'Few first novels attempt so much and even fewer bring it off so well. It is a fluent, compassionate novel which, while it never fails to be contemporary, has also the weight of history's compassion behind it.'
Nigel Forde

Alice Alone
AMANDA BROOKFIELD

On the day that her youngest child leaves home, Alice Hatton discovers two disturbing truths in a matter of hours: the Empty Nest cliché is absolutely true, and she does not love her husband Peter at all.

Horrified by the thought of spending another thirty years with Peter in their North London suburb, Alice embarks on a dubious course of self-fulfilment. When she must cope with loss for the second time, she discovers what even the most respectable woman can be capable of.

'A strong sense of humour, a natural narrative gift and controlled, understated characterisation signify a promising debut'
Evening Standard

'The quality of observation here is so sharp, and this novelist writes so engagingly, that I read *Alice Alone* in one gulp . . . it is rare for a new young writer to have such certainty in her description of a much older woman and her feelings'
The Bookseller